GW00391284

PLATO PARK

Carol Rumens was born in London in 1944. Her poetry is highly acclaimed and she has published five collections: *A Strange Girl in Bright Colours*, *Unplayed Music*, *Star Whisper*, Direct Dialling, and *Selected Poems*.

She has two daughters, and lives in London.

CAROL RUMENS

PLATO PARK

Published by Fontana Paperbacks

First published in Great Britain in 1987 by Chatto & Windus Ltd

This Flamingo edition first published
in 1988 by Fontana Paperbacks,
8 Grafton Street, London W1X 3LA

Flamingo is an imprint of
Fontana Paperbacks, a division
of the Collins Publishing Group

Made and printed in Great Britain by
William Collins Sons & Co. Ltd, Glasgow

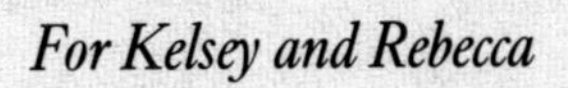

For Kelsey and Rebecca

From Arkady's notebook
Moscow, 1974

Once again we are to be enlightened by visiting Westerners

'An American is really kind of Russian, only richer,' remarked Lev after Lenina Andreevna's party last year. In the tinkling of broken glass he had heard the delicate shattering of his illusions, and he spoke in the steady tones of one who would not be fooled again. A year later, however, the light is back in his childish blue eyes. The British are coming; from the land of Shakespeare, Byron and Roger McGough, with their exquisite manners and the inscrutable, melancholy reserve of the fallen aristocrat, the British are coming to put our illusions together again. Two women, it's rumoured, and one man – a Shakespeare expert who apparently speaks fluent Russian.

As soon as he heard the news, Lev began biting his nails with anguish and delight. If only he were still an English student at the university, if only he knew someone, at least, who could smuggle him into a couple of Mr Lamb's lectures! Even Miss Robinson on Virginia Woolf or Miss Tressel on whoever-it-was would do. So he whined at Lenina Andreevna's feet and she, though unwilling to permit anything so unorthodox as an outsider's attendance at the faculty lectures, magnanimously agreed against her better judgement to give another party for the foreign guests. Of course, she had sworn never to do so again, after the glass-breaking episode with the Hemingway expert from Dallas last year.

So my Anglophile colleague sits all day in the seventh sky, practising under his breath his four English accents (he can do public school, East End, Liverpool and something he calls country soil – in that order of incomprehensibility). As for me, I love the English language, I remain mildly curious about the English soul. But I do not think that teachers, as a species, are excessively interesting examples of the latter. And I prefer to take my language neat, from the page. I shall go to Lenina Andreevna's entertainment with the main intention of making an impression on the guests of honour and remaining, myself, unimpressionable. I shall probably read a section of my poem-in-progress; Ilyusha and the band will sing their parodies of 'Katusha' and 'Kalinka' that we've laughed at so many times before; Miss Tressel and Miss Robinson will succumb to Lev's charms and Professor Z's mysteriously acquired Stolichnaya with blushes and giggles and near-hysterics; Lenina will preen herself, Asta will have a blazing row with her current boyfriend, the token famous person will yawn and leave early and the token African (Maurice) stay and stay, glassy-eyed to the bitter end. We will go home to our hangovers none the wiser about the inscrutable fallen aristocrats/gradgrinds of the British delegation in whose honour, supposedly, the party was given in the first place. And it will be mid-October already, the fogs will have begun, we will forget about the West for another year, or maybe for ever . . .

The shadow of Igor Igorevich, our Responsible Editor, has just passed across my page. It lingered infinitesimally and was gone. My pen continues without a tremor. I am confident that the shadow's owner, though very probably aware that I am engaging, intramurally, in extramural creative activity, has no good reason to complain. Yesterday the new issue was passed at a meeting of the editorial board, so today we can allow ourselves a breathing space before the next act of the comedy, press day. Lev, our best proofreader and most versatile general hack, has been permitted to go to the library to work on his translation; even Kolya, the chief assistant editor, has done nothing for the last half-hour but lounge in his corner, eating yoghurt and perusing the latest issue of *Soviet Sportsman*. I, at least, am making marks on paper (numerously) and occupying my seat. So the substantial, square grey back sways contentedly towards the editorial alcove, unperturbed by the villagelike aroma of illicit distillations. There's no question about it: Igor Igorevich knows that I am writing the short stories, articles and poems that will make the *Literaturnaya Zvezda* the second-brightest star in Moscow. (Second, I mean, to that symbolic star twinkling red above the Kremlin's Spasskaya Tower.)

What I'm writing now, of course, is the story of myself – a story every young writer has to tell, before graduating to telling the truth about something that doesn't exist. I work slowly, rereading every sentence, listening for my own voice. I know that it must be distorted, like the voice I hear when I speak, which isn't the voice I hear on Ilyusha's tape recorder, which, Ilyusha says, isn't my voice, either – at least, not the one he hears. What he thinks my voice is and what I think it is are probably very different things. Maybe his version is the more accurate; my listening is corrupted, no doubt, by my happy delusions about the sort of person I am (as well as one or two unhappy certainties). But what does it matter? Is there really any such thing as my true voice, a voice that doesn't depend on a listener to divine and define its nature? Is there such a thing as a voice? Or as truth? Is there any truth in the Truth? Is there in any truth, the Truth?

Tolstoy's women and just one little capital letter

The day after writing those last sentences (they struck me, on rereading them, as rather elegantly philosophical) a subtle sea-change occurred in the atmosphere at the *Literary Star*. A mere shimmer of a chill, but unmistakable, and liable, at times, to spoil the hot little thought of my date tonight with Luba.

I discovered that the chill emanated chiefly from the eyebrows of our responsible editor. They hung a centimetre closer to his eyes than usual and the point at which they met (the apex of his broad, peasant nose) was a constant in my perception. It was like being looked at by the barrel of a tiny but lethal gun.

When it got to midmorning and he put on, as he usually does at that time, a pair of mock-tortoiseshell spectacles, the gun barrel was replaced by a small strip of yellowish plastic and by something even worse – two sharp, twinkling little stars. They were watching me too.

At lunchtime, Igorevich attended a meeting of the editorial board. He got back late, after 2.30, and his mood was more restive and the two stars more inexorably twinkly than ever. He kept pacing from desk to desk, picking up books and putting them down again, riffling through files, or staring for long minutes out of the window at the singularly uninteresting view of our neighbouring office blocks. Normally, at a relatively slack period such as this, he would retreat happily with his cigarettes and his antacid pills into the editorial alcove to rewrite the ground plan for the next issue but one, confident that there would be many opportunities to review the revisions and the revisions of the revisions. Each time he drifted towards the alcove I fervently wished him into it, but each time he turned away and drifted back, twinkle, twinkle. Although quite legitimately sweating out a review of five new novels about life in the forces (the assignment was passed to me by Kolya, who resents the fact that I went to university instead of doing national service), I felt more thoroughly guilty than if I had been writing a denunciation of our General Secretary himself (perish the thought). It was almost a relief when the little stars twinkled closer, closer and stopped.

Speaking of denunciations, I must make it clear that, even now, I do not wish to present Igorevich as an unpleasant man or even a wholly bad editor. Let me try for a truthful portrayal . . . He has, certainly, a genuine love of books, even though this is at times offset by his assistant's genuine hatred of them. Physically, he bears a luckless resemblance to the late Nikita Sergeyevich: he lacks his bluff self-confidence, however, and though he has a certain quality of peasant cunning, it is inadequate for negotiating the slippery mountain passes of higher literary politics; he flounders horribly between the Muse and the Party, liberalism and puritanism. These vacillations are usefully reflected in his ties. One day the tie will be blackish grey, another, dingy red; sometimes it will be plump and blue and shiny as the breast of a peacock and once a month it will be abandoned altogether in favour of a plum cravat. Cravat days usually follow his meetings with the editorial board. They signal his renewed opinion that the board members are a bunch of philistines and charlatans to whom he is superior in every way and, simultaneously, his extreme relief that the latest issue has been approved by this same bunch of philistines and charlatans.

In spite of everything, the *Star* has a reputation for being lively and innovative and not unfriendly to the more searching creative spirits of our times. That's its strength – and, in my opinion, Igorevich should not be so afraid of his own liberalish instincts. But he insists on playing politics, pretending to be cautious and clever like an elephant walking the tightrope. On blackish grey and dingy red days, the effort steams from his soul in clouds of peppermint smoke.

Wincing discreetly, I inhaled a lungful now as Igorevich stepped towards me with a confiding little smile and made a flat-palmed gesture (of stroking? of erasure?) above the dark-green folder labelled ED. REF: SELF, which contains these very notes.

'Your work – I mean your *own, creative* work – is it going well?'

His hoarse voice was kindly, but the emphases made me start. I thanked him politely for his interest and told him I believed it was going pretty well, the long poem in particular. (He has already published a stanza of this and claims to have been moved to tears by its romantic lyricism, so I felt it was a safe topic to raise.)

Igor Igorevich smiled a fraction less but, still projecting affability, lowered the soft sacks of his buttocks onto my desk, entirely obscuring the green folder with their mass, and tried to come to the point.

He informed me that I had undoubted talent, but that I should be wary of flippancy and immaturity. He had observed in one of my latest works – part of which I had left prominently displayed on my desk so as to allow, perfectly correctly, free perusal by himself or any other fellow worker – both negative and cynical tendencies. In short, I had questioned the veracity of an organ whose veracity is not fit matter for questioning, that organ being the official daily newspaper of the Central Committee of the Communist Party, *Pravda*.

At first, I couldn't understand what he was talking about. Then I remembered the line I had been so proud of – is there any truth in the Truth? I remembered that I had capitalised the P of *pravda*. Well, of course. I am a man of high ideals. I believe that such words as love, peace, life and truth should be written Love, Peace, Life and Truth as a mark of respect for their all-transcending values. Surely the Truth doesn't *have* to become a newspaper when it's capitalised?

I could hear, I swear it, Lev shaking silently behind me. Even I had begun to quiver slightly, but with passion rather than amusement. I was genuinely upset. Warmly I declared my loyalty, my idealism and my admiration for the real (sic) *Pravda*; humbly I made a scapegoat of my impetuous youth. Igor Igorevich heard me out with the utmost sympathy; it was spread over his face like honey over bread. He told me that it was hardly a major issue, and that this was merely the friendliest and smallest of small and friendly cautions. *However* (and Igorevich nervously licked some of the honey from his lips), it *was felt to be indicative* of a certain *general trend*; for example, some of the essays I had recently commissioned *were felt to be* slightly below the *highest literary standards* which the *Star* had always sought zealously to fulfil.

He was no more specific that this, and of course he didn't need to be. I understood at once that he was referring to something written by my girlfriend Luba in response to my request (prompted by Kolya and endorsed by Igorevich) for a fresh view of the works of Leo Tolstoy. Luba's view had turned out to be fresher than expected; she produced what she called a feminist critique of Tolstoy's women. It was a mild enough piece – certainly not an all-out attack – and cogently argued; I handed it to Igorevich, unaltered, and he approved it for presentation to the board with only a few minor changes. Igorevich has always liked to think of himself as a champion of women's rights; besides, he was wearing the plum cravat that day. He had probably since suffered a rebuke from higher up. Maybe Ilya's rave review of the Beatles had not gone down too well in certain quarters either . . . and what if Igorevich had read the bit in my ED. REF: SELF about being the *Star*'s brightest hope? My cheeks burned as I sat with bowed head and racing mind, letting Igorevich's platitudes – they had become flattering again, now he had got the rebuke over and done with – flow over me. The worst thing was that I had already rushed to tell Luba that her brilliant article had been accepted for the next issue. Now I would have to enlighten her, and she would be outraged. I would get all the blame; I always did. It would probably mean that our on–off affair was in for a protracted period of off.

The stars gave a farewell twinkle in my direction; then the two dough sacks were heaved from the desktop, and Igorevich lumbered off to his polluted lair. The green folder – I couldn't resist laying my hand on it to find out – remained, for several minutes, uncannily warm. But I felt weak and cold; the sun inside me had been completely obliterated by menacing clouds. I certainly didn't want to see Luba tonight, and I was tempted to ring her at the polyclinic to plead work – or wife – pressures. But then I'd have the problem of explaining to Tanya why the vitally important evening meeting with my fellow editors had been suddenly cancelled. I'd also have the problem of staying at home.

Family life

'What's the matter with him, then?'

'I don't know, Mama. He's been like a bear with a headache ever since he came home.'

'What's so difficult about putting the kettle on, Arkashka?'

'I've lost my shoelace, damn it! Masha, please turn the television down, I can't think with all this noise!'

'Mashinka, d'you hear your father? He's got a headache again, turn the television down.'

'I haven't got a headache, I just want to find my bloody shoelace.'

'Mashinka, did you hear me?'

'But Mummy, you know *Uncle Robot*'s my favourite! If I turn it down I won't be able to listen, you're all jabbering so much!'

'Masha, that's no way to speak to your mother!'

'It's good to know you still can think, anyhow.'

'Young people these days just say what they like. They talk to their parents exactly like they talk to their friends.'

'Mama, times have changed, they're more honest, that's all. Now, Masha, do as I tell you!'

'If that's being honest, you can keep it.'

'Yes, it can cause a lot of trouble, honesty.'

'What's he muttering about now?'

'Arkashka, she only asked you to make a pot of tea. You can see I'm busy. She's seventy-three years old and you can't be bothered to make her a cup of tea!'

'But I told you, Tanya, I've got to go. The meeting starts at 6.30. It's already quarter past, and I can't be late. Mashka, have you seen a shoelace, a brown shoelace?'

'I think Vaska had it, Daddy. He was playing with something under the settee.'

'I can't see why you have to keep going to meetings in the evening. Aren't you allowed any family life, must you sacrifice everything to the job?'

'Tanya, look at him, he's ruining those trousers you just ironed!'

'It isn't there now. I'll murder that bloody cat!'

'Use some string, Daddy. I've got some in my toy box.'

'Not now, darling. I'll manage like this.'

'Why have you got to go to a silly old meeting?'

'I won't be long, sweetheart.'

'Will you be back before I go to bed?'

'Maybe, maybe. Where's my briefcase? OK, then. Bye, Mashka Pashka, bye, Tanichka, goodbye, Mother.'

Outside in the hall, I quickly re-combed my hair. Then I opened the airing cupboard as quietly as possible, removed a thin Scottish-check blanket, and folded it into my case.

I took a tram, then another tram, then I walked uphill for nearly a kilometre. At the top, Luba was waiting impatiently, leaning against a silver birch. In spite of everything, I was cheered to see her.

As we walked through the crisp undergrowth, twigs and leaves insinuated themselves into my loose shoe, and I had to keep stopping to remove them. 'The forest wants to trap you and marry you,' remarked Luba, and this was so uncharacteristically sentimental that I had to stop and kiss her, though well aware that her patience for what she calls 'physical slobber' is fairly limited. She tried to smile as she rubbed a gloved finger over her lips.

'Don't let's go any farther. Let's sit down here.'

I was surprised; Luba was usually the one who wanted to walk for miles so as to exercise her long legs, fill her lungs with fresh air and avoid the need for slobbery confrontations. Willingly I spread the blanket. We took off our coats, sat down and did our deep breathing and relaxation exercises. Though by now I was lying flat, and trying to feel myself sinking, limb by limb, into a pile of cotton wool (as recommended by Luba's doctor friend), my mind refused to enter into the general notion of weightlessness and was immediately occupied by black memories and forebodings like leaden cockroaches.

Luba lay open-eyed, meanwhile, staring up through her glasses at the leaves. She wanted to discuss their precise colour; supposing, she said, I was writing a poem, how would I describe them? Russet, golden? But those were clichés and not very accurate. There was a coppery pinkness in them, even white, even black, if you looked intently. The words for colours were too simple; colour is always complex. So, Luba persisted, what word would I, a poet, employ to recreate the essence of autumn birch leaves?

'Shit-coloured,' I said.

Luba did not flinch. 'Mmm, perhaps,' she said thoughtfully. 'Some shit. Not all, of course.'

I took a deep breath, and launched two words on the end of it, like black kites. 'Igor Igorevich . . .'

'Darling,' murmured Luba, turning on her side to face me and laying two slim branches, an arm and a pale leg, across my prostrate form. 'Darling, I have to tell you, Borya's coming back from the kolkhoz earlier than we expected. They finished the plan in almost half the time and there's nothing else for him to do, so he wrote and . . .'

'When?' Another cockroach, blacker and more leaden than ever, had plumped itself down on my heart.

'Soon, I'm afraid. Very soon.' Luba caressed me with agile calf and feverish palm. I enjoyed the massage, even while taking in the dreadful conclusion to this unexpected news item. Borya was coming back at the end of the week – Friday, to be exact. Tonight's carnal contact would have to be our last.

Clearly, Luba had decided that she would waive her disapproval of slobber on such an auspicious occasion. She began unbuttoning her blouse and my shirt simultaneously, maintaining all the while an expression of the most wistful, dewy-eyed acquiescence I had ever seen on her cynical little face.

I was willing to be seduced, but not just yet.

'Luba, if you believe that women should have complete sexual freedom, why is it different when Borya's at home?'

'Theoretically it isn't different. But I have to be practical. I've been asking myself how I'd feel if I'd just seen you and then I had to go home to make Borya's supper and go to bed with him – well, I couldn't do it. I'm not a prostitute. I know it's difficult for you to understand, Arkasha, but I really do believe it's different for women. We can't just *compartmentalise* like men. It's our strength, of course, but in some situations it can be a weakness.'

I looked across her shoulder at the wavy lines of birch trees, thinking what depth the forest seemed to hold, what promise, and how illusory it was. Even if you walked for miles, you somehow never really got inside that promise, and finally it would peter out and become a beet field or a track into the town.

'We've been together for nearly nine months. As long as it takes for a child to develop in the womb. It's a long time, Lubovka!'

And yet, I thought, it's always something of a relief when you reach that field or that town.

'I know.' Luba's eyes were clear and round and tearless; it seemed to me that she was acknowledging an emotion similar to my own. 'But I told you from the start we could only be temporary. My marriage is basically a happy one, I've got two small children. I don't intend to wreck it.'

'Fair enough. I understand.' I unhooked the spectacles from her ears; she gave me a friendly smile, friendly enough to show, unusually, a glimmer of neat teeth, and whipped off her blouse. I leaned over and began kissing the thick freckles that covered her back, licking them up like buckwheat kasha. She squirmed slightly but did not complain; she understood that it was part of our bargain that I should finally get my full slobber's worth.

Afterwards, as we hastily and shiveringly dressed ourselves, a sense of loss flooded over me, but I quickly reminded myself that, in our nine months of passion, I had been disappointed by Luba at least as often as I had been charmed. Not only did she view sex as second-rate, animalish and rather boring, she wasn't particularly interested in emotion, either. She would rather talk about anything theoretical – the colour of the leaves, the structure of the isosceles triangle, the use of goat's milk in treating migraine sufferers – than about her feelings; whereas, to me, nothing on earth is more interesting than emotion, mine, hers, even other people's. Believe it or not, I'm not cynical at heart. Once, I had great hopes of married love; when these were worn to shreds, I wove great hopes of love outside marriage. Somewhere, I once read about the knights and troubadours of the Middle Ages, and it was from them that I borrowed the idea of adultery as being love's most perfect form.

Luba, with her strange jokes and abstractions and flights of fancy, her changeling cap of red curls and red-freckled cheekbones, her cunning eyes and her haughty mouth, was well suited to my imagination. But, as I soon discovered, her motives and mine did not coincide.

For Luba, adultery was anything but an ideal. It was a farce, a puzzle, a game, a challenge. An *idea*, above all, to be put in practice only rarely and then with clinical detachment. The only passion was in plotting the moves (she always took a great interest in the mechanics of subterfuge), not in the moves themselves. So you see, I told myself, although we appeared to meet, Luba and I were always far apart. We never met at all – not even when she closed her pale, harebell eyes, wrapped her pale, birch-branch legs around my back (where, I believe, she tied them into a graceful knot) and submitted herself to the predictable little drama of lust – especially not then.

It was no longer impossible to raise the topic of Tolstoy's women, so, as we strolled down the hill to our respective tram stops, I explained briefly the unsavoury new developments at the *Star*. Luba was enraged, of course. What made matters worse was that, considering the first article unfinished, she had embarked on, and almost completed a sequel, wildly assuming we would be delighted to publish that as well. After cursing Igorevich and his lackeys (i.e. me) choicely and at length, she withdrew into a silence that became prolonged and quite intolerable.

The crazy dance of leaden cockroaches began again. In the cold, dreary twilight, as we stood with our eyes frozen to the horizon where no number 8 tram could be seen, I babbled on about anything that came into my head, and suddenly found, to my perturbation, that I had invited her to Lenina Andreevna's English teachers' party.

Luba compressed her lips and, quite against my will, I became persuasive. It was true that Borya would have got back by then, but, I argued, this was after all a public gathering and we would have no reason or opportunity to misbehave ourselves. It would be a real intellectual feast and, by the way, I added, Lenina Andreevna always prepared an exceptional meal on these occasions.

A number 8, with miraculous timing, had now appeared, but Luba continued to compress her lips. The driver was already braking when she opened them slightly to say, 'I might. Then again, I might not.' Frantically I began turning out my pockets in search of a pen and paper to jot down the address. 'Just tell me – I can remember,' said my icy mistress scornfully, so, to the shuddering and panting of the machine, I put my lips to her hot little ear – which I kissed first, for old times' sake. Looking more exquisitely furious than ever, she swung herself away from me, leaped aboard and bobbed down out of sight. Once more, a wave of loss engulfed me. I didn't believe she'd memorised the address, in fact I didn't believe she'd even permitted it to reach her tympanic membrane, let alone the deeper recesses of her fiery-curled skull. Why hadn't I told her that the leaves were colourless in comparison with her hair?

The thought of going home was so dispiriting after that, I decided to walk – at least halfway.

A reconstruction of a conversation that very likely took place between Lenina Andreevna and her daughter, Asta

Lenina poured herself another glass of wine (it was French, I'm almost certain) and sipped it steadily as she jabbed her pencil, like a bird catching insects, at the items on her list. She came to a magic word and the sipping and jabbing stopped. 'Caviar,' said Lenina Andreevna in a conspiratorial voice. 'Professor Z has promised to get me three jars by Thursday. Best grade! He says he can get black olives too.'

Asta, slouching on the Turkish carpet at her mother's shoeless but pleasantly scented feet, merely raised her fine black eyebrows slightly, so Lenina went on, in a more matter-of-fact tone, 'Sour cabbage, smoked fish, salted cucumber, no problem. I'll make the dumplings the night before. Drinks – champagne, vodka, wine, beer, no problem. Flowers – ah – we haven't decided on the flowers.'

'I told you, Mummy, paint dried leaves and grasses silver and hang them from the ceiling,' said Asta, yawning irritably.

'But, darling, you can't beat fresh flowers. Chrysanthemums, for instance.' Lenina's rather protuberant brown eyes became hooded and saintlike. 'Cool and curly and crisp and smelling of freshly chopped wood. Darling Volodya, he filled the dacha with them for our honeymoon – everywhere was *swimming* in them – purple, bronze, yellow . . .'

'You've forgotten our colour-scheme, Mummy,' Asta scolded. 'Red and silver – remember? Yellow chrysanthemums would absolutely wreck it!'

Lenina had opened her eyes; she was admiring the handsome, angular blaze of her daughter's face – like a painting by Modigliani.

'All right, dear,' she said soothingly, 'I'll leave the flowers to you.'

'And you will wear your red kimono, won't you, Mummy?' Asta persisted. She had by now woken up completely; she sat bolt upright and her usually lazy, drawling voice was animated though her gestures remained stiff, puppetlike. 'And let me do your makeup – I've got the most wonderful idea. You ought to have red shoes, too, *and* black stockings.'

'I don't think – ' Lenina Andreevna began.

Asta interrupted her. 'Oh yes, Mummy, they'd be perfect – and I think I know how to get hold of some.'

Lenina decided to assert herself. 'It isn't a matter of life or death, you know. It's the people who count, after all. They're the main ingredient of a party. And the most unpredictable.' She drained her wine glass; Asta obligingly filled it for her, and she continued, 'Of course I like them like that. Of any privileges I may have, the privilege of having interesting friends is by far the most precious. These people are my art, Asta, darling! To cherish their individuality, to foster their creativity, at the same time gently restraining it from getting out of hand and landing them in trouble – that's as delicate and difficult and rewarding a thing as your painting, darling. I understand them so well – of course; I was a rebel, too, before I met your father.'

'Isn't it funny, Mummy,' said Asta, with a shrewd, ironical look, 'that a rebel should have a name like Lenina?'

'Well, of course, not a *real* rebel – not even before I met Volodya. I always had a sense of duty to my country. Mother and Father made certain of that!'

'Mamochka, d'you think they deliberately *planned* it so you'd be born on 22 April?' Asta made round, innocent eyes at her mother, then modestly studied the carpet.

'I'm sure they did, as far as it's possible to plan such things. they were genuine revolutionary idealists,' said Lenina earnestly, ignoring her daughter's sudden high-pitched giggle. 'You don't remember them, do you? They were teachers – we've always been teachers in our family, since long before the Revolution. More's the pity for me.'

'I don't know why you hated teaching so much, Mummy. I love telling people what to do.'

'But, darling, that's not real teaching. Real teaching is teaching people to think for themselves . . . It can't be done any more, of course. That's why I switched from literature to language. You can still teach facts – grammar, syntax, punctuation. But I'll tell you something interesting; it isn't just our students that are conformist. Last year the Americans were telling me that it was the devil's own job to get their literature students to think independently and not follow some fashionable line of rebellion. Blue jeans, long hair and J. D. Salinger – they're all obsessed with a writer called J. D. Salinger, apparently. It's probably the same with the British.'

'I hope the British won't break all our glasses, Mummy.' Asta twinkled maliciously.

'You mean you hope they do! Well now, back to business.' Lenina turned the page of her notebook. 'Replies. How many definites have we got? The guests of honour, of course. Professor N and Doctor P – he can't stand crowds and will go home early, with any luck. I suppose I'll have to ask Doctor G as well. Then there's Professor Z. Did you know he was working on a satirical novel? Fascinating man . . . Well, that ties up the university. Family – only Rina and Uncle Bobo and your Steva . . .'

'You don't call Steva family, do you?' said Asta scathingly. 'I'll probably have ditched him by next week!'

'Really?' Lenina gave her daughter a sharp look. 'I thought he was such a nice young man. Now, let's see. Lev. Marvellous, he'll be able to amuse the British if nobody else can. Arkady Petrovich, yes, of course!'

'Arkasha!' snorted Asta, tossing her black hair. 'Every year you invite him and Tanya, and every year he arrives without Tanya and with some dopey girlfriend.'

Lenina smiled. 'Well, it's difficult for him. Tanya doesn't exactly get on with intellectual types, does she? And she can't stand to be in the same room as Lev, specially when he's rattling on in a language she hardly understands one word of, while Arkady doubles up with laughter. They should never have married: I always told him it wouldn't work. A more artistic type would have suited him much better.'

Asta's vivid colour darkened a shade. 'You shouldn't encourage him to be unfaithful though,' she muttered priggishly.

'I don't! I'm always scolding him about it,' cried Lenina. 'But he's completely incorrigible. And maybe it's for the best if their marriage does break up – best for him and Tanya too.' Lenina was staring thoughtfully at her daughter's hot face. 'He's a wonderful poet, anyway; we have to forgive him.'

'We certainly do not! That's romantic twaddle!' said Asta violently.

'Well, perhaps. Now, back to the party. Ilya, yes. Ilya's band – I can't remember their names but there are three of them, right?' Lenina made three small ticks. 'Maurice, yes. Rivka Simonovna, mm, perhaps.'

'Rivka who?'

'I hope she'll manage to come,' said Lenina musingly. 'You know who Rivka is, I told you. My best graduate – then she goes and applies for an exit visa and makes herself unemployable, silly little girl.'

'Oh yes, teacher's pet!' Asta knitted her fine black brows.

Lenina ignored her. 'Actually I'm curious to see how she'll hit it off with Ilya,' she said confidingly. 'Of course they'll clash, they're as different as fire and water, on the surface. But deep down they might just spark each other off in a big way. He might even persuade her to withdraw her application.'

'Mother, you're such a schemer! I suppose you want her back in the Language Department.'

Lenina smiled. 'You know me so well, darling. But it'd be tricky, very tricky.' She brooded over her list again. 'No reply yet from Bella, Andrei or Bulat. I suppose I'll have to chase up Bulat. I must have at least one great writer to show off to the Brits.'

'They've probably never heard of him.' Asta got up from the rug, yawning. 'I'm sleepy, I don't know how you can drink wine and stay awake.' She stretched her excellent body like a ballerina and pranced on tiptoes to the door.

'Practice, darling,' said Lenina.

Asta paused. 'I wonder what Daddy would think of all these parties. And all these people. D'you think he'd say we were betraying his ideals?'

Lenina looked at her daughter uneasily. She flushed slightly. 'My parties have nothing to do with politics. It's a social, cultural, *aesthetic* thing. For me, a party's a work of art, mixing the people's like weaving a tapestry, so of course I have to have different colours. Anyway,' she went on, 'it's a great Russian tradition, a great Russian art. We owe it to socialism to keep such an art alive!'

When Asta, yawning assent, had closed the door softly behind her, Lenina Andreevna stood up and, after all, did find her balance slightly unsteady.

'Socialism with style, that's what we need. We can build communism but still have beautiful architecture, can't we, Volodichka?' She spoke to her husband in a whisper, seeing him exactly as he must have looked the moment before he collapsed in the snow outside the Big House in Djersinskaya Square. He had been smiling and talking to his colleagues at one minute, dying the next. And he looked so strong and fit and rosy in his grey coat with the snow-speckled fur collar (how she had loved to bury her cheeks and fingers in that collar) and his ear flaps raised to show wisps of tender, boyish, fair hair.

Oh Volodya, Volodya, dead at only forty-nine!

She sat down again, and quickly swallowed another glass of wine. She forgot about Volodya and began to think about beautiful architecture. She raised the bottle high and let the last drops trickle slowly between her lips. She had closed her eyes, the better to see her vision of the ideal – a mirage, confused and seductive, in which swam the Turkish rug, the red velvet curtains, her kimono, her Chinese jar, little, dimpled, gilded putti from heaven knows where, twisty towers, golden domes and a distant, tall whiteness that was the Parthenon.

Outside the window, an office block ordered by Comrade Stalin and a lamppost erected at approximately the same time stared into the room as if they saw the mirage too, and wished to unite in condemning it.

We all live in a yellow submarine

Writing those last pages, I discovered the honesty of fiction. At first, I was confident that I was bringing a great deal of imagination to play on the characters of Lenina Andreevna and her daughter; then I began to suspect I was telling all kinds of little truths. And when I read it through, I was certain of one thing at least: my desire to be the object of the real-life Asta's sexual interest. I had to stop writing, I was so irritated and fascinated. It was as if I had stirred a pool of clear water and suddenly suffused it with the secrets, the dark excitements, of its rich and muddy depths. The prospect of the party became both more interesting and more alarming.

I dreamed of making an entrance, of declaring myself instantly, by my sheer presence, a young man of talent. I dreamed (I admit it) of a parrot on my shoulder, a velvet cloak or a Don Giovanni hat with a snowy plume. Naturally, these are not the usual props to be found in a Soviet citizen's wardrobe. I poked about frantically in mine. At last, in order both to calm myself down and to impress on Tanya the sobriety and officiality of an occasion which once again enforced my departure, I chose the suit I usually wear to work and a pale, very pale, green shirt.

I have a nervous habit, whenever I'm on my way to some out-of-the-ordinary social event, of taking the slowest and most tortuous route. I add extra streets, an extra block or two, even, when desperate, an extra few stops on the metro. Having arrived – as I somehow eventually do – at the fateful door, I hold up my head and stroll carelessly past. There are various targets, my watch tells me, that I must fulfil first – such as reaching a certain set of traffic lights or distant tree – before I enter. All this nonsense started once when I arrived at a party so early that no one else was there – to the dismay of both my timid young hostess and myself. But I admit I've taken the ploy too far, and now carefully make myself late even when I'm late already.

Everything, needless to say, was in full swing when I arrived, dampened and tousled by my long detour through the night winds of autumn. Lenina Andreevna greeted me in a flurry of silk and scent and exasperation. She wasn't wearing her red kimono but something gold and one-sidedly draped to reveal a plump shoulder and the deep pucker of a vaccination scar. 'Asta,' she cried, as if, like Igorevich, she had been peeking at my notes, or as if the words were in my eyes now instead of on the page, 'Asta, the little wretch, has run off to the theatre with a new boyfriend – an avant-garde film director, would you believe?' She'd be back soon – she'd certainly better be back soon if she knew what was good for her, the little imp – but in the meantime I must come and meet the guests of honour. Lenina Andreevna's heavily braceleted hand gripped mine, lifted it high, and danced me through the crowd like a puppet. People fell back and stared at our progress (Professor Z actually giggled and pointed his finger at me) so my entrance was not negligible, after all, and I thought longingly of the bare, windy, anonymous stretch of Akademikov Street I might have been casually strolling for the fifth time.

Miss Robinson and Miss Tressel were standing side by side, looking cheerfully bemused. They had almost identical brass-buttoned blue suits and almost identical busbies of fluffy grey curls, and they sipped their Crimean champagne and goggled at me as if I had been a Martian – yet another. I admit that I too felt the universe to be subtly altered – everything was so bright (even after one glass), so noisy, so spacious and full of eyes. 'Isn't the food wonderful and doesn't Lenina Andreevna look lovely?' was the breathless refrain of the ladies as they sipped and pecked, while the third member of the delegation nodded his head in time to their sugary music and concentrated on feeding his wrinkled parchment jaw from the plate of sour cabbage with which Lev, flushed and obsequious, had just presented him. He was clearly not to be hurried; but when at last the jaw was sufficiently appeased, Dr Edward Lamb became all charm and attentiveness. He questioned us in detail about our work on the *Literary Star*, his mind as keen and darting as his yellowish eyes (by the look of him he was at least seventy), his Russian elegant. Cruelly ignoring Lev's groans of disappointment, I steered the conversation towards poetry. Dr Lamb recited the opening stanzas of *Eugene*

Onegin most creditably, after which I tested his knowledge of more recent literary history with some Mayakovsky which he recognised at once and countered with a passage from Yevtushenko's *Babi Yar*. During this performance, Lev, Miss Tressel and Miss Robinson were rescued and hustled away by an agitated Lenina to meet the newly arrived famous person (or, rather, very famous person; all of us there were at least slightly famous). I was about to pitch in with some verses of my own when, politely but forcefully, Dr Lamb interrupted me. 'Do you speak excellent English like your friend?' he asked.

Of course I was delighted to tell him, in English, that I had studied the language, both inside and outside academia, for the last sixteen years and how privileged I felt myself to be in sharing the great literary heritage. 'This royal throne of kings, this sceptred Isle,' I began, as Dr Lamb nodded his long head, gobbled up a last mouthful of cabbage and shot needly glances around the room. 'I'm looking for my daughter,' he explained. 'Oh, there she is. Elizabeth!'

She was examining a vase on one of Lenina Andreevna's shelves with a minute and, I supposed, not very sincere interest. There was a leaf-shaped clip in her hair which sparkled as she turned, a shy, neat schoolgirl in a loose-hanging rust-coloured dress with puffed sleeves. I noticed now that several more clips were doing their best to restrain the fine, wheat-coloured, somehow coltish hair that wafted round her shoulders. A daughter, so young, so light and pale – how could such an old man? I took her hand, which was cold and unmarked as a pearl. I was astonished to hear her father saying that she was a philosophy student at university; I really had considered her to be about fourteen.

'So have you come here to study?' I asked, suddenly absurdly self-conscious about my English (I even hesitated over the verb 'to study,' and very nearly made it reflexive).

'Oh no, I've just come for a few days' holiday before term starts. I like Moscow,' she added, 'it's very interesting.'

'So how do you like Moscow?' The inane question had rushed out before I could retrieve it. 'Apart from its being very interesting,' I went on, making desperate efforts. 'Have you been to the Kremlin Gardens, for example? They're especially beautiful at this time of year.'

Elizabeth, looking worried, was explaining that she was afraid she hadn't, when my peripheral vision, always highly alert when I am embarrassed, warned me that Luba had arrived, and that she was accompanied by someone small and navy blue. Meanwhile, Ilya, still strapped to his guitar and looking ferociously romantic, was weaving about with an empty beer glass somewhere in our vicinity.

I decided to abandon my role of walking guide book and get down to serious conversation while there was still time.

'Do you enjoy your philosophical studies? Who's your favourite philosopher?' I hoped it would be someone I had at least heard of, and preferably knew something about – Plato, Schopenhauer, Bertrand Russell . . . She hesitated.

'I don't like any of them much. I find it really, really difficult to concentrate on abstract ideas for more than five minutes. Even for two minutes,' she amended candidly. 'And I hate logic, it's like algebra – really, really boring!'

There were pink, passionate flames on her cheeks, and I had to smile. 'In that case I won't introduce you to Professor Z. Look, over there. He's Professor of Logic at Moscow University.'

Elizabeth glanced anxiously over her shoulder and shuddered slightly. 'No, I don't want to meet him. Did you study with him?'

'No, no,' I reassured her, 'I did literature and languages.'

'I wish I'd taken English literature.' Elizabeth sighed. 'It was always my favourite subject at school.'

Words of approbation and delight were bubbling up in me when I was enveloped by a familiar scent cloud and a bare arm crawled around my waist.

'The young ladies you invited are here,' hissed Lenina Andreevna importantly in my ear. 'They want a word with you.'

'What young ladies?' I hissed back in alarm.

'You should know. They say you invited them. I'm merely the hostess! So come and talk to them, you wicked boy!'

I groaned and grimaced, apologised to Elizabeth (who was at least gratifyingly amused by my facial antics) and allowed myself to be escorted away. Ilya stepped obligingly into my place. He bowed low to Elizabeth, strummed a chord and began to serenade her with 'We all live in a yellow submarine'. I promised myself to strangle him at the first opportunity.

'Arkady Petrovich, Maria Borisovna,' announced my ex-mistress formally, and a girl whose head came no higher than Luba's narrow waist stepped up in a smart, frisky, jokey way like a clockwork soldier.

'Please call me Boba, everyone does!'

'Hello, Boba.' I forced a bright tone. 'Did I invite you?'

'No, Luba did.' Boba continued to grin like a cut melon.

'Boba's from Irkutsk,' said Luba, in a vague attempt to urge on the conversation.

'Hello, Boba-from-Irkutsk!' We grinned at each other inanely.

Luba frowned at the note of satire – but how else could I respond? Boba was so small and quaint and comical with her moon face and Mongolian eyes and chopped-to-the-ears brown hair, her dainty little voice and toothy grin, her technician's dungarees and the row of pens stuffed into her breast pocket.

'But I live in Moscow now. I'm doing a radiography course at Luba's clinic. You're a writer, aren't you? I write a bit too, journalistic pieces mostly, in fact I was hoping . . .'

I have not quite advanced beyond the stage of feeling gratified if someone calls me 'a writer', but, on the other hand, I am not so inexperienced that the smile doesn't glaze on my lips when that person goes on to add that he or she wants to be a writer, or indeed *is* a bit of a writer, too. Involuntarily, I found myself backing away: I caught the words 'feminist' and 'journal', and also the look of disappointment that momentarily turned down the edges of Boba's plump, candid little mouth (her eyes were black glints of sly, oriental profundity, but the Slav mouth could sulk and grin and twist and surely kiss with the best). At the same time a hand had fallen onto my shoulder like a huge leaf, a rosy-ebony hand with pale pink fingernails. Although I can guiltlessly deny my presence to aspiring writers, I feel a deeper sense of responsibility towards my fellow workers from the developing nations. So I let Maurice guide me with his weighty, undeniable, African hand away from these girlish intensities and excitements, and off we drifted on the turbulent, twisting river of party time that was now the Nile, reflecting the vivid jungle flowers of Maurice's shirt and the sinewy jungle trees of his bare arms.

But, though externally caught up in these eddies of party space, I was inwardly detached. I didn't even care that Luba would never pretend to let me pursue her again. I had formed the image of a little, peaceful, sandy island, and I clung to it while the waves rolled over and round me: it was a boat, a life belt, a straw, an oyster shell, a yellow submarine, a rust-coloured dress.

I watched the reel move faster, heard the soundtrack bang out echoes: Maurice, who had vanished from my side a few minutes earlier, now a great deal more blurry in outline as he waves his arms and shouts belated charges of imperialism at Jean-Paul the Parisian; Lev dancing something like a tango with Miss Tressel: Ilya's imitation of Elvis Presley; a girl called Keloway who says she used to be married to the Moscow correspondent of the *Dublin Times*: Miss Robinson telling me her address twice in a loud voice and saying I must visit her whenever I come to Birmingham; Lev almost crying because of something Miss Tressel, Linda, has said about Roger McGough; Rivka Simonovna singing resoundingly in Hebrew; Keloway soothing Maurice by unbuttoning his shirt and putting it on herself; Miss Tressel reciting 'The Inchcape Rock'; Dr Lamb proposing a toast to Solzhenitsyn; Asta phoning to say she'll be very late; Ilya's impersonation of Tom Jones; Lenina Andreevna sobbing that she is husbandless, daughterless and unloved; Luba telling me that there are more important things in the world than sex (and storming out); me wondering if I have inadvertently made a pass at her; little Boba staring back at me with her anxious melon grin as she follows Luba through the door.

And I rose and fell and rolled with the tide of events, drowning perhaps, or already drowned, but keeping the image of a sweet, sandy island in my head, confident that I would reach it eventually, without even trying.

I woke up sitting on a bench in the Kremlin Gardens, in bright lunchtime sunlight. At first I didn't know where I was. I had a blazing headache. I looked at my watch, jumped to my feet and then sat down again, my heart racing. A girl in jeans and a black velvet jacket was walking towards me. Her hair flickered like summer lightning.

'I'm not late, am I?' said Elizabeth.

So we did have a date, I wasn't dreaming. 'Your timing's perfect.' I shook her hand and dared to keep it for a moment.

Smiling, self-possessed, she perched on the bench beside me. 'Only the tsar's family was allowed to come here once, but now everyone can enjoy it,' she said in an approving but somehow official voice – she was probably quoting her guide book.

I nodded and rubbed my eyes and my aching forehead. Why were there so many people around – had we brought the party with us? No, these people were sadder and somehow smaller and more earthy, trudging with their children and dogs through the untidy autumn shrubbery of brown beech and green azaleas.

Elizabeth suddenly nudged me. 'Look who's here!' I turned: so we had brought the party with us, or some of it. Lev, accompanied by the stately Luba and her two little lubas – tiny, scrawny girls with fluttering red curls and bare, pale legs – was strolling down the path with a broad smile. Plump as a wood pigeon in his freshly pressed party suit and silver-weave tie, he bounced himself onto the bench next to Elizabeth, gathered up her hand as carefully as he'd gather mushrooms, and placed it to his lips.

'How utterly charming to see you again,' he said in his upper-class voice, 'this is the life, eh, what? How's your head?' he added to me in Russian.

'Not bad at all.' And this was true, oddly enough: although I had felt so terrible five minutes ago, I now found myself completely rehabilitated.

At once we all began to boast how well we felt. It was imperative, we agreed, that we should carry on the party spirit and do something to entertain our English guest.

'What would you like to do?' Lev asked Elizabeth.

She blushed. 'I don't mind. Only not sightseeing, I'm going to have rather a lot of that next week.'

'I know, then, let's go back to my place,' said Lev. 'Ma and Pa won't be there, they've gone to the country for a few days. We can have a bite to eat and a swallow of something, and after that go on to Ilya's.' He patted my arm. 'Is that all right with you, Arkashka? Will

Tanichka let you off the hook again?'

I frowned; I didn't want to think about Tanya. I had invented a continuing work crisis to cover myself and avoid giving her pain and that was that: for a while, she didn't exist.

'No problem at all,' I said.

Luba looked at me severely. 'It's out for me. I've got to cook for Borya and the kiddies.'

She called the girls, who had been hunting quarrelsomely for beechnuts and acorns. We walked together to the gate. 'I might manage to drop in for half an hour later this afternoon,' said Luba thoughtfully. 'I'll try. But don't wait for me after six.'

'Husband problems?' Lev asked, after she'd gone, and winked.

Lev had all of Elizabeth's attention as we walked down towards the bridge. She seemed to find his English impersonations hilarious. I was mildly piqued: I had wanted her to myself, and yet there was a kind of security in his presence. I was half in love with Elizabeth and half terrified. She wasn't a real girl but a goddess, and there is always a mortal danger of offending the gods. I had a peculiar feeling she might suddenly just disappear. She was out of her element in this coarse world. Maybe I had only imagined her.

At the same time I felt a ravenous hunger for *her* world. It wasn't just that I wanted her physically, though of course I did: I wanted her past, her dreams, her whole mental life. I wanted to bury my face in her hair both because it was beautiful and because I wanted to know what English hair smelled like (I imagined grass). I wanted to fly away with her when her plane rose above Moscow and turned west.

Not really, of course. But if only I could establish just a little bit of validity, of Truth, to our relationship! Then it wouldn't just disappear when she went back to London; we'd both have a little souvenir of each other to keep.

It's the same when you write the kind of story or poem that no one must ever read. You're asserting that something of yourself has a life outside history and society – perhaps what old-fashioned people mean by the Soul. That piece of yourself, never corrupted by being made public, will live for ever.

So I was terrified that day – and almost wild with hope. For the first time in my life the broad streets and tall buildings and even taller sky of my native city did not make me feel insignificant: on the contrary, my small human flame was capable of leaping to twice their height.

It was another windy day. The wind loves grand architecture: a plain of tarmac to sweep across, a block of concrete against which to sharpen itself, and Elizabeth, though laughing, looked scared and small as it beat at her jacket and tossed her hair like a piece of the sun it had broken off to play with. I told her I was afraid she'd blow away (it wasn't a joke, the wind seemed to me to be rehearsing the laws of aerodynamics) and caught gently hold of her arm. It was the first time I had touched her, apart from shaking her hand. She laughed, and allowed her elbow to nest in my palm.

We crossed to the other side of the river. The wind had dropped and the sky was lilac as we walked through the Simonovsky district where Lev's parents lived. I felt something menacing in these narrower streets, a force more crushing than that of those great buildings which openly displayed their power. Here, power crept and snarled and pounced. I'd never felt such a thing before; it was as if I'd caught some electric tremor from Elizabeth. A sudden gabble of voices; we were passing the entry of a drab thirties block of flats where three men crouched in the shadows, sharing their half litre from a single paper cup. Their eyes glared at us out of the darkness and one called after us, 'Go on, playboys, get lost!' I tightened my grip on Elizabeth's arm. We would soon turn the corner and then she would know that Lev also belonged to these dreary blocks. As we climbed the unlit stairs and sniffed the dank, cabbagy air I convinced myself that she hated us for bringing her here.

I had been in Lev's kitchen many times before, of course; it was not very different from my own. But now I could see with absolute clarity how drab, untidy and even ugly everything was. The cupboards looked rickety and home-made. Exposed pipes crept around the walls. Battered knives, ladles and other odd bits of equipment hung on nails, and from each nail trickled a thin rust streak. The lace-patterned oilcloth on the dining table was pocked with little burn holes.

Lev was innocent of his surroundings. He bustled happily with plates of salted cucumber, radishes and glasses. The bottle came out of the refrigerator white with frost. He put one of the little glasses in front of Elizabeth. 'What are you doing? She can't drink vodka on its own,' I said angrily. 'Haven't you got anything to mix it with?'

'No, I haven't.' Lev looked crestfallen. 'But ask her, maybe it's all right as it is – with a snack?'

'Can you drink this stuff on its own?' I said.

'Could I have it with lime, please? Or orange would be fine if you haven't got lime.'

'What's *lime*?' muttered Lev to me.

I hated Elizabeth at that moment. 'Whatever it is, you haven't got it,' I said.

'Maybe I could borrow some mineral water from Mitya,' he suggested, brightening.

'Would mineral water be OK, Elizabeth?'

'Yes, fine.' Elizabeth looked anxious. 'I'm sorry to have put him to so much trouble,' she said, as he clattered up the stairs to the flat above.

'He doesn't mind at all.' We sat in awkward silence.

'His parents must be very poor,' murmured Elizabeth, peering at her fingernails. I didn't know what to say: the Ivanovs were certainly no poorer than Tanya and I. 'What do they do for a living?'

'His father's a chauffeur. His mother's a cleaner, I think, in a school somewhere.' I lowered my voice. 'We needn't stay here much longer, if you don't want to.'

'But I do,' said Elizabeth enthusiastically. 'It's really, really fascinating to see how the ordinary workers live!'

'We're all ordinary workers in the USSR,' I told her with a grin.

'Are you?' She looked perplexed. 'I didn't think that Lenina lady was very ordinary.'

Lev bounced in. 'He's got some lemons! Can you drink it with lemon juice?' Elizabeth said she could, though I was doubtful. Lev, on his knees, fumbled at the back of the store cupboard and brought out a small tin of meat. 'It's a deal,' he said to me in Russian. 'Six lemons for some sausage-filling – not bad?'

'Not bad,' I agreed. 'Tanya says there hasn't been a lemon in the shops for months.'

'Ask no questions.' Lev grinned. 'He's got a whole boxful under the bed!' He hurried out again.

'What did he say?' asked Elizabeth anxiously.

'No problem! He's fetching the lemons. Let me get you another glass, that one's going to be too small.'

Elizabeth's Moscow night

The first toasts were gulped, and the kitchen gradually lost its squalor and became cosy. Elizabeth looked flushed and happy. She had taken off her black jacket and was no longer shy. Lev and I hopped round her like pigeons, bickering over whatever crumbs of fine, white London bread she could feed us.

Pubs, tea bags, the Thames, Sebastian College, nasty Dr Stewart and crazy Professor Somebody who took something called LSD and tried to fly from the top of the cyclorama, broke both legs and has since been suspended. Lev had heard of LSD, but we were both baffled by the cyclorama. A kind of tower with murals of London going all round the walls, said Elizabeth, and giggled when I asked if it was the latest thing. Victorian, she said, like everything else in Plato Park, including the regime at Seb Col.

Plato Park, Plato's *Republic*, the Queen, the weather, Chinese take-aways and a socialist government. We strained our brains to imagine it all, particularly this last. Gamely, Lev took on the task of explaining to Elizabeth that a bourgeois democracy cannot, *ipso facto*, be socialist. Elizabeth looked sad, so I changed the subject and told her how much I liked her jeans. Lev, of course, knows all about jeans – etymologically, at least. He was earnestly explaining 'gene fustian' and '*serge de Nîmes*' when the doorbell chimed.

It was Luba, self-consciously chic in a black jacket not much inferior to Elizabeth's, a black plastic handbag with a sparkling clasp swung over her shoulder. She was in a good mood, I saw to my relief, not disposed to cast meaningful frowns at me or make pious remarks about her marriage. Lev was attentive to her, and at last I could talk properly with Elizabeth. Everything was going smoothly, till Luba murmured something to Elizabeth and got to her feet.

'We want to have a private word,' she announced.

'Go ahead. You know where the bedroom is. Just leave us the bottle,' said Lev cheerfully. 'Shout if you need our protection, Elizabeth!'

Luba looked at him witheringly. 'It's not *your* protection she needs.' She took Elizabeth's arm. 'We won't be a minute.'

'Women's solidarity,' said Lev with a grin when they'd gone.

I didn't think it was a matter for grinning. I was convinced that Luba wanted to warn Elizabeth what an old ram I was. They would leave together in a blaze of self-righteousness, and I'd never see Elizabeth again.

'It's a character assassination, I'm afraid.'

'Nonsense, old chap! Luba's not malicious, you ought to know that. She probably wants to buy some clothes off her or change some money. You'll be all right with Elizabeth, I can tell she likes you. Really; you've got it on a plate if you want it. And if you don't there's others as do!'

'You're so crude sometimes, Lyovka!'

'I'm just being honest. You're keen, aren't you?'

'Of course.'

'Well, then, listen to me.' Always benign, Lev after a few drinks is sunlike, a beaming, radiant life force. 'After they've finished in the other room, we'll all go on to Ilya's. I'll give you the key to this flat' – he lowered his voice – 'and you and the kid can leave early and come back here. I'll hang on at Ilya's for a couple of hours. Fair enough? But listen, don't forget to leave the key with Mitya when you go.' He gestured towards the ceiling. 'Mitya's OK. But don't be too late – he goes to bed about twelve.' He slipped the front-door key into my palm. 'Go on, put it away, they're coming back.'

'You're a friend.'

'You'd do the same for me. If only Luba . . .'

They came in together, looking contentedly inscrutable. Two tall, strange, secretive girls from opposite ends of the earth, divided in almost every experience except that of being pursued and misunderstood by men. (Of course, we try to understand them, and maybe it's mostly their fault that we don't.)

Luba shook hands with Elizabeth and kissed her lightly and quickly on the cheek. Her goodbyes to Lev and me were more casual. To my great relief, Elizabeth sat down at the table. She was smiling; she obviously knew nothing of my ramishness and caddishness, though these qualities, even to myself, are indisputably mine.

A blue cigarette haze and a scratchy, subdued moaning of saxophones floated up to us as we filed down the narrow stairs to Ilya's cavern. But the scene inside was disappointing – no live music, lots of empty tables.

Ilya greeted us with a gloomy smile. The militia had dropped in last week, two nights in a row. They'd tapped their feet in time to the music, sent the band bits of paper with scribbled requests for Beatles and Stones numbers, and warned Ilya that his was a charmed life, he'd better not put a foot wrong. It didn't mean anything, probably, but it had been enough to frighten off a number of the regulars and generally dampen the atmosphere.

Ilya was downcast: he'd have liked Elizabeth to see the place at its best. 'Have you ever been to the real Cavern, in Liverpool?' he asked her anxiously, fearing an unfavourable comparison. But Elizabeth hadn't; she said she didn't know for sure but it may have closed down by now. Ilya smiled wryly. 'You can tell them when you get back it's moved to Moscow. We haven't closed down – not yet!'

I decided that the place was fine, half-empty. I even liked the old gramophone music. I drew Elizabeth towards a secluded corner table for two.

'Hey, Arkasha, that's not fair,' called Ilya.

'Leave them alone. They want to have a serious conversation.' Lev draped his arm over Ilya's disappointed shoulders. They moved off in the direction of two girls who were sitting by themselves, playing cards: one of them, I think, was Rivka Simonovna. I took from my pocket a small bottle which I had accidentally forgotten to relinquish at Lenina Andreevna's party. I put it to my lips, then held it out to Elizabeth. If she takes it, I thought, I'll know she really likes me.

'Cognac. It's good stuff,' I said. Elizabeth took the bottle, sniffed it cautiously and drank.

We must have spent more than an hour over that small bottle. But it's hard to tell; drink and desire do strange things to time, stretching it out wide as the universe, or rolling it up to a tiny silver pearl of mercury. Tonight, the pearl rolled away before we realised. We drained the last of the cognac and licked our sticky lips. 'I'm so thirsty,' sighed Elizabeth.

'Let's go and find some cups of coffee,' I said. For some reason, we found the phrase hilarious, and snatched at imaginary floating coffee cups as we stumbled up the stairs, almost crying with laughter. As we staggered out into the blue-black night, Elizabeth swayed against me, giggling. 'I can't think what Daddy will say if I go back to the hotel like this!'

The sky had opened up above the square; it had a rosy light in it, and dozens of stars. We stopped as the big, gold-rimmed clock began to chime.

'Where can we get our coffee?' Elizabeth asked.

At that moment, a chequered door sailed past us. 'Over there, come on!' The taxi had pulled up, and a happy crowd of drunks was pouring out of it. The driver shouted after them about their unruly behaviour. He looked at us meanly as we approached, about to put his foot down and speed off.

'Please, comrade, don't go without us. My friend's a visitor from England. Her father fought with us against the German fascists. He won a medal for bravery!'

Seeing I was in earnest, the driver calmed down.

'That's a fine thing, yes. Where are you going?'

I gave him Lev's address.

'Where are we going?' asked Elizabeth.

'To find some coffee!'

'But where? Is anywhere still open?'

'Very nice peoples,' remarked the driver, straining to get a good view of Elizabeth. 'Very nice English peoples, yes.'

'Don't worry, I know just the place.'

'The Russians are very nice too,' mumbled Elizabeth without conviction.

'I thought Lev might have got back by now. Never mind, let's make ourselves at home. I'll do the coffee. Why don't you go and take a look at his book collection. He's got hundreds of English books – they were his uncle Misha's. Uncle Misha used to teach English in a boarding school in Cornwall. Maybe you know it? I can't remember what it was called, now.'

I babbled on as I rummaged in the cupboard for the tin of coffee I was almost certain not to find.

'They must have run out. We'd better have tea instead. Is that OK? I'll light the samovar.'

I lit the gas and put the kettle on. A look of disappointment had momentarily passed across Elizabeth's face: a small shadow, followed by a pale smile.

'Is anything the matter?'

'No. I've got a headache, though, after all the brandy.'

'You should lie down for a bit. Go on, I'll bring the tea when it's ready.'

I flavoured it with the fragrant lemon shells that Lev had carefully saved, and rinsed the grime from an old tin tray I found under the sink. The bedroom was in darkness when I went in, though faintly lit by the lights of the opposite flats coming through the uncurtained window. There was a musty but not unpleasant smell from the stacks of old books. Elizabeth had stretched out on Lev's divan.

'Are you asleep?'

'No, I'm looking at that shadow on the wall.'

It was a cross-shaped shadow, cast by two entangled coat hangers that dangled from the curtain rail.

'It reminded me of that poem in *Dr Zhivago*. D'you know the one?'

I handed her the tea, and crouched beside her on the edge of the divan. 'No, I'm afraid I don't. I've never read *Dr Zhivago*.'

'Oh, but you must. It's really, really wonderful.'

'I'm sure it is, but you see, it's not published here. We're not allowed to read books that denounce the Revolution.'

She peered at me to see if I was being ironical. 'I didn't realise. Oh dear, how ridiculous!'

'D'you think so?' I asked lightly.

'I'm sorry, I didn't mean to offend you,' she said quickly.

'You didn't. It may well be ridiculous – how can I tell until I've read it?'

'It's a whole vision, really,' Elizabeth went on. 'I think it's an attempt to see everything and not make judgements. After all, however good something is – like the Revolution – it's such a drastic change that some people are bound to suffer. Nothing's really black or really white!'

Everything is here, I thought. I imagined England, and the greeny greyness which is the essence of England and Englishness drifting over everything – the buildings, the people, the countryside – like fog. And then it lifted and there were all kinds of pale, shining colours I'd never seen before, and I plunged my hands into them like a child into a heap of New Year toys.

I found myself listening to a small, songlike voice: the candle on the table burned, the candle burned.

All great poetry has that feeling of inevitability. I knew at once I had been robbed. 'It's beautiful, go on,' I said, when the voice tailed off.

'I'm not very good at memorising. But there's something about a draught, it blows the candle flame and the flame divides, sort of. Yes, I remember: like the heat of temptation, it forms two wings in the shape of a cross.'

'The heat of temptation – that's good,' I said, and touched Elizabeth's hair, calming myself, losing my sense of loss in the warm strands.

Hair's supposed to be dead, I thought, yet it's always warm, even at the tips.

I suddenly felt anxious, guilty about my own manipulativeness. In my pocket lay Lev's key and my wedding ring, wrapped in a handkerchief for safekeeping. I was too slick, too banal; Elizabeth deserved something better, or didn't she?

It wasn't as if she was completely inexperienced. She'd told me she'd had boyfriends, one of them serious. She came from a decadent society where girls could have sex with the same freedom as men . . . If she hadn't wanted something to happen, she wouldn't have got into the taxi with me . . .

I stood up. 'It's getting late, Elizabeth. I think you ought to go back.'

I walked over to the window, astounded and bitterly disappointed with myself. First one of the lights in the opposite flats went out, then another. They're all going to bed, I thought enviously, all drifting away to their wedded or unwedded bliss. Then I turned round. Elizabeth was holding out her arms to me.

'Not just yet. Daddy won't expect me till quite late. I'm not a schoolgirl, you know.'

I turned quickly back to the window and closed the curtains, obliterating the shadow that had grown fainter with every bedtime, turning everything to shadow.

How I almost became a parasite

I didn't go to work the following morning, Tanya, Mother, Masha and Vasya tried various methods of getting me out of bed – mostly unsubtle, and stopping just short of assault and battery. I remained obstinately comatose and, one by one, they drifted away, except for Vasya, who has no other duties in life to attend to, unfortunately. He devotedly set himself to massaging my chest with his claws, purring all the while like a pneumatic drill. At one point, I dislodged him and telephoned the office, but nobody answered. So I went back to bed, and indulged myself in the pleasing idea that an epidemic of lovesick hangovers was raging through Moscow, and that all my colleagues – even Igor Igorevich – were similarly prostrated.

It was after midday when I finally dragged myself out of doors. In love or not, hungover or not, my fellow citizens were working. Not merely working, but demonstrating the work ethic, I should say, with twice their customary zeal. My vague, headachy euphoria began to wilt. If Vasya's purrs had resounded in my sensitised membranes like pneumatic drills, imagine what real pneumatic drills sounded like, as they bounced in unison outside the Lenin Library. Construction workers shouted, cement mixers churned, rooftops echoed with hammers, trucks panted, bricks cascaded, cranes trapezed in the dusty, diesel-saturated air. I walked a path of sagging boards through a birch forest of scaffolding, and came out into the relative quiet of

Herzen Street. Here, not far from the Conservatoire, I was almost mown down by a scurrying Ilya.

This, I must emphasise, is a most unusual sight. Ilya is one of nature's saunterers. 'Where are you off to, you Jewish parasite?' I asked him affably.

'Again this kibitzer! A trolley bus should run through his intestines, God forbid!' Bright-eyed, out of breath, Ilya clapped me on the shoulder and began to propel me in the direction I'd just come from.

'Where are we going?' I asked, happy to have been relieved of the decision whether to put in a late appearance at the office.

'Don't ask questions.'

'Rivka's?' I suggested hopefully.

'This is work, my dear boy, not pleasure. To everything there is a season!' He patted his cardboard attaché case and looked at me knowingly.

Work! Couldn't anyone in this place ever stop thinking about work?

'I'm indisposed, you know,' I pleaded.

'Sure, who isn't? A bit of private enterprise will make you feel better.'

He steered me off the kerb, oblivious to a changing light. And then he did the unthinkable – he ran, and made me run too. True, it was to avoid getting killed. But in the usual way, he'd have just stood still and hoped the car would go round him.

We stopped outside a shop called World of Music. Ilya brushed his hand nervously over the lock of hair that dangles on his forehead. Suddenly, I saw him just as he used to look in the old days when he walked onto the concert platform to give a recital: the same neat suit, the same nervous gesture, and then, the utter poise and assurance of the first notes.

'I hope you know what you're doing, Ilyuska,' I said.

'I hope so too.'

He looked round furtively and motioned me to take the case. I unlocked it, and he removed a large brown-paper package.

'So, what are you selling?'

'It's the Beatles' latest! I taped it from Voice of America and recorded it on X-ray film. Look!' Ilya's eyes shone as he held up one of the flimsy discs so I could see the ripple of white ribs.

I shuddered admiringly. 'So you're a technological genius as well as a musical one?'

'Not really, it was easy. With a little help from my friends at Melodiya. And Luba – she raided the polyclinic dustbins. It was her idea, actually.'

What a girl! A pang of regret went through me. Why couldn't Borya have stayed on his blasted kolkhoz a bit longer?

'They don't sound perfect, of course. But better than you'd think. I'm charging one rouble fifty. D'you think that's a fair price? They're worth more, but I'm not just doing it for profit, I want to give people the chance to hear some real rock and roll, for a change.'

He nudged me as two men came out of the shop, carrying packages. They were suspiciously smart and clean-shaven.

'No,' I whispered, drawing Ilya back.

'No, you're right,' he agreed. 'Definitely the wrong sociological type.'

'Now there's a possibility,' I said. A young woman, not much more than a girl, was wheeling her pushchair towards us.

Ilya pounced. I stood back, watching the street, not close enough to hear the transaction. The girl and Ilya were smiling, and Ilya's hand went to the packet in his pocket. Afterwards he came rather breathlessly towards me.

'She wanted to take two. A copy for her cousin. But I told her, limited stock. Only one per person!'

I don't think I'd ever seen him look so excited.

We stuck at our posts for several hours more. But the record shop was not attracting a great deal of custom, and, with Ilya's caution about sociological types, his sales did not amount to more than a dozen by the end of the afternoon. He wasn't disappointed; he'd try another area tomorrow, he said, where he expected business would be better.

As we walked home, he tried to persuade me to accept a share of the takings. At the risk of patronising him I refused; I knew his financial position was even worse than mine. He flushed angrily but put away the crumpled notes. 'At least let me give you a free record,' he said irritably. I accepted it, trying not to show my reluctance. We parted on the corner of Herzen Street, not far from the Conservatoire where he had once been star pupil, carefully avoiding one another's eyes.

I had just put the record on the turntable when the phone rang. I rushed into the hall, expecting the worst from Igor Igorevich.

'Arkasha, what's wrong with you?' demanded Lev. 'D'you intend coming to work tomorrow?'

I told him that though I was in love I had no further plans to default on my duty. 'Where were you all this morning, anyway?' I asked.

'In a meeting.' He lowered his voice so that it seemed to issue from deep inside the earpiece. 'Developments,' he breathed boomingly.

'What developments?'

'They kicked out you-know-who!'

'They what?' I almost dropped the handset.

There was a pause; then a new voice, crisp, businesslike, rattled off a list of typesetting instructions.

'Yes, sir, no, sir, anything you say, sir,' I muttered, as the phone clicked and purred. I cursed whoever had interrupted Lev, and reeled back into the kitchen.

He must have meant Igorevich, poor old bugger. What dreadful thing had he done? And who else was implicated?

I began to slice some carrots for Tanya's stockpot, and in my agitation cut my thumb. I looked at it in surprise and admiration; I had not seen my own blood for ages. It somehow gave me a bond with my unhappy editor. For a moment I felt more cheerful. I made a bandage of a size suitable for eliciting wifely sympathy, and ate some of the tepid soup as a strengthener. My only comfort was that I now had a superb justification for all the emergency editorial meetings I'd been attending at strange hours over the last few days. I didn't like making capital out of Igorevich's affliction, but it *was* for the sake of a severely ailing marriage.

I presented Tanya with the news as soon as she'd opened the kitchen door, before she could demand to know what time I'd finally deigned to get out of bed.

'Of course I'd seen it coming all along,' I said airily, by way of conclusion.

Tanya plumped herself down at the kitchen table without so much as removing her coat. She kicked off her stubby-heeled shoes, stuck out her feet, rolled up her eyes and began to utter laments in that peasant way she has – which may be OK in the fields of Yasnaya Polyana, but in the enclosed space of a small Moscow apartment is both sinister and inappropriate. Whatever would become of the Polyakov family now? Masha clung to her sleeve and burst into tears. 'Whatever's going to become of us?' she echoed.

'For goodness sake, anyone would think it was me who'd been kicked out!'

'How do you know it isn't?' Tanya was suddenly steely.

The thought had already occurred to me, of course. I had combated it with the humorous image of Igorevich and me wielding mop and bucket on the office stairs, competing like two babushkas for a brighter finish.

'Rubbish, Tanichka, they might even appoint me as the new editor.' I swung Masha high into the air. 'You'd like your daddy to be the big boss man, wouldn't you, darling?'

'No, I would not!' wept Masha, struggling.

She cheered up when I told her the tale of Ilya and his X-ray records, but Tanya refused all comfort. In fact, it seemed to make her feel worse. She hit her forehead with the flat of her palm and begged God to tell her why she had been so stupid as to marry into the intelligentsia.

Where have I been for the last three days?

When my grandmother died and they took me to her house shortly after, I expected, since I was only four years old and this was my first experience of such things, to be greeted by a personage who was still my grandmother, still alive and kicking, only dead. I tried to picture it. In the usual way, my grandmother was white and violet, her eyes were turning to water, she had a twisted violet scar like a serpentine brooch on her pleated neck. Dead, she would be more fiercely white, more ripely violet. She would be colder and bigger and not able to talk to me or see me. She would fill up the house like the smell of burning pancakes. Would she try to kiss me? I hoped not.

When we got there I was very disappointed. There was no smell of pancakes, even burnt ones. The windows of the little house were open, letting in fresh breezes from the country outside and I thought that grandmother must have got blown away. Her things were there, but they were lost and crying. Clean sunlight poured through the rooms. The bed was made. The dishes were washed and stacked. The floors had been swept. At first I wanted to laugh – so this is Dead Grandmother, nothing at all, big deal! But I found, as the day wore on and the grown-ups busied themselves elsewhere, that death was here after all. Death was this tidiness and cleanness, this spring sunlight and fresh air and gleaming floorboards and white linen. My teeth began to chatter with the coldness of death, my head to ache with the light of it, and I fell ill that evening from pneumonia, and nearly died myself.

I remembered my grandmother's house when I saw my desk this morning. Or rather, when my ghost saw its desk – the newly tidied desk of Arkady Petrovich. No scribbled sheets wandering from a fat file marked ED. REF. SELF., no copies of *Krokodil*, chewed pencil stubs, empty matchboxes, bird's-milk pastilles, paperclip sculptures etc. jostling for the roaming creative attention, little eager servants of the Idea, the Word. All that inhabited that dustless veneer was a neat stack of slips printed: 'The Editor regrets' etc. The in-tray held another neat but substantial pile of papers, each clipped to an envelope. A single writing implement sat forlornly by the pile of slips. And that was all. The wastepaper basket was not overflowing, neither were the ashtrays. The other desks were tidy, too; a great deal of filing had been accomplished by Valya, who still wore an overall and looked cheerless. No clouds of smoke and peppermint emanated from the editorial alcove, merely the crisp chatter of a typewriter.

The ghost of Arkady Petrovich shuddered at the sound. It sat itself down on the grey upholstered chair which was supposed to swivel but didn't. It picked up a rejection slip and turned it on its back so the printed message beginning 'The Editor regrets' became itself a ghost seen in a mirror. It wrote an idle first line: 'Death, you are so tidy.' It added another: 'Death, you are so Kochekov.' The ghost of Arkady Petrovich abruptly returned to its corpse, which sat up and giggled. Then all at once the clattering typewriter stopped. An invisible chair creaked. The piece of paper hastily crumpled itself and dived into Arkady Petrovich's pocket. Bristling with what might easily have been rage, though it turned out to be his own untrustworthy, choleric variety of good humour, Kochekov marched out of the alcove and glared about him.

Having not yet brought myself to read the great man's memoirs, I have no idea why General Kochekov abandoned his reputedly brilliant career as a soldier in order to churn out novels. I suspect he was wounded, though he shows no physical signs of this; very possibly he was mildly brain-damaged. All I know for sure is that during the course of twenty-odd books he has written more pious clichés than he could ever have killed Germans. Veteran of the Great Patriotic War against the Imagination, our new responsible editor has drilled platoons of vivid, fresh young words to a grey, obedient mass. He heads the triumphal march of mediocrity. Death to the enemy talent! is his cry.

Already, it seemed, he had drummed and trumpeted his way through an editorial. He placed the manuscript on Valya's desk and commanded her in his most affable bark to get up from her knees beside the filing cabinet and start typing a fair copy – *at the double*, because there was still Kolya's piece, 'The Timeless Genius of Leo Tolstoy', to redo, and this time don't forget the triple spacing and the one-and-a-quarter-inch margin on both sides of the text, he added humorously; old soldiers like to see every button polished!

With that metaphorical sally, Kochekov returned in glory to his alcove. He had not glanced either in Lev's direction or mine. There was no need; he had already satisfied himself in a short, sharp meeting between the three of us that we were in full accord with the *Star*'s progressive new policies, and that I, in particular, would ensure that from henceforth my creative efforts struck a positive note. I would not, for example (at this point, to my alarm, he had seized the July issue, lifted it to a great height and let it crash like a shot pigeon into his wastepaper bin) concentrate exclusively on the expression of personal emotion in my poetry and reviews. He remembered one review in particular, a review, in fact, of his own award-winning novel, *Vanya and Lenya*, during the course of which I had made the preposterous comment that he had dwelt too briefly on the love affair between the hero and heroine, and given the sunflower-growing agriculture of their kolkhoz an unwarranted narrative supremacy. It was perfectly correct that he, Kochekov, had elevated the sunflower-growing agriculture to narrative supremacy, and he was perfectly correct to have done so, for it was honest labour, not animal passion, which was the heart and soul and lifeblood of the revolution. At this point Kochekov became so enraged he lost the power of speech altogether; after a few spluttering attempts he began to cough, and had to content himself with hammering his fist on the desktop instead.

'Read and learn,' Kochekov exhorted me finally, after I had apologised for my absurd misunderstanding and he had calmed down. He dumped on my desk a pile of manuscripts that were to be returned to their authors as unsuitable. 'Even rubbish can be instructive to a young writer.' He permitted himself a thin smile at the thought of my spending the next two days reading rubbish and learning about rubbish and putting rubbish into envelopes. His relish was heightened, of course, by the knowledge that I would find something of value among the rubbish, but be powerless to retain it.

Lev had got a milder scolding; his sins chiefly consisted of the translation of faintly unsuitable imperialist texts, admittedly in the absence of the necessary editorial guidance on these matters, and an occasional touch of sarcasm or whimsy in his reviews. Penance would take the form of a 5000-word appreciation of the general's early novels, recently reissued.

As a further step in our re-education, we were assigned the joint project of visiting the Stretsky auto-plant to talk to the workers about the hopes and triumphs of the Soviet car industry. 'Facts, and no flummery,' said Kochekov, handing me a set of production figures for the previous year. 'That's the spirit of the *New Literary Star*!'

I was alive again, but I'd become much smaller, wormlike. I preferred being dead after all. I even felt a twinge of envy for Igorevich – truly, honourably dead.

In fact, he has been demoted to the position of assistant editor on one of our sister magazines, *Soviet Technics*. (I found this out from Valya, whose husband knows someone who works there.) I imagine he is not altogether unhappy. He knows nothing about technology, of course, but that's my whole point: innocence of any kind is bliss in our society. Just think of it – no more weighing up of literary v. political merit, no more soul-wrenching decisions and brain-jangling revisions. He'll be able to write an article claiming our radio technology to be the most advanced in the world, and he won't even know it isn't true (if it isn't, I mean. It might be true, for all I know or care).

Lucky, dead Igor Igorevich!

But what brought about the recent purge? Lev, Valya and I are agreed that it was initiated from very high up – perhaps, even, the Ultimate. And thus the stone tablet was passed down from hand to hand, gathering momentum, crushing a minion or two on the way, and finally coming to rest upright on the *New Literary Star*'s editorial chair. It looks, at this moment, almost like a human being. But the important thing to remember is that it isn't. At any time it could turn back into a stone and roll around the office, grinding anyone it doesn't like to a fine, invisible powder.

If football is the poetry of the workers, what is the New Year Plan?

Lev and I were having lunch in the auto-plant canteen. We'd spent the morning being shown round by a particularly self-righteous little foreman, who fortunately had now absented himself to attend a lunchtime training session of the football club. That was why the canteen was three-quarters empty; the real joy of these workers, we had discovered, wasn't cars, but football. How to hint such a thing in our review would be a delicate matter.

'To the Stretsky carworkers, football is poetry,' I offered, as a trial sentence. 'But doesn't that imply that they can't appreciate real poetry? And what about the New Year Plan? If football is poetry, the New Year Plan can't be. And it ought to be, don't you think?'

I groaned. 'I don't feel I'm a writer any more,' I confessed. 'I'm just a pen now, in the hands of the Party. When future literary critics look back on the writings of today, they'll be reading autobiography. Not poems, stories, novels. Just the story of the Party, in its own words. The fact that the names of individual writers are attached means nothing. I hope they realise that.'

'Cheer up. There are worse things about scientific communism than the way it treats writers. What's it done to the humble sausage, for example?' Lev prodded the gravied article on his plate. 'Come on, you little rat!' Urged by the flat of his knife, a small clot of meat emerged reluctantly from the plastic skin. 'What I want to know is why, if there isn't a shortage of pigs – and there can't be, or we wouldn't have sausages – there's a shortage of guts to stuff 'em in. What do they do with the guts?' Chewing with a good deal more vigour than the size of his mouthful seemed to deserve, Lev stared at me sternly.

'They mince them up and add them to the sausage meat,' I suggested. 'That way, everyone gets a rotten sausage every day instead of a mediocre one every other day.'

'Very concisely said, young man. Very Kochekovian, in fact. Though perhaps you should improve your adjectives before you put it on paper. Substitute "excellent" for "rotten", for example. However' – he engaged in a particularly energetic bout of mastication – 'I think you may be wrong. My theory is that they now use minced gut entirely in all but a small proportion of the sausages, naturally reserved for the elite. The elite gets twice as many twice as good sausages as a result.'

'Bloody hell, this is a depressing conversation.'

'Nevertheless, life isn't without its perks. Tell me about your little adventure the other night. I've been meaning to ask you all week.'

'Very pleasant, very satisfactory,' I said gloomily.

'You don't look particularly pleased or satisfied.'

'Well, what was the point of it? Elizabeth's gone back, and I'll never see her again.'

'You're a bit of an ungrateful bugger, aren't you?' said Lev cheerfully. 'I mean, *some people* sacrificed themselves out of sheer comradeliness so that you could have your bit of fun.'

'All right, all right. My humble thanks and serene condolences! But you're lucky really – you can't miss what you never had.'

'Can't I? Want a bet?' said Lev.

I rapped my temples in a gesture Tanya would have understood. 'It was such a crazy evening! I must have really been pissed out of my mind. D'you know, I didn't even get her address.'

'That's easy. Luba's almost certainly got it.'

'Luba?' I took my hand from my head and gazed into Lev's candid, bright blue eyes. Ever since our student days, Lev has had the knack of seeming to know less than I while secretly knowing more. Though I was the brilliant one in class, in exams he always beat me by a grade. And when I produced a good bit of gossip he would listen as if deeply impressed but, later in the conversation, casually come out with a further and infinitely juicier revelation. What was between Luba and Elizabeth? And how did Lev know?

It turned out that Luba, the obstinate bitch, had asked Elizabeth to smuggle out an article she'd written, entitled 'What Soviet Women Are Fighting for'. Worse still, she was planning to start an underground journal of feminism. Boba was in on it too. Lev boasted that, so far, he was the only male who had been asked to contribute.

'Are you jealous, by any chance?' (I grimaced silently.) 'Boba wanted to ask you to write something too, but you seemed so preoccupied with other things. Anyway, she probably thinks you're a bit of a traditionalist where women are concerned. Seducing virgins, that sort of thing!'

I leaned across the table, spilling half my glass of kvass, and seized him by the collar.

'Hey, steady on.' He contrived to look sweetly unperturbed.

'That's slanderous. I don't seduce virgins. If you mean Elizabeth, I can assure you – ' I spluttered.

'Wasn't she really?' Lev's mouth opened in genuine astonishment. I relaxed my hold on his collar and slumped back. The tabletop was swimming with kvass.

'No, she wasn't. So what? Let's get out of this dump.'

'Permissive society and all that, I suppose.' Lev got gloomily to his feet. 'But I'd never have thought it, never.'

'Anyway, if she had been a virgin, you played a part in contriving her downfall,' I told him, as we tramped along the corridor to the factory gym, where the workers were still exercising.

'That was before I realised,' muttered Lev.

'Realised what?'

'That she wasn't a stuck-up little cow after all. That I quite fancied her myself!'

From Elizabeth's diary, London, 1974

5 June. Excitement in the Greek phil seminar! Pelican strolled in halfway through (bare feet, blue tie-dyed kaftan, ponytail), delivered us all a furious lecture about the 'murder' of Socrates and how the Romans were better than the Greeks because they didn't persecute their philosophers (Dr Stewart, blinking, tried to argue that they didn't have any worth persecuting), and marched out again. It was electrifying! No one dared to giggle, not even Soraya. Pel was sitting in the flowerbed when I came out. Am I *mad* or *glad* to be associated with this guy?! We then strolled round the Park, in fits of mirth at his Dramatic Entry.

7 June. Pel in a bad mood because he got an E and a red line through his 'essay' (only the second he has ever written in two years!). I wasn't exactly surprised. He was supposed to write about Empiricism, but wrote about Imperialism instead – which is intimately related to Empiricism, he says, only Stewart's too thick to see it. It was a typical Pelican diatribe, the basic premise being Everything Stinks. The University stinks, because it is is a bastion of privilege and class antagonism. British philosophy stinks because it takes no interest in universal concepts, merely in the logical analysis of statements, and is therefore just a kind of jumped-up grammar. (He's got a point there.) Even the Park stinks, because it's Royal and Regency and the Prince Regent represents all that's sickest about the monarchy which is still thriving (tho' less ostentatiously) and drinking the lifeblood of the working classes. Et cetera. He walked me home along Fox Crescent and I tried to see it through his eyes, but really I think all that stately goldeny-white architecture is very beautiful. Of course I'd be ashamed to live there. At least the rectory isn't Georgian, although Pel says Early Gothic Revival is just as disgusting.

'But you are the pearl in the oyster shell.' (He was slightly stoned, I think.) 'You are the reincarnation of Mary Anne Bradley, timeless and blameless, etc.' I wish he wouldn't go on about this, I should never have told him. The story (Daddy's – and I'm sure he's romancing) is that, when our house was a proper rectory in the 1820s, a radical clergyman lived there with his daughter, Mary Anne, and she was not only the King's occasional mistress but one of the first Chartists! Pel of course was thrilled by the story – I think that's the main reason he asked me out. Now, though, I've started to get bad dreams again through thinking about it so much. He says I should write them down and make a study of them instead of trying to run away from them. But he doesn't realise how frightening it is. The dreams started years ago, *before I knew about the story*, just after Auntie Bonnie died.

When he called me Mary Anne this afternoon I told him to shut up, and he got offended. Now I suppose I am part of everything he hates: privilege, property, rationality etc. He sloped off saying that he intends to drop out of college and join this commune he's heard about, in Wiltshire.

20 June. Pel didn't turn up for the end-of-year exams. I thought he might make an entrance, at least, if only to rip up his papers or symbolically burn them. But he's disappeared; no one has seen him for a fortnight. I supose he really has gone to Wiltshire. I think it's really mean of him not to have said goodbye.

Life is going from bad to worse – on top of everything else, Daddy's got this girlfriend. He met her at the Pushkin Circle, she's a courier with Lenitours. She gave him a ghastly photo of herself posing beside a huge cannon. She's got frizzy hennaed hair and she's at least fifty and her name's Josephine (she likes to be called Joey, but Daddy says it makes her sound like a budgerigar, so he's changed it to Seph). I think he's planning to take her to Moscow when he goes on the Lang. and Lit. Teachers' freebie. If he does he will make himself a Laughing Stock.

12 July. 'It' happened: the 'dream'. Daddy was at the NFT with his Beloved and I was making notes for one of my hateful vacation essays: 'Aristotle's View of the Good in the *Nichomachean Ethics*'. I was copying from the text, that bit about how the Good varies from one art or action to another: in medicine, it's health; in strategy, victory; in architecture, a house, etc. – and getting more and more bored and sleepy – when it began. The words swelled up from the page, sank back, swelled up again. I forced them back into place, and went on reading.

'Since there are manifestly more ends than one and we chose some of these, e.g. wealth, flutes and instruments in general for the sake of something else, it is clear that not all ends are final. But the supreme good is evidently something final . . .'

I tried to keep my mind on the supreme good, but I couldn't think of anything but flute players. The words came out at me and played flutes; little men in gold-trimmed scarlet suits – not ancient Greeks at all. Their flutes were ebony and played tiny screams. The light round me got brighter and brighter. The dressing-table mirror caught my eye; it was almost on fire, incandescent, sending white shafts straight at me. He always used to come out of the mirror. Only before it didn't shine like that.

'The supreme good.' I tried to go on reading, but I could feel something behind me. It lifted the little hairs on my neck, and smarted at the back of my nose like the beginning of tears or a sneeze.

I flipped over the pages, looking for any word that could save me. A single sentence halted me: 'Whereas every good is the product of an art, there is no art of pleasure.'

Horrid vibrations went through me. There was a weight in the room, like a ton of scented bath water. Auntie Bonnie! Her smell: lavender water, brandy, something decayed. Teeth maybe. Did he have bad teeth? Then a babble of voices and a loud, high giggle.

'Nonsense, my dear Philosopher. There is no art but the Art of Pleasure!' Suddenly the voice was much nearer, hot and moist on my cheek. 'Are you the maid whose name was to me once this very same Pleasure'? He had never spoken to me before! Words surrounded me like eyes: you, you, you, they said.

I was terrified and began to read at a mad, jabbering rate, understanding nothing but somehow keeping him at bay with the barrage of senseless words. An intense coldness crawled over me; the room began to twist about and sob. I got up and ran to the door, but it took me ages because of all the heaving, swamping water. And all the time his voice echoed behind me (it came from different directions, as if he was searching for me): 'You are she that rose with the mob at Peter's Field to charge me with their hunger. You refused to pay me the price of your lover's freedom: so he hangs, so he hangs.'

I ran downstairs and turned on the TV. I put the volume high and yelled with laughter and terror until I heard the key in the door and immediately composed myself.

30 July. Daddy and Mummy's wedding anniversary. Daddy didn't go to the grave – again. He has become a complete atheist over the years. When I was a child we always seemed to be taking flowers there. He said later that it was for my sake, not his, so I shouldn't feel she had abandoned me by dying – children sometimes get these ideas. But I thought that deep down he had gone on loving her. Now I realise he hasn't. He's probably even had other girlfriends. If I ever love someone it will be total and for ever and nothing will affect it, not even death. I almost think I love Pelican like that. I think about him all the time.

6 August. A hot day. I felt tired and feverish and aching. As I dozed in the chair a breeze came through the window with The Voice. It was very sweet and gentle. He wanted me to come to the park with him. He said he would gather herbs to cure my wound – lavender, rosemary, sage, camomile, hellebore. I smelled their sweet fragrances, then a stink. Hellebore is a poisonous herb. The thought and the stink came together, rushed at me and knocked me out. It was Daddy who woke me. At five o'clock with a cup of camomile tea! I wanted to tell him, but didn't know how to begin. He'll be fed up if he thinks he's got to go through *all that* again, like when I was sixteen.

12 August. The Auntie Bonnie 'dream' – with new developments! It began the same as always. She was lying in the bath, drowned (that wasn't how she really died, she had a heart attack, but I'd seen her in the bath, by accident, a few days before, and I'd been very frightened of her huge white body and angry red mouth with the teeth like little bits of coal). This time, she metamorphosed into the King, who was also fat as a seal. He stood up, bare and dripping, and I was his servant and had to dry him with a towel that was the furry skin of some animal. I nearly vomited!

Then we were at a banquet. Flutes were squealing in the background. All over the table were large silver tureens; they had no lids and I could see there were human heads in them. The salver nearest to me contained Dr Stewart's. It bobbed about and mouthed at me like a fish: 'Is, ought, is, ought, is, ought.' And then the whole table seemed to catch fire. There was pandemonium. I could hear Pelican's baying laughter, frightened cries and the beating of horses' hooves, and found myself in a field full of people.

I knew I had to get to the front of the mob so I could see John. He was making a speech and I could just get a glimpse of the top of the of his black hat. I pushed my way through the hot, sweating mass, while the cheers got louder and louder until they became a single stormy howl. Suddenly I was spinning in a wall of frantic, screeching faces. I fell, and hooves pounded over me like a rain of black rocks.

John's body lay on a cart. I watched them place his black hat on his breast, the red ribbons flying, paler than his wounds. All he had done was to speak up for the poor and disfranchised, and plead for their representation in the Mother of Parliaments. The King's soldiers had thrust their swords into his heart, but they couldn't kill his unarmed truth. Democracy is a human instinct, as natural as the sun! All at once I was absolutely sure that he wasn't dead. I tried to call out to him, but my voice was a terrible pain that made me fall to the ground.

Today I feel different, somehow light and free. It's because I dreamed of my death last night, I think. I'm more of a soul now, less of a body.

19 August. I told Daddy about it. All of it. He sighed and said, 'Are you thinking about Auntie Bonnie again?' When I said I wasn't, he said he supposed I was still upset because my Layabout Boyfriend had, just as he always predicted, let me down. I said, 'How can you think I care about a twit like that?' but he didn't believe me. Then we had our old conversation about the house being haunted. As usual, he got angry and said did I want him to call in an exorcist, and all that nonsense? He calmed down when I said that I knew it was really I that was haunting it. Anything psychological is fine with him. But I told him I absolutely wouldn't go to psychotherapy again. Psychiatrists are so banal; you can't help knowing what they're thinking, and saying what they expect you to say. Daddy sighed and sighed: in the end he said what about trying a more traditional 'cure' – such as a holiday? If I could hold out till the end of September he'd take me with him to Moscow. 'Instead of the Budgie?' I asked, amazed. 'I never had any intention of taking Seph,' he said indignantly. 'She can go to Moscow whenever she likes – she's already been three times this year!'

20 August. This was what I dreamed after talking to Daddy about Moscow. I was in a huge room with a curtain at one end and a throne in front of it. I walked towards the throne feeling rather small and yet fiercely determined. I spoke to the throne about John, how he was to be hung for treason, and that he was innocent of any crime but the desire for liberty and bread; those things, I said, which you have never lacked yourself, Sir.

A horrible giggle broke out from behind the curtain. I shrank back in horror; I knew he'd come out and demand his payment and I couldn't bear him to touch me. Somehow, though, I made myself step forward. I heaved the throne aside and dragged back the curtain.

There was a table with a white cloth and hundreds of ornamental snuffboxes and pepper pots. I almost laughed, they were so pretty. The Kremlin was there, and the Brighton pavilion! As I stared at the pavilion, a little key turned in its side, the door opened, and a tiny figurine stepped out. It was the Prince.

He gazed about him with a self-satisfied expression and sniffed the air. I had a tremendous urge to pick him up.

Of course I knew it wasn't just a clockwork ornament. It was alive and might have horrible powers. But I had to smash it. If I did I'd smash the chains that John was in, I'd smash hunger and poverty and terror. I snatched at the figure, expecting my hand to be severed at the wrist, or a dagger to fly into my chest. Nothing happened. The figure was cold and light – just hollow porcelain. I flung it down and it burst into a galaxy of splinters. There was a tiny part of a rouged cheek near my foot, with a scrap of blue eye in it. I lifted my foot and ground it under my heel.

I felt very calm and happy when I woke up. I thought: I'm going to Russia! There are no princes there. I feel as if he knew it was all over for him; there have been hints of weeping on the windows, blood drops on the carpet, coffins in the wallpaper, etc. Of course it's only my imagination. Only!

When I go to Moscow I shall leave my imagination at home and maybe it will have vanished by the time I get back. Let's hope!

12 October. Am writing this in a tacky pub off the Euston Road. Ye olde oake radiators (but the oak veneer is peeling off), mud-coloured plastic seats and pink doors. Lovely view through the window of a concertina-shaped office block. I'm waiting for Pel – I bumped into him yesterday in Albany Street. He's just got back from the States. I said I'd just got back from Moscow and he said, 'Great, let's meet up and swap travel notes.' I thought, Why not? I still like him, after all, though not in the same way. I'm not afraid of him any more, either. I'm not even afraid of being here on my own, the first time I ever went into a pub without Male Protection. Of course, you get a few looks. But I know how to shrink into my coat and make myself look anonymous and middle-aged and eccentric – like some old anthropologist taking notes on Homo Intoxicatus. Moscow has changed me *for the better*.

Ilya. Everything to be said and nothing to be said. (That's from this beautiful song he tried to teach me, 'Moscow Nights'.) All we ever really talked about was music. He's not a pushy type like Arkady . . . he's quite shy, except when he's playing the guitar and singing. Yet he talked his way past the doorman and the grumpy old *dejurnaya* to get to my room – anything for music! I'd mentioned some tapes I'd brought with me, and he was desperate to hear them.

My things were spread out on the bed because I was packing, and he said, 'I wish you could find room for me in your suitcase.' His ambition is to see London and Liverpool and marry a nice English girl like me.

(Seriously – that's what he said!) 'Why don't you come for a holiday? You could stay at the rectory – we've got loads of room,' I said, blushing furiously. He made one of those sad, empty-handed gestures of his and raised his eyebrows. 'Perhaps . . . but travelling's very expensive for us here, and we have to get special permission – it isn't like it is for you in the West.' 'Maybe you and the band could come on a tour,' I suggested. 'Yes,' he said, 'maybe – if we make ourselves a bit more respectable! But you'll come and see us again, won't you?' (Just try to stop me – I've already started saving.)

Before he left I gave him the Dylan tape. He said he didn't have anything for me (that sad gesture again), then he remembered something in his pocket, a little medal he'd found. It was a hero-mother medal – for women who've had ten or more children! He told me not to show it to anyone until I got home because it's state property and not really his to give away. It's beautiful – Pelican will be dead jealous when I show him.

I know we'd have kissed each other if Daddy hadn't come flustering in to say we'd be late for the Leaving Party if I didn't hurry up. He almost had a coronary when he saw Ilya. So we just shook hands, very solemnly, our eyes saying Everything.

I whispered that I'd write to him, but he whispered that it was better not to, his mail is usually intercepted.

'That young man's heading for trouble,' Daddy said afterwards. 'And you'll be partly to blame!' He was furious with me for mixing so much and having a good time – which was the whole point of the holiday, I thought. He said he'd never be invited again, I behaved so badly. I told him he ought to apply for a job with the Supreme Soviet, he'd really be at home among those grey old geriatrics!

He was cross about Luba's article, too. Even more cross, really. I wouldn't have told him but he's the only person I know who can speak Russian. He said that if I'd got caught it wouldn't have been me that was in big trouble but Luba and all those others I care so much about. I don't think there was any risk at all, I hid it so well. I'd bought these nesting dolls at the Beriosky and I folded up the pages very small and tucked them down inside the fattest doll! I thought it was a great idea. 'The customs men know all these tricks,' said old

Doomjoy, but I don't think they search people who are obviously tourists – Luba said so and I believe her. Now I'm waiting till he cools down, and then I'll ask him to translate it. I'm really, really determined to get it published.

It's peculiar, the Russians took all the first steps in emancipating women, then they seemed to come up against a brick wall and turn back again. Luba said, 'How can women be liberated in a society where no one is, not even men unless they're in the *nomenclatura*?' It seems to me, though, that the men do have more freedom than the women. All the women who've got children are doing two jobs, for a start, and the men only one. And they still think it's OK to beat their wives!

Of course, a woman could get a job on a building site and no one would whistle or catcall like they would here. Luba said, 'So what?' But I think it's quite important.

13 October. Got B minus for my *Nichomachean Ethics* essay – a Minor Miracle, considering the circumstances under which it was composed.

But gloom and doom in the philosophy of history tutorial – Stewart gave me a D and said sarkily, 'I hoped you would be starting your second year on a brighter note, Miss Lamb; it seems my optimism may have been misplaced.' Pel was right – why did I ever come back to this prison?

I've been looking at the small ads for an affordable flat. Found one (third girl wanted, o.r.) the other side of the park for £25 a month, so I rang up and the girl (Eve) said you can come round and see it tomorrow morning. That'll mean missing aesthetics and logic, but I'm so behind anyway I can't see it'll make much difference.

14 October. The room's nice – really huge – though it rattles a bit when the trains go by. But I don't suppose I'll get it. There were three people in front of me and four more arrived while I was there. We went round in turn, like a relay race. Or a beauty contest. Do I look the type to burn the baked beans or leave spittings round the basin after I've cleaned my teeth? The two girls (Sue and Eve) are older than me and a bit snotty. When I said I was a philosophy student, Sue said she thought it was a waste of time doing a degree, specially an arts degree; she knew this girl who got a first in philosophy and she ended up selling central heating. She and Eve are both trainees in an advertising agency. They looked me up and down and Eve said, 'The chemistry's so terribly important, don't you think?' I said, 'Yes, absolutely,' thinking she meant everyone ought to be doing science in the space age, but then she looked meaningfully at Sue and said that that had been the problem with Lindsay, the chemistry wasn't right; and then they both looked meaningfully at me and I suddenly felt positively toxic.

'We'll let you know,' they said, but they haven't yet. Oh, it would be so nice to get out of this dreary old place and have a life of my own! Sometimes I feel as if everyone's died in our house – including Daddy. He'll be furious if he finds out I'm looking for a room. I mentioned it once, in my first year, and he said in amazement, 'But you've already got your own room!' He couldn't understand when I said, 'But that's not the same!'

17 October. Met Pel for a Chinese. He says why don't I move into the squat with him; there's loads of space and no hassles with the neighbours or the Bill – they've got electricity and water and everything. I don't want to – it's too far from college, and Daddy would be wrecked if he found out. But our relationship's really nice now. Pel thinks he's gay; he met someone in the US and now he thinks he's in L. I told him I was too – not gay but in L – yes, with the guy who gave me the hero-mother medal! Pel said I should go to Moscow and have ten children with him if that's what I want! He's a Romantic like me, that's why we'll always be friends. I don't desperately fancy him – I realise that now. I never fancied anyone before Ilya, apart from an occasional pop star and Professor Berne, of course, like all the other first-years! Oh, dear dead innocent days! We all cried when they suspended him, and Soraya said we ought to have a sit-in, silly cow!

The most unequal thing, in my opinion, about men and women is that women can have sex without enjoying it, but men *have to* enjoy it. It's geared to them completely. Pel said once that if women are supposed to have Os, why didn't God put the C inside the V? He wasn't being sarky about women having Os. He really wanted me to, but it just didn't fit in with what he had to do to get his.

It was the same with Arkady, really. Nice but not Magic. If it seemed a bit special at the time I realise now that it was because of where we were and who he was. My first Russian, my first poet and my first communist (Pel's only a textbook anarchist)!!

30 October. Doing Tom Paine in Hist. Phil.

> We hold these truths to be Self evident: that all Men are created equal and independent, that from that equal Creation they derive rights inherent and unalienable; among which are the Preservation of Life, and Liberty, and the Pursuit of Happiness; that to Secure these ends, Governments are instituted among Men, deriving their just Powers from the consent of the Governed; that whenever, any form of Government, Shall become destructive of these Ends, it is the Right of the People to alter or to abolish it, and to institute new Government.

(I'm Moved and Trembling, but determined not to give in to any 'dreams'.)

TP was a staymaker, exciseman and pamphleteer who gave up on his fellow Englishmen and went to America. Cobbett said that the real cause of the American Revolution was 'some beastly insult offered to Mr Paine when he was in the Excise in England'.

'What happens if you remove the concept of a creator?' Stewart asked, blinking rapidly in my direction. 'How, for example, would a man or woman reinterpret that passage in terms of present-day thought?'

'We hold these truths to be self-evident; that all men *and women* are endowed *by the fact of their humanity* with certain inalienable rights, that among these are equality, life, liberty and the pursuit of happiness.'

'Very good. But tell me, Miss Lamb, does this modern, secular Tom or Thomasina Paine *really* have the authority to say that every human being is endowed, ipso facto, with these rights?'

'No, I suppose not.'

'But if they themselves believe it and think it, that makes it a fact,' said Soraya.

'And if they don't?'

'You could just as well say they have no rights at all, I suppose.'

'Very good.'

'Getting rid of the concept of God has made a lot of things more difficult, in my opinion,' I said.

'Quite so,' said Stewart, and everyone in the tutorial laughed.

'Would you say that this was one of the problems that modern Marxist-Leninism has tried to solve?'

Stewart knows I went to Moscow and he keeps trying to trap me into conversations about Soviet politics. But I had to admit he was right. Socialism is a kind of god. It's a very religious society in a way – their eyes are on higher goals all the time.

'A teleological society, would you say?' Stewart wrote 'teleological' on the board. No one else knew what it meant either.

'Anyone can tell you went to Catholic schools,' said Soraya afterwards. 'Do you still go to church?'

'Not any more. I believe that the kingdom of God is of this world!' (That shut her up.)

15 November. Letter from Moscow. My hands were shaking so much I could hardly open the envelope. I looked at the signature – it had to be Ilya! But no, it was Arkady. Typical of him to write such a screed. He says they've just had October Revolution Day, which seems a bit weird as his letter's dated 8 November. He watched a parade, got drunk and thought about me (sounds riveting). And he wants a long letter back – all about me and my life and college and the park, so he can see it just as if he was here. Well, he'll have to wait – I've got all these essays to write, plus flu.

30 November. The Budgie came round for lunch on Sunday and stayed till ten in the evening. Daddy talked Russian with her and got out the Best Sherry. I was hoping things had cooled off between them, but apparently not. If he marries her I'll definitely move out, even if I have to go to Pel's.

She's crazy about Russia and reckons she's a great expert. (She's been there twelve times!) Maybe I ought to be nice to her – she might be able to get me a cheap ticket.

She got back from her latest tour a week ago. I'm furious I didn't know she was going, or I could have given her a lovely tape for Ilya. She says there has already been snow in Moscow though it's thawed slightly now. Soon they'll be hosing over the paths in the parks to make ice tracks. You can skate for miles, even at night, when they light all these little lamps. It must be so Magic. And then the real snow comes – nine foot, twelve foot deep. The English don't know what winter really is, says Joey. But you've got to go to Siberia to really experience it. Once she went on a picnic with some hunters. They had reindeer meat, pepper vodka and roasted apples – they had to roast the apples because they'd frozen into solid balls!

When she was saying all this my ears began to tingle. 'I remember once the ice on the Thames was so thick they set up market stalls,' I said. Daddy and Joey stared at me: *when*? 'No, I mean I read about it,' I said quickly. 'I don't remember it, of course.'

I hope my Imagination hasn't decided to make a return visit!

1 December. Rows! I was slightly later than usual (I'd been to Pel's and had a little grass) and when I got in, there was the Budgie mooning over Mummy's photograph. Heaven knows why Daddy had to show her. It was taken not long before she died, and she looks very thin in it, though pretty. I hate the picture, because I imagine the cancer spreading its horrible knots under her skin and eating her alive. How could she smile like that, knowing she had It? The Budgie looked straight at me with big, pitying eyes, and back to Daddy. 'Your Lizzie's just like her, blah, blah'.

'I'm not like her at all,' I said, but Daddy said, 'She doesn't remember, she was only two when Rosemary died.'

The Budgie went all tragic, of course, as if I was a Poor Little Orphan, and I was a bit rude, I suppose; I said, 'Why don't you throw these pathetic old photos away – it's only geriatrics who live in the past!'

Then Daddy started grousing: no manners, dirty jeans, straggling hair, out till 10.30 (10.30!!), no studying for weeks, going about with the Great Unwashed, etc. The Budgie said, 'Come on, Ed, I'm sure she's a good girl really, the modern kids have to do their own thing, you know,' and I said, very dignified, 'I suppose you know the origin of the phrase you used, do you, Daddy?' 'No and I don't want to,' said Daddy, but I told him anyway; it was when the government tried to suppress all radical publications after the six acts of 1819 by charging a stamp tax which the radical editors couldn't afford, so they brought out their publications illegally, and they were nicknamed 'the Great Unstamped'. 'They were a powerful force for social reform,' I said, quoting Stewart. 'So it's a compliment to be called after them! Actually!'

And guess what the Budgie said? 'Good on you, Lizzie! She's got spirit, Eddie, and brains to go with it, you should be flipping well proud of her!'

She needn't think she'll get round me as easily as all that – it was a good feeling, though. 'Sisterhood is Powerful,' I thought. There was a book called that, and I suddenly knew exactly what they meant, because Daddy shut up and put the photos away and poured us all a drink – including me.

10 December. Eve rang up out of the blue and said was I by any chance still interested in the room? The girl they'd originally got had suddenly decided to go to Spain and teach EFL, and she was leaving straight after Christmas. I could hardly believe my ears. 'What about the chemistry?' I said, because I couldn't think of anything else – yes and no are too definite for me when I get taken unawares – and Eve said she reckoned it would be all right, but if I did want the room could she please have a month's deposit a.s.a.p.? I said OK, I'd take the room and call round with the money at the end of the week. When I put the phone down I was shaking with panic. But now I've had an idea. I'm going to ask Joey to lend it to me. I'll pay her back when I get my job on the Christmas post. She's quite rich, after all. And I know she wants to get me on her side.

12 December. Joey coughed up to the £25! I went round to her flat, and she was really nice. She even gave me a necklace – she says its amber from the Baltic Sea. And she said I'd better break it gently to Daddy about leaving home; it would be better if she had a little chat with him first, and explained how important it was for a girl to learn independence. 'Your daddy's a very lonely man,' she said, 'but he's got no right to stop you doing what you want.' She said she'll tell him next week, after the carol concert. I was so pleased I actually kissed her!

I took the money straight to Eve and Sue's and we sat round with mugs of coffee and talked about their jobs in advertising. One of them's training to be an account executive, the other a copywriter. The life sounds quite fun, and you don't even need a degree. But I think it's wrong, persuading people to buy stuff they don't need and can't afford and telling them it'll work miracles. I didn't dare say so; chemistry, chemistry.

Now I'm going to type up a fair copy of 'What Soviet Women Are Fighting for'. Pel knows someone who knows a girl on the Red Rag collective, so I'll maybe try it there. The trouble is, though, they might object to an attack on socialism – even one by a feminist!

The only thing I'm sad about is Daddy. Maybe it's selfish to leave home when he's so lonely. But he's got Joey – and I need space! Anyway, it's only just across the park. We can visit each other any time. I'm dreading Saturday, though, when I've got to break the Big News.

Moscow
2 June 1979

Dear Elizabeth,

It's so long since I wrote to you. Forgive me – it isn't that I ever stopped thinking about you, simply that over the past few years I've accumulated so many experiences that seemed especially difficult to share by letter. And when you stopped writing to me, I felt that your life, too, must have changed in unimaginable ways, and that perhaps you would even prefer not to be reminded of a certain Moscow night?

But now I've seen Joey, and feel greatly encouraged. She says she's sure you'd love to hear from me, and she'll be happy to take back a letter.

We had a very jolly evening. Then Joey left to pack for her trip to Novosibirsk, and I sat up till four in the morning, my brain firing on all cylinders! I wrote a score of false starts – there was so much to say if I was really to deliver you a piece of my life and heart – then I had a brilliant idea. (It seemed brilliant in anticipation; perhaps it won't be so in execution!) I would invent a new form – the *story-letter*.

So that is what this is going to be – I think. (My hand is actually trembling – I feel like Gagarin must have felt as he clambered inside Vostock on launching day.) I hope you won't be overwhelmed. I shall try to entertain you, as well as move you. I shall tell the truth – but only at its most interesting. If I bore you, you're welcome to throw me in the wastepaper bin. Don't feel you have to reply (though, of course, I'll be delighted if you do. I'd love to know about the workings of a London advertising agency. Can you send me some of your adverts?).

To tell you the truth, I'm in the mood for a little reflection, probably because I'm getting married this Saturday. Joey will get back from Novosibirsk on Friday, and leave for London the same day. So I have three nights only in which to tell my story – 997 fewer than Scheherezade.

The first thing I ought to confess is that I'm two people. I don't suppose you realised that when we met; I hardly realised it myself in those days. If you want a convenient way of separating us, call us Arkady Petrovich and Arkasha. The Russian language gives voice so naturally to this schizophrenia I suspect it's one of our deepest national characteristics!

So what about these two fellows, AP and Arkasha? Well, to put it most simply and obviously, AP is official, Arkasha unofficial. (The Petrovich, by the way, comes from Piotr, which was my father's name. Piotr made an attempt at being an official sort of person himself, then ruined it entirely by disappearing when I was nine years old, but that's another story.) AP is a respected Soviet writer. He attends meetings of the Writers' Union and has published a rather successful book of poems which not even Glavlit (our board of censors) could find fault with, although it tried. Arkashka (the 'k' is optional, denoting merely a shade more familiarity and contempt) wrote poems too, but he didn't publish them; he also kept a journal until things started to go well for him and he began to feel guilty about soiling the paper with his real thoughts.

Arkady Petrovich, I have to confess, has been married before and has an eleven-year-old daughter, Masha. Arkasha was never married: he loved to be in love, and spent a lot of time pursuing the ideal woman and not quite finding her. (One night, he did find her, but she went back to England and eventually forgot all about him; he never forgot her but he learned not to think about her too much. Sorry: Arkasha is an incurable romantic – be patient.) Arkady Petrovich is rather a lonely figure. See him sitting, dark of suit and white of cuff, behind his only slightly untidy desk at the *New Literary Star*, writing in his elegant longhand politically impeccable articles and reviews, or writing other people's articles and reviews so that they become politically impeccable too. Follow him as he leaves his office at the unlikely hour of 11 a.m., and sets off smartly towards the Lenin Library, briefcase in hand. He will disappear into the reference room where he will spend a long time taking notes on the Astrakhan gas-pipeline project and other similarly elevating topics in which he has learned to take a professional interest. He dines at the

Union sometimes, but only for politeness' sake; he doesn't get drunk, and leaves early. Sometimes in the evenings he types out a comic story – he's rather good at these, you'll be surprised to hear. He sends it to Masha, who lives with her mother and stepfather, and whom he rarely sees any more, to add a little laughter to her serious young life as a grade-A physics and maths student and medal-winning Young Pioneer.

Arkasha, on the other hand, rarely thinks about his daughter. (Which is your signal not to imagine he is a thoroughly good sort, nor to imagine that Arkady Petrovich is a total villain.) He is a heavy drinker, a gregarious all-nighter. He and his disreputable friends have pickled and stored their souls in that converted underground warehouse you once visited, known formally as the Moscow Cavern, and nicknamed variously the Hole, the Village, the Dive, the HQ, the Little House, the metro, Nirvana, the Pink Eye, the Indian Reservation.

Arkady Petrovich often lectures Arkasha about the unsuitable company he keeps, and advises him to pull his socks up unless he wants to become an endangered species too. Arkasha is indignant, morally appalled, though he knows it's shrewd advice. Arkasha, however, has a streak of fatalism. Anyway, he believes he has a lucky line in his palm; an old gypsy woman once told his mother so. He tiptoes dancingly across this cotton wisp, waving his parasol (white with red stars) and whistling the 'Internationale'. Far beneath is a frozen lake, but the gypsy woman said he'd never fall. (His mother doesn't believe the gypsy, by the way; she's sick of holding her breath and watching her son's silly balancing act. That's why she's run away to live with her old school friend, Alla, in Leningrad.)

So, Elizabeth, now that you've been introduced to us, there's no need for you to ask who the author of this narrative is. Arkady Petrovich certainly doesn't pour out his soul to women he hardly knows – least of all, foreigners. No doubt you're glad to hear it. But I'm afraid you'll be meeting him from time to time, though I'll do my best to keep his appearances to a minimum. I hope you won't judge him harshly; after all, he's only an ordinary man. No one demands great sacrifices of ordinary men in your world, Elizabeth. Your writers don't have to be heroes to tell the truth. (Or do they? You must tell me if I'm wrong.)

The last I heard from you was your lovely postcard from Marrakesh. So I'll begin my story with the postcard which, I remember, filled me with a confusion of feelings – envy probably being the strongest. But hope was there too, and the thrill of imagining, as I ran my finger over the familiar, rather childishly candid loops of your handwriting, that I was touching your soul. 'A magic, filthy village-city, with walls as red as the sunrise': you see, I've never forgotten your description – which shows why some people are afraid of the power of poetry.

I'm watching the sunrise from the south side of the Moscow River.

The water is grey-blue and shadowy, and breathes out a misty cold from all over its surface. I take the card from my pocket thinking: maybe she'll spend the whole year travelling – that's what young people in the West sometimes do. And there's the sky above me, the wide open sky, and the river flowing at my feet – and I'm still young, but I must stay here, shut up in the land where I was born. However big the USSR is, it isn't the world. It's minutely small by comparison. So how will I ever be anything but a small writer? You'll forgive me – there are various mitigating circumstances that I'll explain later – if I confess that I crushed the postcard in my fist and hurled it into the river? It didn't actually reach the water; it floated gracefully downwards, despite the force with which I'd sent it spinning, and settled itself among some muddy stones on the bank. That made me feel even more trapped; I would have felt better if I could have watched it being carried off on the tide. Well, I'm glad I've confessed; I've always kept that crumpled postcard with me, lodged in my conscience. Now it can float free at last.

You'd like to know more about those so-called mitigating circumstances? In that case it's necessary to put the clock back to the morning I discovered that my marriage had ended. Another sunrise, three weeks chillier: panes of wet ice still slithering underfoot. I'm hurrying along Bitter Street (Gorky) but my mood is so far sweet because I've just won five roubles playing cards. Although a bit filmy-eyed with lack of sleep, I'm happy enough to be whistling the

'Farewell of the Slav Woman' as I stride. My guilt at having stayed out all night at the Cavern is minimal; after all, I wasn't with a woman; after all, I won; after all, Tanya knew where I was going; after all, five roubles is over halfway to a bottle of her favourite cognac; after all . . .

Masha hadn't left for school. She was sitting in the kitchen, her eyes black and sulky, drawing spirals with her spoon in her bowl of rice kasha. Mother was making tea, every gesture an expression of stifled rage. When I asked what was the matter, she jabbed the teapot in the direction of the bedroom door.

Tanya was still asleep, lying on her back with a face flannel spread across her temples and her mouth open. She didn't stir when I called to her. There was a sweet, heavy forest smell in the room that reminded me curiously of my childhood.

I ran back into the kitchen. 'Tanya's ill. Haven't you sent for the doctor?'

'She isn't ill.' Mother lowered her voice because of Masha. 'I'd have thought you of all people would recognise alcoholic poisoning when you see it.'

In an instant I understood the smell in the bedroom. And I understood it because of something mother herself had done, when I was about ten years old, a short while after father disappeared. As well as drinking the gin and half-drowning herself in the bath, though, Tanya had swallowed half a bottle of pills.

'Only herbal pills, perfectly harmless,' Mother said. 'Raisa next door gave them to her, the silly cow! I've taken them myself for my rheumatism. They don't do any good but they can't hurt you.'

I found the half-empty bottle on the draining board, and read the contents. Just alfalfa and a few vitamins, thank God.

Mother was muttering angrily.

'Why's she so afraid of going to the clinic, the big baby? It's all over in a few minutes, and nothing like as bad as what she went through last night. If only you'd been here you could have put a stop to it!'

'Put a stop to what? Why are you two whispering?' demanded Masha, languidly stirring her bowl of slops.

I scooped a handful of kopecks from my pocket and jiggled them in front of her.

'Did you win, Daddy? Did you win all that?' The cloud lifted from her face.

'Little capitalist,' I said, and tickled her under the chin. 'Look, watch this!'

I put a five-kopeck piece on a saucer and made it float up and up till it reached the top shelf of the dresser.

'I'll fetch it down for you when you've cleared your bowl!'

'That's shameful, too – calling the child dirty names and bribing her!' Mother picked up the tray with a jerk, spilling long blood-red fingers of tea. 'You're not fit to be a parent – I have to say it, although you're my own son!'

'Why should Masha have to be made unhappy?' I muttered as I followed her into the bedroom.

'You tell me! You tell me why the whole household has to be made unhappy – apart from Mr Wonderguy, of course!'

Tanya was sitting up now, her face white and her fringe stuck to her forehead in wet black stripes. I ran over to her, but I couldn't kiss her; her stare stopped me like a glass wall.

'Tanichka, how could you have done such a horrible thing? You might have died.' And really, I felt as if she had, and that this was her corpse, washed up from the bottom of the sea.

Her face relaxed and took on a faint colour. She shrugged her shoulders.

'Anyway, I was sick. It was a waste of time!'

'Of course it was,' snapped Mother. 'These old wives' remedies never work. I'm surprised at you for listening to that idiot Raisa, that peasant!'

'Maybe because I'm a peasant too,' said Tanya. Her voice was almost inaudible and she had shut her eyes again. To my surprise, tears were rolling from her shut lids, squeezing themselves insistently between her fine lashes. I took her hand but she didn't open her eyes. I'd never seen anyone cry like that, with closed eyes, and so silently.

Mother wasn't going to let herself be melted by a few tears. 'Stop whining and drink your tea. Who's taking the little one to school? Me, I suppose, although my ankles are all swollen again. Well, that's that; we old ones seem to be twice as tough as the younger generation. We've just had to get on with things all our lives, and so we do!' She went out to the kitchen, muttering self-righteously.

Tanya opened her eyes and gave me a cold look as she edged her hand out of mine.

'I suppose the poor little beggar thinks it's got a future with us!'

I didn't know what to say. I felt as if I was stepping in and out of a cinema screen; I was a villain, a tragic hero, a spectator all at once. I must confess, Elizabeth, I hadn't even known Tanya was pregnant. It seemed incredible that the child had anything to do with me. Yet while I was watching her cry I began to feel part of her again, bound heart and soul to the sad weight of our joint existence. I forgot how many times I'd stayed out all night recently. I forgot that there was no wedding ring on my finger. I forgot that on the rare occasions we made love I pretended it was you. (No, I didn't pretend; I believed. Every woman in those days was a manifestation, a mode, of you.) When she cried, pushing her forehead into her knuckles, she reminded me of some small, rooting, half-starved animal. This animal moved me with its blindness, hunger and insistence; I could only bow my head to it.

I protested that the child did have a future; I defended its right to life. I said how pleased Masha would be. I promised to see the housing officer about a bigger apartment.

Tanya's blue eyes went narrow, inky. 'You stupid bastard, Arkady Petrovich! What's the good of all that when we're finished?'

Tanya and I finished: yes, of course, how obvious, how simple. But the child said we weren't. The child is the strongest one, the truth of the matter, or rather, the Truth. Truer than love, which is just a trick of the imagination.

A real child. Already with a heartbeat of its own? Maybe – I hoped not.

'You've never loved me and never been faithful to me,' said Tanya. 'I'm sick of your girlfriends, your nights out, your laziness and your lies. I want a divorce. I'm going back to the country; yes, it's all arranged,' she said quickly, as I opened my mouth to protest. 'But I can't have the responsibility of another child, and it wouldn't be fair to Mum and Dad anyway, on top of Masha. If the only way to get rid of it is to go to the public slaughterhouse, then I will. Because I don't love it and I don't want it. Understand?' She wasn't shouting, but her voice was hard as an old kitchen cloth.

I flinched, imagining the child inside her hearing every word. I wanted to hold her in my arms, but only to rock the child to sleep.

'Give me the compress again and then leave me alone,' she said. She shut her eyes and this time they stayed tearless. I spread the flannel over her hot forehead. 'I shouldn't have married you,' she whispered in that dry, baked voice. 'I wanted to get to Moscow so much! And to be married!' She gave a small groan and laughed. 'I shouldn't have chased after you, Arkady Petrovich! But it was all I'd ever wanted since I was a little girl. City lights and a white veil! What a little fool!'

Two weeks later she went to the abortion clinic. I had tried to pull strings with the help of Lenina Andreevna and get her into one of the top-drawer places, but these things take time to arrange, and she was already over twelve weeks gone. She went off alone. Men aren't allowed in, and anyway she didn't want me, not even to see her to the bus stop. Raisa, though, had promised to meet her and bring her home.

I left work early that day, but when I got to the flat she still wasn't back. I couldn't bear my own thoughts. Don't think I'm just trying to impress you, Elizabeth, with my womanly compassion. The baby had been real to me, although it had no sex or name. And if, deep down, I had wanted to cause the death of my marriage, I certainly would never have done so if I'd realised it would mean killing my own child. It was like slaughtering a little god of life, or home, or future. I paced the empty flat, hearing women screaming, wanting to scream myself. I dreaded the rattle of the key in the front door and Raisa's sharp little looks, telling me what a dirty, heartless goat I was.

And then, I was saved. Maybe the magic line in my palm isn't a tightrope but a little passage marked 'exit'. Because at that moment the phone rang and it was Asta; she was having a few friends round for a drink, an impromptu flat-warming: nothing grand, but she'd be pleased if I would join them.

You never met Asta, did you? But you must have heard Lenina Andreevna going on about her. To understand her, you have to realise she spent much of her childhood in Canada (her daddy was a 'diplomat' at the embassy there); she also travelled in Europe quite a bit. But all this was before she was fourteen, when the family was recalled to Moscow. Asta, I believe, has created her adult self out of her childhood impressions of the West. Even her pictures are paintings of the paintings she saw in Paris, Munich and Barcelona (she can do Picasso, Matisse, Cézanne, Kandinsky and de Chirico, according to her mood). She is perfectly artificial, perfectly unlocatable. A walking dream of the West, a transplanted orchid. How can an orchid survive the Moscow winters? you may ask. Well, perhaps, if you look closely, you'll discover the orchid is made of silk, or even tin – the finest tin imaginable. Very cleverly and fascinatingly made, though, there isn't a doubt.

And why should this orchid have taken an interest in me – a humble Russian potato?

The simple fact is that, whatever the mess and muddle of my private life, I publicly carried at this time a certain aura of potential. No, more than that: of potential in the process of becoming actual. A champagne aura to many noses, male and female, great and small. Hadn't I that very week had six poems printed by Karambaev on page one of the *Moscow Gazette*? (Karambaev: famously plump and jolly and easy-going in society, and famously hawk-eyed as a poetry editor, giving no quarter to the backslider, the bluffer, the egoist.) Asta had probably just got around to reading her copy, and had thought: Aha, here's someone who would enhance my salon, provided he comes without his wife. (Merciless, aren't I? But it's my job to understand human weaknesses, including my own.)

I said I wouldn't be able to stay long, Tanya wasn't well. 'What a shame,' said Asta daintily. Then I had a shower, and set off for Universitetsky Prospekt.

Asta enacted delight at seeing me. Maybe the delight was genuine. Her little flat was superb (by Moscow standards) but the social atmosphere that night was scarcely electrifying. Professor Z had decided to exert his wits at the chessboard and had commanded Lev to be his opponent. (You remember Lev – the perfect English gentleman in almost everything but his love of vodka and chess?) Both were hunched immobile over the coffee table and scarcely even grunted an acknowledgement of my entrance. An elderly distinguished artist was absorbed in explaining his highly unoriginal theories of composition to a middle-aged art teacher (one of Asta's colleagues at the Repin Institute), whose heavy lower lip sagged like a pelican's beak to enable her to gather up every word. I had no choice amid such polarities, but to latch on to 'the young people'; Asta and her film-director boyfriend, Taras.

My first impression of Taras was that he looked a bit like me, only bigger and better. For example, my slightly Mediterranean complexion and hair density were magnified in him to a full-blown Georgian swarthiness, complete with black moustaches and lustrous, rolling tresses. He was taller than me and broader-shouldered and whiter-toothed; he wore an azure blouson with NASHVILLE printed on the top pocket flap, whereas I wore a nylon anorak with tears in both armpits. An embroidered sweatband round his temples was the ultimate statement of – well, whatever it was, it left me out of the running.

We sat at the Swedish dining table, drinking an abrasive pineapple liqueur he had smuggled back from one of his unimaginable locations west of the Black Sea. Wisely, the other guests had declined it.

Asta talked rapidly. Splinters of green light seemed to shoot out of her eyes. Taras yawned at me. A docile beast, I thought, and a stupid one. He insisted that the liqueur had extraordinary aphrodisiac and rejuvenating properties, and was gulping it by the tumbler.

'Is he going to make a star of you?' I asked Asta conversationally.

'She's already a star, aren't you, baby?' Taras stood behind her chair and massaged her breasts, oblivious to the glares of the pelican and the distinguished artist. I rolled in my hands imaginary icy globes of stainless steel, and made them glow.

Asta writhed coyly. 'What about a part for Arkashenka, darling?'

'Sure, anything's possible. Would you like to have a screen test?'

'No, really, thanks all the same – ' I broke off in alarm as a paw like a black-whiskered cactus fruit floated towards my head. Another cactus fruit approached it from the other side. And now it was being held in a vice and gently rotated. 'Good skull, supple neck,' Taras grunted. 'Can you dance?'

'Not a step,' I said eagerly.

'That's a real pity.'

'What part were you thinking of, Tarasik?'

'The Man with the Broken Neck, of course.'

'And why would I need to be able to dance?'

'He dances. All my characters dance. It's an allegory, isn't it?' Taras yawned at the necessity for such elementary explanations.

'I play the Woman without a Womb' said Asta helpfully. 'It's science fiction, really.'

'Darling, it is *not* science fiction!' Taras's hormone-rich baritone squeaked with pain. 'In fact, that's the whole point.' He leaned towards me confidentially, as if this was men's talk and Asta had better go and do the dishes or keep quiet. 'It's about the *fiction* of *science*!'

'That's what I meant,' said Asta fiercely.

'You see, my film depicts a world in which biochemical engineering has eradicated all that makes us human – lust, creativity, mother love, patriotism and so on. It begins with a group of scientists deciding to put an end to the problem of war. And it ends with the very thing they set out to prevent – the annihilation of the human race. Aggression, you see, is essential to survival. It's the root of everything good, as well as evil. In the first phase of the experiment everything's bliss. It's like the flower-power thing they had in California. Peace and lerve, man,' drawled Taras in ludicrous Amerenglish. 'Here's a daisy, you fuzz, let's kiss and be friends. All you need is lerve, man. But it ends' – Taras's voice went deep and sinister – 'with *total stagnation*. Because the *hormones of aggression* are vital. To both men *and women*. Otherwise, the whole damn human race simply *freaks out*.'

'Very interesting,' I said. 'I'm sure there's some truth in that.'

'Some truth? It's total truth, comrade! Everyone'll relate to it. It tells where the West is going wrong, see? In a way even a child could understand.'

I nodded assent, though it seemed to me that the West was considerably less pacific than Taras painted it. And I couldn't help smiling as I imagined the Man with the Broken Neck and the Woman without a Womb performing a slow-motion tango in front of a bemused and slightly bristling board of censors.

'So you're a poet?' Taras suddenly said, with a definite undertone of his beloved aggressiveness. 'Nastenka says you're having a book published.'

The pelican and the distinguished artist had pricked up their ears and were staring round at me with ballooning eyes.

'It's not definite' I said, embarrassed. 'I submitted it, I haven't heard yet.' My head throbbed like jungle drums, my mouth felt like a fruit crate. I got to my feet, staggering slightly, and apologised to the liqueur bottle. 'I really must be going now, my wife's not very well, you see.'

'Wife? I'd like to meet your wife.' Taras stood beside me and pawed me, I think with benevolence.

'Come on,' said Asta, taking my arm and leading me to the door.

'Will you be all right, Arkasha?' I was pretty sure I wouldn't be but I didn't want to bother her with that.

'Will *you* be all right?' I countered, summoning up a feeble vestige of gallantry.

'Of course. I can handle Taras. The big oaf! I only put up with him because of the perks. Like films at the Goskino! And he's taking me to Belgrade for the summer film festival.'

'Good for you.' My stomach rose and fell on nauseous waves of envy.

Taras tottered into the entrance hall, and called out that there was a part for a poet in his film.

'The Poet with the Wooden Leg?' I managed to quip, though reeling in the gust of fresh night air.

'No. Just a poet. The guy's already crippled, if he's a poet.' Taras neighed with laughter.

Asta rolled her eyes and indicated a screw loose. She kissed me in a friendly way and told me to come again, but I still went out into the night feeling as if I'd really lost a limb.

At any rate, I noticed the recurrence of an old hereditary disease which, for want of an official medical term, I shall call *domophobia.* Though the broad streets were rearing and swooping and swirling like circus horses, though I had to concentrate hard on putting one foot in front of the other, there was still a tiny, clear, uncontaminated part of my brain that registered horror at the thought of going home. I found myself in a phone booth, talking to mother; I learned that Tanya was safely back, all right and in bed, and that it would be appreciated by my mother if I did not make calls at one in the morning. I swam out of the phone booth, and then all the horrors converged in a wave of nausea – broken necks, doctor's knives, bleeding wombs, pineapple liqueur, Taras's sweaty face. I sobered up enough to find a quiet street and an anonymous doorway. I sat down, vomited convulsively, and then stretched out and fell asleep.

I woke up to pummellings, buffetings and exhortations – insistent, but, to me in my condition, only dimly alarming. 'Come on, get on your feet, time you went home.' I allowed the two men to balance me in a roughly vertical position between them. 'Where d'you live, comrade?'

Even in such a condition, my domophobia asserted itself. 'Simonovsky,' I gasped.

'Get going, then,' said the younger and stockier of the two men, giving me a shove.

'It's a long way. He'll never make it,' remarked the other.

'Yes, I will,' I said, not at all convinced, but not wishing to give my helpful vigilantes any further provocation. After all, it was their duty to deliver me to the nearest drying-out cell.

The older man gave me directions. He was mild, friendly, amused. The younger seemed to me less inclined to be indulgent, and I think if he had been by himself he would have tried to set me on the path of correction. I left them with grateful thanks and a show of sobriety and purpose which, as I walked, became at least partially absorbed into my true state. Dawn was breaking when I got to within sight of Lev's. But I realised I didn't want to talk to him or anybody else. I simply wanted to be by myself.

The area sweepers were already out, a first tram rattled by. I went down to the river and leaned on the parapet; I took out your postcard. You already know what happens next. The postcard floats downwards, and I am slowly engulfed in great harsh waves of envy, and in smaller, warmer, teary waves of pity – not only for myself, but for Lev, Tanya, Ilya, Mother and all ordinary citizens of this socialist republic of ours. How does anyone ever succeed in finding his or her own authenticity in its stifling maternal embrace?

Some people never even manage to leave home.

And even if you succeed in leaving home, you remain a child. The army, the university, the factory, the office, the yard committee all extend the smothering arm as you try to totter free, and overwhelm your conscience with ersatz mother love and ersatz fatherly advice. Even the walls in the streets are peppered with commands and wise suggestions. Spiteful literary critics, heavy-booted militiamen, friendly vigilante squads: everyone everywhere telling you what to do and threatening you with what for if you don't do it! Publicly, you're the eternal child. And inwardly, the eternal adolescent, straining at the leash, obsessed with mirrors, diaries, bodies, alcohol, passion.

Where else could I have found my poems, except in those private rooms and foreign countries of booze and sex? Forgive me, Elizabeth, Tanya, but where else?

I left the embankment as the first sunlight stirred the water to a blaze and the air seemed quite suddenly to be filled with the roar and dust of daily life. Passers-by stared at me with faintly scandalised expressions. I knew they saw only my dirty clothes and hair, but all the same it was as if they looked right through my jacket and shirt and into the rose-red postcard in my heart. My domophobia expanded from that moment on, and filled the whole city.

There was a happy, almost holiday atmosphere about the morning Tanya left for the country. She radiated it herself, although she tried not to, for my sake. (I had worked hard, from motives I cannot explain even to myself, at persuading her during the last few weeks to change her mind about leaving, and now, though I certainly did not deserve it, she felt sorry for me.) She was wearing a new, primrose-coloured suit, and there was a round glow in her face which suggested she was already breathing country air. I could hardly keep myself from flinging my arms round her and peeling off the yellow jacket. This was the girl I'd married, the girl who'd once held in her broad, friendly hands and gentle eyes all the ideals of my Tolstoyan adolescence. False ideals, perhaps; I could no more have lived in harmony with the earth than she could be entirely happy among noisy streets and factory machines. But at least she had woken up from her nightmare and struggled free. She was going home to become a child again and make a fresh attempt at growing up. I envied her because she had a place to go back to. I had never left the house of my childhood; perhaps that was why I couldn't love it.

I helped her father load up the Moskvitch. He was a cheerful countryman, one of the few collective farmers I've met with a genuine dedication to the land. He smelled pleasantly of linseed oil, and wore a cornflower in his buttonhole. 'These things happen,' he said as we stowed assorted goods: Tanya's favourite pots and pans, a spare mattress, skis, a dinghy and Vasya, cowering in his basket. 'No point in blaming anyone. In my opinion, nature arranged it all wrong. By the time folks are old enough to get married, they're too old to have children.'

What was the marriageable age he had in mind?

'Oh, maybe fifty-five,' he chuckled, showing yellow hamster teeth. 'My age, roundabout!'

Tanya got into the back of the car with Masha, who was bouncing with excitement. She'd been begging pumpkin seeds off Granddad all morning, and now she had made herself a beard with the dribbled husks, just as he told her the old peasants used to do.

'That's not nice manners,' said Mother, but Tanya cooed indulgently as she took a handkerchief to Masha's chin. 'Already a little country girl,' she murmured, and flashed me a proud, defiant grin.

I leaned in and we kissed formally. She smelled of Red Moscow, her favourite perfume, together with a faint trace of that burnt, rubbery odour she used to bring home from the Aeronautical and General Instrument plant. She wasn't a country girl yet; maybe it wouldn't be so easy to shake off the city after all.

As an afterthought she said, 'Good luck with the book. Send me a copy – not that I ever understood a word of your poems!'

Then the car was inching out of the courtyard, with Masha waving excitedly at the back window; my Masha, who would never be mine again in quite the same way.

When the advance copies of *Notes from a Hurrying Train* arrived, there was no one to show them to, not even Mother, who was staying at Alla's for a holiday. But I wished the book a happy birthday by myself, and drank a toast to it. I had no wish actually to read it. I even had to force myself to check that the pages were cut and numbered properly, I was so nervous of bumping into the frail little naked bodies of my thoughts.

A week later, there was a stack in the middle of the window of World of Books. I felt my first excitement. There I stood, rooted, staring through the glass like a father in a hospital nursery, blushing if anyone approached, wondering absurdly if it could see me as it lay there so innocently. And then, right in front of me, someone went inside and bought a copy. A woman of indeterminate years and appearance – but to me an angel. How decisively her rosy hand descended towards the pile. She scanned the cover – purple with a band of yellow rectangles to represent the train, and the title superimposed in grey – flicked through the first pages, and knew at once it was the book for her. I was deeply impressed by her intuition. I decided that, as a reward, I would offer to sign my name for her as she came out. I managed to restrain myself, as it happened, since she peered at me in a rather unfriendly way, as if she did not associate me in any way with the touching words she has just been reading. I waited on, in the hope of further customers, but none was in the offing. So I gave up and went to work – not much downcast at this early stage.

My sense of importance expanded wonderfully over the next few weeks. The pile in the window went down and had to be replenished – I lost count of how many times. Mother brought Alla back for some return hospitality, and the two old ladies larded me constantly with comfortable, fat, uncomprehending praise. Lenina Andreevna arranged for me to give a reading at the university: about 800 people came (nothing, compared to the size of the audience a poet like Yevtushenko draws, but not bad for a beginner). There was a tedious celebratory dinner at the Union, and several even more tedious visits to factories, clinics and schools. The reviews were unanimously favourable. My own editor wrote a pleasantly ingratiating 'Profile' for the *New Literary Star*.

Perhaps the most satisfying result was the blossoming of my affair with Asta. It was an asexual blossoming, true, but we ate supper and had intellectual conversations together at her Swedish table several nights a week, and went with Taras to the latest imported films at the Goskino. Asta was proud to be seen around with me, a published poet, and even prouder, I have to admit, to be seen around with both a published poet and an avant-garde film director at the same time.

Among my Cavern friends, however, I found myself embarrassed by my new respectability.

In fact, I had been embarrassed ever since the Union had decided to honour me with membership. And that sweetest of writerly moments – the acceptance for publication of one's first book – had, for me, the unmistakable tang of the flypaper. I was in prison, though the bars were coated with honey. It's perfectly true that I was not asked to change more than a word or two of the typescript: perhaps if the censor had seriously challenged me, I would have been inspired to make a stand. The fact that I wasn't challenged proved to me how thoroughly I had absorbed my earlier lessons in self-censorship. It had become part of my technique – even part of my talent.

But my friends were no strangers to such necessities, and did not condemn me. They were simply glad to see me prosper, whether inside or outside the system. And they claimed me back for themselves, my dear, brave friends, by giving me my own, unofficial launching party at the Cavern.

There was music, of course. Ilya brought his guitar, Maurice his tenor sax and Keloway a little silver Irish pipe that flutes away at a pitch barely audible to the human ear – a makeshift ensemble, but what they improvised together was weirdly beautiful and, I am sure, though I am no musician, touched by genius. Lev was there too, of course, and Rivka, and Maurice's friend Valdai – a young, heavy-jowled, docile white ox who practised law by day and, it was rumoured, wrote pornographic stories by night. Luba, accompanied as she always was these days by Boba, turned up eventually.

'We've done it, we've done it,' Boba cried, dancing about with bundles of flimsy typescript. Luba was more restrained, but she looked like a cat who'd just licked up a bowl of smetana.

'The first issue of the only feminist magazine in the whole Soviet republic!' Boba grinned.

I felt a little upstaged: this was my celebration, after all.

'Are you sure it's the only one?' asked the literal young lawyer.

'Wonderful,' I said, trying to mean it. I leafed nervously through the manuscript Boba had thrust at me, pausing briefly at an article entitled 'Sexual Initiation'.

'And your book, too – congratulations,' Boba offered kindly. 'Would you sign my copy?'

She was wearing her usual gear – dungarees, if you remember, with a bib pocket which she rather affectedly stuffs with pens and pencils to make herself look like a real writer. Tempted by a slightly irritable impulse (book-signing was something official, stilted, stamped with Writers' Union respectability), I snatched a bright, tinny little pen from Boba's bosom. I scrawled the usual banal message, and tried to replace the pen.

'No, please keep it, I've got hundreds!' She edged away from me, a frightened look in her eyes, as if I might assault her.

For a long time afterwards my face would turn warm whenever I thought about this trivial incident. I'm clumsy with women, I know. Was I with you, Elizabeth? Forgive me if I was. It's worse when I'm nervous, and Boba for some reason always makes me nervous. I slipped the pen into my pocket, and eventually gave it to Luba to return. I still feel as if I had done something horrible to Boba, in stealing from the pathetic little armoury on her breast.

We listened to the 'band' for a while longer; then came the moment I'd dreaded. I admit I was trembling as I stepped onto the orange-box platform. This was a test far greater than reciting to 800 people at the University!

To my surprise, the words I heard – my words – calmed me down almost at once. Dropping them into the pool of that generous, intimate silence my friends spread out for me, I sensed a transformation – passed by the silence to the words, and by the words to the silence. I remembered how once, when I was a little boy, father had tried to explain to me that, each time I threw a stone into a pond, the wash of ripples didn't cease at the pond's perimeter but went on into the field, into the town, into the world. And, one day, thinking it over to myself, I realised that the ripples must ultimately change the stone too, the stone that had started them all off. This was what was happening now. I heard my voice become more confident and expressive; I no longer buried my head in the pages, but drew the rhythms up from my memory and stared my audience in the eyes. And they, my audience, were giving me back irony, satire, intensity; they told me I did not lie. Luba, Ilya, Rivka, Boba – you who lived in the truth – you told me I did not lie. (Perhaps I didn't – I was younger then, after all, and could have been more honest than I realised.)

'To poetry. To the revolutionary potential of the word!' cried Ilya, lifting his glass towards me as I stumbled back to my seat. 'To Petrovich the Poet!'

Everyone drank.

'To music. To the revolutionary potential of the Moscow Cavern. To Ilya!' I returned, hoarse and breathless with the alcohol and a gathering of thick tears at the back of my throat.

Everyone drank; vodka and tears. Lev on my right, Ilyusha on my left, arms overlapping across my shoulders, a hand gripping my shirtsleeve, another ruffling my hair, till the swimming rainbows shrank and neatened themselves to small ovals of candle flame, and I could see Rivka's face in front of me again, black-eyes and glowing with the harsh compassion of a saint in an icon.

Why had I cried? Of course I was moved by the loyalty of my friends. But it wasn't only that. I was thinking of Asta, wanting her with me, and at the same time remembering how she had come to the Cavern only once, and then belittled it. 'I love sleaziness,' she declared, bumping into chairs and almost tripping over Ilya's guitar case, and 'How quaint' when we offered her vodka in a thick china cup. And afterwards she said, 'I don't like your crowd much. Why do you hang out with scruffs and weirdos like that? The Irish girl looks like a junky. And where did you dig up that mothballed Jewish hag?' Oh yes, the daughter of the KGB boss lives on in the marrow of Asta's fine bones and sprouts out like a flick knife whenever she's angry or jealous; even though at other times she likes to think of herself as an artist and rebel – and, in her manufactured way, genuinely is. I knew at that moment that the time would come when I would have to choose between Asta and my friends.

At the same time, Elizabeth, I was thinking about you. You'll think I'm being sentimental if I say that no gathering ever seems quite complete without your face, your voice, your moody, Slav flashes of feeling. I remembered how many colours there are in your hair, like the stripes in the jar of different sands we used to have in our classroom, and how your nose pulls your top lip upward so you always look slightly indignant with the world. And I wanted to boast to you that I'd published a book. Well, now I have – boasted, I mean. And I wish you could read it. As I said, it isn't all falsehood. I'll give Joey a copy for you anyway, and, if I've got time, I'll even add some translations at the end of this letter – to save you from having to learn Russian.

I finished my recitation with a poem called 'The Ant Parade'. It's nothing much on the page (you'll see) but in the context of that night it acquired a sort of subversive comic power. Everyone laughed; the applause lasted whole minutes. Such a warm sound, Elizabeth, and the memory goes on warming you – maybe even when you're dying.

'I loathe parades,' said Rivka passionately, as I sat down again.

Everyone round the table agreed. 'And yet,' said Maurice importantly, 'man is a collective animal. There's a certain satisfaction in marching in step, feeling the same emotion.'

'Particularly if you're united *against* something,' Boba put in. Her voice, soft, rapid and precise, made me think of a typewriter pattering away quietly to itself in the small hours of the morning, its roller stuffed with secretive carbons. 'I think it requires the focus of an enemy to bring out real solidarity in people,' Boba said, with a nervous glance at me.

'Exactly,' said Valdai, and he began to tell us about his experiences as a soldier in Prague in 1968. His voice was quite emotionless, although the scenes he was describing – of traffic stopped in the streets as the people surrounded the tanks, explaining, lecturing, chattering, holding meetings, singing songs, tearing down street signs, handing out bunches of leaflets and flowers – seemed full of emotion.

Rivka leaned towards him excitedly, unaware that her blouse fell open, exposing the pale roots of her breasts to Ilya's shining stare.

'Did any of the soldiers rebel? Did any of them decide to take the part of the Czechs?'

'Well, as a matter of fact, yes. I heard about this corporal who refused to go in on a raid. He went and told his officer that he thought that the Czech brand of socialism was better than the Russian kind. He shot himself before the firing squad could do it for him.'

'That's what I admire – the courage to stand up alone for what you believe in,' cried Boba.

'But what good did it do anyone?' asked Maurice stubbornly.

'Exactly,' said his friend, but Rivka butted in excitedly.

'That's not the point! Listen, I was fifteen when the army invaded. I joined in the demonstration in Red Square. I hadn't planned it, but as soon as I saw these women just standing there with their banners, quietly saying no, I went over to them, I simply had to. One of them tried to shoo me off, but I wouldn't go, although I was pretty scared. And then the militia came, it was all over in a few minutes. They took me away and began to question me, but when they saw I was only a tongue-tied kid with wet knickers and tears streaming down my face they just said, "Oh, get out, go home, and behave yourself in future." I don't know for sure what happened to the others on the demo, but I can imagine. As for me, I came to see that day as the best and most revealing day of my life, the first time I ever breathed real air!'

'Oh, I can believe it, I can believe it!' said Boba. Her chin rested on her clasped hands and she stared at Rivka as if she were praying to her.

The rest of us said nothing: our eyes darted covertly from one to the other. None of us knew anything about the demonstration. The only one who did, it turned out, was Keloway, who had been in Ireland at the time and read something about it in the paper.

Then Valdai cleared his throat.

'Your demonstration was simply another kind of parade,' he told Rivka. 'Of course, it was only a miniature parade. But it was still a collective act. There's no difference. It's purely a matter of scale.'

'The difference was that we were standing up to a dictatorial authority on behalf of true socialism,' Rivka blazed.

Valdai was determined to remain calm and unimpressionable. 'And when we march on parade we're standing up to world imperialism. I'm not arguing morality, or even politics. I'm simply saying that psychologically it's the same phenomenon.'

'You're just playing with abstractions,' said Luba irritably. 'I'm sure the women on Rivka's protest had thought out the matter for themselves, and were obeying their consciences. But when we march on parade we don't think, we just do it because everyone says we ought, or it's a tradition. There's no conviction behind it.'

'But there was once,' Valdai argued. 'It only shows how the spirit of the October Revolution has degenerated if people march mechanically, without anything in their souls but cynicism.'

'Why shouldn't people feel cynicism if their leaders have betrayed them?' asked Rivka dangerously.

Even Valdai flinched and blinked his white eyelashes. 'Betrayed? That's a very serious accusation!'

I looked at Ilya and he at me: we were both thinking that the conversation had gone on long enough.

'A year and a half ago our leaders signed the Helsinki Final Act. Since then they have not honoured a single one of the agreements on human rights. If that isn't betrayal, tell me what is?'

Ilya broke in gently. 'OK, Rivka, but this is a party, after all. We should save these arguments for another time.'

Rivka shot angry glances at him and Valdai, but said nothing more.

'Sometimes I feel women have so much power when they're together it almost frightens me,' said Boba suddenly. 'It's like plugging yourself into pure energy. I believe we could make something happen if we tried – something really tremendous!'

Both Luba and Rivka lifted their glasses in her direction and Luba said, 'We will, we will!'

'Read us another poem, Arkasha,' said Lev, nudging me. 'What about a sexy love poem, to take our minds off politics?'

I left the Cavern that night of my recitation and supposed triumph feeling that after all I had achieved nothing in airing the trivial privacies of my poems. It was all very clever to hit at the system so softly it didn't know it was being hit at, but what was the point?

And if I had hit it so hard I made my knuckles bleed, what would have been the point of that?

One thing was certain: if you hit the system, it was you who bled.

In a sudden rage at my own helplessness and cowardice, I grabbed a small serrated knife from the kitchen drawer. This knife, I should explain, was not an import but the product of a factory in the Urals (Goods for Common Use Department) and therefore made of the lowest-grade steel, the better grades being reserved for the manufacture of arms and heavy industrial machines.

Holding my breath, I ran the blade backwards and forwards across the little blue tree in my left wrist. After numerous attempts, it finally etched a line of blood spots. Disgusted, I slammed the pathetic item back into the kitchen drawer.

That night, however, my wrist ached quite badly and kept me awake, wondering if I would need to go to the polyclinic next day for an anti-tetanus injection. There was another ache, too: for Ilya.

You've met Ilya, of course, and heard him play. He liked to borrow a saying of the Beatles: 'We're just happy little rockers.' But Ilya isn't just a happy little rocker – I mean, apart from the fact that no one could be, here, for very long. Ilya, you see, was going to be a concert pianist, and all that ambition and talent are smouldering inside him still.

He attended the Conservatoire, and everyone said he was the best student they'd ever had. Then came trouble. One of his fellow second-years, a talentless but highly influential Party brat called Tolya, lost his girlfriend, Lara, to Avram, also a student at the Conservatoire. Ilya was going out with Avram's sister at the time, and knew the family quite well. They were a shade disreputable, specialising in black-market and foreign-currency tricks. Tolya grabbed his opportunity and began trying to persuade Ilya to inform on Avram. Ilya refused. And then, to make matters even worse, Tolya discovered that Lara and Ilya had once gone out together too. Tolya now exerted his influence against Ilya in a variety of unpleasant ways; I won't go into all the details. You'll understand that being Jewish in our society – as in yours, too? – gives an additional vulnerability. The result was that Ilya failed his exams that year, quite inexplicably. He could have sat them again, but he was too proud. He walked out in disgust and promised never to play another note of classical music. Only street music from now on could speak to his soul, he said. (You're surprised he could be so extreme? Ilya's a very complex character, though in those days he liked to give the impression of careless good spirits and even, sometimes, calm reasonableness.)

That's how he came to start the Cavern. He had a few useful contacts; the authorities quibbled but then decided to permit him to exist, as proof that they're not such a bad lot after all. They even let him be filmed once by a Western TV company.

I was worried about him mainly because of Rivka. He could take risks and do crazy things well enough by himself, without her to spur him on. Her intensity seemed to bring out an answering intensity in him, even while he was calmly denying it. I remembered how bright his eyes had shone when she talked about the demonstration, and how he couldn't stop gazing at her. What would he do if she got her visa? Apply for one too and try to follow her? I couldn't imagine him anywhere but Moscow; he was a night child, a child of dim lights and jazz and vodka and smoky blues, a Russian far more than a Jew.

Rivka was trying hard to raise his consciousness, on every front.

'D'you know,' she said to me one day, 'he didn't even realise that the Americans had put a man on the moon? And what's worse, he didn't care about not knowing.'

'Well,' I said, trying to dredge up a few dim adolescent memories, 'I don't think we were told much about it; I'm sure a lot of people didn't know – and probably still don't.'

'Precisely!' said Rivka. 'And it's our duty to fight this disinformation at every opportunity!'

Ilya, who had been listening to the conversation with an expression of innocent amazement, suddenly began to strum and sing:

'There are footprints on the moon, but the moon still shines
There are drunkards in the streets, but the grapes still grow
on vines
There are troubles in our lives, but life is just a game
There's anger in your eyes, but I love you just the same!'

(Excuse the translation – it was better in Russian, though not much.)

'That just about sums up his philosophy,' said Rivka, but her eyes had softened, and she let him kiss her. I got up and left the room, no doubt to their surprise.

On another occasion, Rivka gave a Passover supper, extending invitations to her maverick friends – the unorthodox, the goyim, the atheists – as well as her fellow refuseniks. In such a setting Arkady Petrovich's palms began to sweat. The refuseniks were discussing their plans for a demonstration outside the Lenin Library.

'It won't get any Jew to Israel but it will get you to a labour camp, if that's what you want,' I said, surprised at my own anger.

Rivka looked at me with contempt. 'Two people got visas after the protest in '73,' she said. The others nodded consent. She turned to Ilya and murmured caressingly, 'You'll be there, darling, won't you?'

Ilya looked frightened. 'No, I agree with Arkasha,' he said quickly. 'This isn't 1973. Things are much tougher now.' My relief was short-lived; Ilya's days of liberty, as it turned out, were numbered.

About a week later, he suddenly went missing. He simply didn't turn up at the Cavern for three days, something quite unheard of. Rivka was on holiday at a friend's dacha, but we knew he hadn't accompanied her; since the party they'd barely been on speaking terms. Lev and I decided to go to his – not flat, because Ilya didn't have a flat, or even a room – his corner.

This corner Ilya rented was in a room belonging to a Jewish couple. It was in one of the old, communal blocks, not more than a minute's walk from Lev's. No one ever visited him, partly because there wasn't the space (with Ilya, the Blavatskys and another woman tenant distantly related to them, there were already four people struggling to eke out the 'sanitary norm' of eight square meters apiece) and partly because the couple was rather antisocial, self-concious about their living conditions and especially liable to be hostile to any non-Jew. Both of them had done time in Stalin's camps.

The doorbell didn't work, so we were forced to rap with our fists; not as Lev remarked, a promising start. When we said we were Ilya's friends, though, Mrs Blavatsky opened up immediately, and drew us eagerly into the cluttered, heavily furnished little room.

She gestured towards the crimson curtain which screened his corner. 'Ilya hasn't slept in his bed for four nights!'

Lev and I looked dismally at each other.

'I'm sure he'd have told us if he'd planned to be away.' She twisted the hem of her apron and gazed searchingly into my face. 'One morning he just goes out as usual to that music-shop job of his, and then he never comes back.'

Her husband shuffled in, a tiny, bent, white-faced man with a permanent, anxious half-twist of a smile. 'Gone,' he said mournfully, pointing at the curtain like a child.

'I told them, Yasha, they already know it. Please, sit down over there and I'll make some tea.'

The old man sat down, too, and smiled anxiously at us, massaging the palm of his left hand with the knuckles of his right.

'Prison,' he said with a mournful smile, 'that what. I don't tell the old lady, though.'

'You can't be sure,' I said.

'Prison,' repeated the old man sharply. 'Them records he was selling was stolen property. He made them himself, from hospital X-rays. Yes, he showed me! Can't tell the old lady, though.'

I didn't reply, but what Mr Blatvatsky had said was true. Of course, Ilya did have a line in selling pirate records, though he'd been getting away with it for so long I thought he must have had a private order from some rock-and-roll-hungry young KGB man.

To register an official enquiry would have been risky, so I spoke to Lenina Andreevna, who has a number of contacts among the police and magistrates. But before she could discover anything, Ilya reappeared. He had been away a fortnight. And now here he was on my doorstep – thinner, sunken-eyed but grinning. He held up a string bag with three bunches of speckled ripe bananas in it, trying to claw their way out.

'That's how it was in our cell,' he said wryly. 'But it's an ill wind, et cetera. I made some good friends, including a bootlegging greengrocer. They let him out at the same time as me, so now we're in business. He wanted to do a deal in turnip vodka, but I said I'd rather have fresh fruit.'

Ilya seemed jaunty, and I hoped he wasn't holding down a deep, smouldering rage. The twelve-day prison sentence had been for petty hooliganism; the militia had ignored his record-selling activities, and picked him up when he was strumming his guitar to entertain a cinema queue (he was always giving impromptu concerts on street corners, and sometimes made a few kopecks at it). Of course he should never have been sentenced, but I was relieved that it was nothing more serious. All I hoped was that it wouldn't drive him to some more serious act of rebellion.

He didn't stay long; he wanted to go and make his peace with Rivka. He left a bunch of bananas on the kitchen table.

'Don't do anything silly, will you?' I said as I saw him out.

He laughed. 'But my whole life's silly.'

'You know what I mean. The protest march next week, for example.'

'Oh, that. I'd forgotten all about it.'

On impulse, I pulled a 20-rouble note from my pocket and handed it to him.

'Please take it, it's just to keep you going for a bit – I know things can be difficult at times like this.'

To my astonishment, he smiled, folded it neatly into four, and slipped it into his pocket.

'There you are, I'm a jail-bird now, so I needn't be proud any more!' He laughed, and shook my hand warmly. 'Don't worry. Take care of yourself, poet Petrovich. I'll see you soon!'

I went back into the kitchen and ate a banana, dissolving the creamy chunks slowly on my tongue and trying to focus the nostalgia that indescribable flavour stirred in me. The slim metal wheels of a child's pram drew parallel lines in the dewy grass, but I couldn't remember if the pram was mine or little Masha's; only the grass smell and the fragrance of the banana and the silvery trails passed me by like a childhood – anyone's.

We celebrated Ilya's release with a party at the Cavern. Even the poor old Blatvatskys came for a short while. Only Rivka wasn't there. Ilya excused her, saying she was busy. But there was something blackly satirical about his mood that made me wonder if there hadn't been a serious rift between them.

It was Keloway who told me about the demonstration outside the library. She hadn't joined in but she'd been a spectator, drifting with the obscurely curious or obscurely hostile flotillas of passers-by.

It had been drizzling quite heavily, she said, as the protesters unrolled their banners. They lifted them high, and walked at a funereal pace in the middle of the pavement. Ilya was at the front with Rivka. There was also a middle-aged couple and a young man of eighteen or so. Ilya's banner read: LET MY PEOPLE GO.

A headscarfed babushka shouted, 'So go to Siberia if you don't like it here!' She raised her fist, then hurried away.

The little procession walked the length of the library façade, turned and came slowly back again. The bright-blue Stars of David inked onto the banners were beginning to weep. Everyone had their heads down and their coat collars up. The four men who ran out of the library to wrest the banners from the marchers' hands were wearing raincoats which flapped like broken umbrellas; they hadn't had time to do them up. Whoever tipped them off had obviously fallen short of perfect, split-second accuracy.

From this point onwards, I can verify Keloway's narrative. I didn't tell her, but I had been in the library all the time, researching an article on the Zagorsk monastery. I'd completely forgotten about the demonstration. When I heard shouts from outside, I hurried over to the window. At once I covered my face with my hands, I couldn't help it, though it was indiscreet to show such obvious distress.

Through my sweating fingers, I saw Ilya glance wildly up at the building, almost as if he knew I was watching from the window. His hand moved quickly over his drenched lock of hair.

Rivka seemed to whisper something to him; she was shaken hard by her officer and obviously told to shut her mouth. But Ilya had begun to smile and I saw, when he looked up again, that he was laughing. They were both smiling as they were pushed into the second of the two gleaming police cars that had just screeched down the middle of the road, stopped with a horrible convulsion, and discharged another contingent of militiamen.

The officer who had dealt with Rivka was obviously a tidy sort. He gathered up the broken banners and arrested them too, hustling them into the back of the Zhiguli, cursing the bright-blue tears that had dripped onto his shirt cuff.

At this point, Keloway said, one of Rivka's friends made a sign at her from the car window. She made a returning sign as unobtrusively as possible, lifting her finger as if to scratch her nose, and hurried away. Keloway's ex-husband, you see, is a journalist, and she was hoping to be able to transmit a report through him to the West.

That was when I sat down again with my books. For ten minutes I pretended to read, blood pounding in my ears, my vision blurred. Then I went home and sat motionless for an hour or more, not even able to pour myself a drink.

If I could have been sure that Ilya had acted from his own strong convictions I would have been less afraid for him. But I suspected that he had acted on a hurt but fairly trivial impulse, and it was Rivka, to whom such convictions were fundamental, who had provided the powerful booster thrust. If that was so, he would be far more vulnerable to whatever punishment he received. If there is anything I wish for Ilya now, apart from his release, it is that he has come to believe in the rightness of what he did. Such a belief is a few hundred extra calories a day, a couple more ounces of blanket, an extra inch of heart muscle, a half-hour less of shovelling icy stones.

None of their friends was allowed to attend the trial. But I found out via the network that Ilya and Rivka had been accused on the serious charge of anti-Soviet agitation and propaganda. Ilya was sentenced to ten years' hard labour in Mordovia, followed by five years' internal exile – to Siberia, of course. (Where would the tsars have been, where would the Soviets be, without Siberia? Perhaps everything is all Siberia's fault; perhaps there's a little piece of the subarctic in every Russian soul?) Rivka's sentence, for some reason, was slightly shorter.

Keloway wasn't successful in contacting her ex: he'd run off to the Caucasus with a girl who'd wooed him with legends of Colchis and Mount Kazbek. Mount Kazbek, you'll remember, is where Prometheus was chained by the gods for his theft of fire. And do you remember why he stole the fire? It was because Zeus had ordered him to create human beings out of mud and water, and he felt so sorry for them. Prometheus overreached himself not out of conceit but pity, so proving himself a nobler being than the gods. (But, of course, if they had been noble and compassionate they couldn't have been gods.) He wasn't an ordinary being, by the way, but a Titan. That titanic pity – it doesn't exist in the world any more. But how we need it, we people of water and mud, we empty-hearted gods.

Is there any chance, Elizabeth, that you could make Ilya's story known? You managed to get Luba's article on the Soviet feminists into print. I don't need to tell you that our gods are sensitive to Western opinion. These things can help.

Darkness is closing in on my friends' lives, Elizabeth, and I can do nothing: I want to survive, that's the trouble. To survive and write. But it's time I brought this story-letter to a close. The bedroom curtains are already faintly grey. My third night is becoming daylight; so we can end, as we began, with the sunrise. Have I succeeded in entertaining you – or at least not putting you to sleep? I'm sure by now your patience must be running out. So, a few last points, before I forget.

Luba's very grateful to you for getting her article published. She thinks it's very important for Western feminists to understand that socialism isn't the cure for all their ills. Concerning the *Noviye Domostroi* – which Joey has also promised to take to London – Luba has written her own letter explaining everything to your father (or whoever translates it – I believe Dr Lamb hasn't been very well. Forgive me for not mentioning this before: I hope he's in good health now, Elizabeth). One of the problems will be the title. The original *Domostroi* was a seventeenth-century book about household management; it included advice to husbands on wife-beating. Luba says any title your father can come up with is fine by her, as long as it conveys the message of a fresh view of women's rights. Maybe you will have some ideas? Joey says you're very good at *le mot juste* – it's part of your job.

I'm not sure, but this letter probably marks Arkasha's last public appearance. As I told you, I'm getting married on Saturday. And after that, there'll be no more nights in the Cavern. Keloway is planning to take it over for the training of a children's Irish pipe band – she's getting the pipes sent over from the Emerald Isle and it's all official – the USSR loves the Irish peasantry, it seems.

You'll want to know the name of Arkady Petrovich's bride-to-be –if you haven't already guessed. It's Anastasia Vladimirovna – more affectionately known as Asta.

I hope it doesn't offend your sense of propriety if I confess that I still don't know whether her undoubtedly beautifully designed body is constructed of steel, arcrylic, porcelain or some other sophisticated, man-made substance. She has so far not revealed it to me, despite my pleas, rages, sobs and acts of desperate cunning. 'You must wait till our wedding night,' she says pitilessly, 'if I can't be a true virgin, I will at least be a virgin to you.' Do you think this proves how much she loves me, Elizabeth? It may be clearer to you as a woman than it is to me.

Asta has made another condition to our marraige, one I dislike even more than the last, which at least is only temporary. It is that I permit her to continue her affair with Taras. Apparently, he is not much good in bed. But he is still her pet, her slave, her punchball, and does things for her which she could not possibly expect of anyone else – not even her husband. What these things might be I'm too delicate to ask – but I suspect they may have more to do with her professional than her erotic interests. Taras is vital to Asta's new career. Although the Woman without a Womb failed, unsurprisingly, to reach the public screens, there have been other films and other parts which have encouraged her to dream of becoming a 'real' movie star. She can't precisely act, of course, but she has an intensity, a presence, that seems to be right for Taras's films – which are, in a strange way, rather like her paintings. So we could make Hollywood yet, Elizabeth. Perhaps Taras isn't a bad price to pay for such an escape. You'll come for a holiday, won't you? There'll be a swimming pool in the garden, naturally, and a chauffeured Rolls-Royce at your disposal.

As you must have guessed by now, it won't be me but Arkady Petrovich who stands beside the white-robed Anastasia Vladimirova in the Palace of Weddings on Saturday. So what's going to happen to Arkasha? I hear you ask.

Arkasha is only yours now, Elizabeth. Only yours.

PS. These are the only poems I've had time to translate. I've put the page numbers at the top so you can identify them in the book. I'm sorry I haven't got any new ones but I don't write much poetry any more. I'm working on a novel at the moment, a fantasy – it's strange, but as I get older I find the truth less and less interesting, particularly the truth about myself.

Page 50. The Ant Parade

They scramble over the (red) earth at my feet,
a hundred at least, perhaps more.
The big, ripe, Georgian sun doesn't make them sweat.
They run and run, these tireless little workers
in their polished-up uniforms,
each carrying his own tiny banner
– a grass seed, a crumb of (red) earth.
Weaving and zigzagging, running all the time,
it's the strangest, most scatter-brained parade.
They don't know what a straight line is.
No discipline, that's the trouble,
no sense of common purpose.
I focus my dizzy gaze
on just one of them, to pursue him
and find out where he's going.

But it's always the same story
– he weaves about, turns circles, drops his banner,
searches for another – quite pathetic –
then races off in the opposite direction.
And yet, some people say
ants are intelligent and well-organised
in their own crazy way
– and that ant hills somehow get built
no honest observer can dispute.

Note. Red is in brackets because it's the one word I was asked to change. I substituted pink – I did so because I actually think it's a more accurate description of the colour of this kind of earth. (That was all I was trying to do, paint the earth in its true colour.) But now I've decided that pink sounds too flowery, so I've reinstated red!

Page 6. Mushrooming.

The Special left Gorsky Station
at midnight, wild with adventure.

It tore into the one-lamp villages,
into the black woods,

bouncing the baskets, the fruit juice
and the shrieking, unstillable children.

By the time it yawned, they had toppled
gently into its corners.

I carried our daughter, curled,
through the rose-blue dawn

till the air, clean as an icicle,
cooled her face, and she woke

and struggled to be put down.
Her hands closed like rescuers

on the swimming heads of the mushrooms.
She ran where she wanted to,

and we drifted after her
slowly, as if recollecting

something we had once dreamed,
touching the field like snowflakes.

Note. 'Mushrooming' is one of the poems in the sequence that gives the book its title. They're all about various train journeys, personal and historical. (There's one about Lenin, of course.) But I like the personal ones best. I dedicated the sequence to my ex-wife, Tanya.

Page 42. Practising

I remember the Practice Room.
It had sanded floors, sash windows,
and a smell of lilacs, blown in

with the curtains. (It was always spring
of course in the Practice Room.)
I came one day with my girlfriend,

the one you fancied, too.
She stood by the door, shyly
turning a loose button on her coat,

while I beat time knowingly,
pretending to have heard it all before.
You looked up from the keyboard,

nodded a wry blessing,
and played us out of the room
to a white-wedding march.

And when we had gone, you kept on playing,
while the curtains of your life
blew out towards the stars.

Note. You've probably guessed it's about Ilya.

From Arkady's notebook: resumed February, 1984, Moscow, in anticipation of fresh adventures

To reassume my unofficial self at a time like this may not be the wisest thing to do, but happiness, even mere optimism, demands freedom of expression. So, for the first time since my marriage was sealed in ink, Kodachrome and Crimean champagne and I stepped cheerfully into the prison of this huge, airy, beautiful Soviet flat, furnished with imports (official and unofficial) from every luxury life style of Western Europe, the Orient and Tsarist Russia, I have unlocked the bottom right drawer of the walnut escritoire and removed the file marked ED. REF: SELF.

We are alone: me, my file (its green cardboard felty and ragged from once frequent thumbing) and my glass of iced lemon vodka. My wife is still at the Film Institute with her lover – our fellow tenant Taras, who, I have to admit, has made a small contribution to the glamour of our lives: some of the furniture, the hi-fi, the Volga and – oh yes, the dacha. (Not that he has done it for nothing. This very flat has cost me half [at least] of my wife, but I don't find the price exorbitant. Asta does not consider herself exploited – on the contrary, she feels her sleek head positively heaped with laurels of womanly desirability. And I have learned that sexual jealousy is easily overcome if one maintains a few extramural interests of one's own.) So where was I? Alone, yes, and certainly not wanting to stray on to the subject of my past casual lusts. They all had a grey tint of officiality and, in retrospect, seem more a part of my career than of my private life, the perks awarded to a Soviet author for writing a hugely popular anti-British, anti-American satirical novel. Only two women have ever been really important to me in my secret sexual life; it is their radiance that bathes me now, as if they were two angels standing, tall, delicate and distantly benign, on either side of the walnut escritoire, keeping watch over me, my glass of vodka and my ragged green folder.

In fact, it was surely their mingled influence that led me to unlock the reluctant, wise old drawer, inhale for a moment its dark, wood-dusty fragrance, and steal back the words I had meant for it alone. ('Are you sure, are you sure?' it hissed, as I slid it shut again.)

At last I opened the folder. And what did I find on top but – a good omen, surely? – Elizabeth's letter? I mean, of course, *my* letter, written at some length and intensity in the June of four and a half years ago and intended for personal delivery by an obliging Lenitours courier, Joanie (?), but never sent. Why didn't I send it? Even as I sealed the envelope I understood that I had only been pretending to write to Elizabeth. It wasn't at all that I was ashamed of my confessions. The problem was Joey (?) – the sort of woman that I instinctively distrust. She seemed generous and warm-hearted, yes, capable of giving you the shirt off her back, and not without wit or courage. But she struck me from the moment our paths first crossed as being someone who loves a scandal, and who has an unconscious skill in provocation. I am not suggesting that she'd have waved my envelope in the customs man's face, nor concealed it with anything less than perfect propriety: she told me all about the pockets sewn to the inside of her panty-girdle, indeed she would have gladly displayed them to me, I'm sure, if I'd given her a word of encouragement. No: I was far more afraid that she'd get safely onto the plane and open the letter herself.

Another thing: I was sure she was jealous of Elizabeth. In my experience older women always are jealous of younger ones, and it occurs at every age: a twenty-five-year-old is jealous of a nineteen-year-old, for example, a fifty-year-old of a forty-four-year-old. I don't blame them. There is such a demand on women to be young and pretty that every additional year is a wound, at first psychological, later, both physical and psychological. I have learned this chiefly from my mother, but Asta too shows the symptoms. So I felt I could not trust Joey's intentions towards Elizabeth, even though I could trust them implicitly concerning myself and my dissident friends (whether women or not), whose persecuted status brought out all her motherly goodwill. When she extended an eager hand for my envelope, all it contained was a postcard from the Hermitage, and all that the postcard said was – I don't even remember – the usual stuff I suppose: Dear Elizabeth, I'm well and hope you're well too, drop me a line, etc.

She didn't drop me a line, but I shan't dwell on that; it was a take-it-or-leave-it kind of communication, after all, its chief aim to say nothing that would fascinate Joey as she slipped it out of the envelope and pierced it with her burning cornflower eyes.

Never mind. I have no regrets any more, I shall read the real letter through without a pang. Elizabeth is no longer a distant wonder I am afraid to think about. She reaches out her hand to me: I shall place the letter in it myself.

Ssssh, Arkasha! You haven't even got a visa, yet.

True. But you've got to admit the signs are hopeful.

Well, OK. The signs are hopeful.

It must have been a good six months ago that Lev and I were first told there was a possibility that we would be invited to take part in the London Socialist Writers' Congress in the April of this year. We didn't take it too seriously, of course: we simply offered up a small, ashamed, un-Soviet prayer and left the machinery to go on revolving our names with those of any other young writers it considered fit to represent it abroad. Then we heard that Kochekov would definitely head the delegation, and that he had an important say as to who was on it. For me, at least, that was a sign of hope. Relations between us have been most genial for longer than I care to remember. And finally, today, both Lev and I were summoned to appear before the Foreign Visits Commission. Our so-called 'applications to travel' had been approved in principle, we were told, and, pending the results of our medical examinations, we would be issued with the necessary documents.

'Aha,' said Asta knowingly to the mirror this morning (she was painting her eyelashes as I stood behind her, fixing a pair of opalescent studs to my shirt cuff). 'It's not like you to get dressed up for work!'

'Lunch at the Union,' I lied. 'Delegation of technical journalists from Belgrade.'

'How bloody dreary!' Asta frowned a sharp little frown.

'They're all men,' I reassured her.

'Why should I care what gender they are?' She pursed her lips haughtily, and glossed them.

I draped myself in my best Turkish cucumber tie.

'Are wives allowed?'

'Only beautiful ones!'

Asta was never sure how to take my banter. She narrowed her eyes at me.

'Would you really honour us dreary old fellows with your presence? I'm sure it could still be arranged,' I went on, enjoying the very slight frisson of danger.

'Pity, but I can't today: I've got to audition through lunchtime.'

I nodded suavely.

'But I'd like to meet them some other time!' I raised my eyebrows, genuinely surprised: she returned a scowl. 'Really, Arkasha, anything for a change. I'm bored to tears – even filming bores me – and as for auditioning twelve-year-olds! I'm desperate to do something exciting.'

'Such as have a torrid affair with a technical journalist from Belgrade?'

'Possibly,' said my wife seriously, teasing small curls onto her forehead with a tortoiseshell comb. 'But what I'd really like to do is to go abroad!'

She looked at me with her cold green eyes, her nostrils flaring. As always at such moments, I could imagine her giving a wicked flick of her comb and turning the carpet to marshes in which I sank slowly to my neck. I was convinced for a second that she'd somehow found out about the projected trip – concerning which I had still not uttered a single word. But then I decided she'd have said so: when she really wanted something, she was too impatient to be subtle.

'We'll find a nice resort for the summer,' I said placatingly.

'But I want to go away long before then, Arkasha! If I have to put up with another slushy city March I'll die!'

'We could have a week or two in the country, work permitting,' I offered.

'You mean Borodino? Ugh!' (Taras's dacha is just outside the village, in fact, but Asta detests the whole atmosphere of the place; she considers war memorials to be morbid, and, besides, the dacha itself is fairly primitive and uncomfortable.)

'No, no, somewhere nice,' I told her vaguely, and hurriedly put on my topcoat. 'I've got to run, I've masses to see to in the office first. We'll talk about holidays tonight.'

Asta pouted. 'We'd better. Otherwise I might really have a torrid affair, you know.'

I kissed the top of her head. 'You're a wonderful animal, Nastochka. All your rampant desires shall be granted!'

As I crunched through the bright snow towards the metro I brooded darkly on my own wickedness. A selfish bastard like me surely didn't deserve to go to London. For, I must confess, I have no intention whatever of taking Asta with me. I want to be free, in so far as a Soviet delegate can be: free to look up Elizabeth, to get drunk, to write, if I want, an ode to the Queen. It is bad enough that Kochekov will be watching over me: two bodyguards would be perfectly unbearable. This is *my* trip, whatever Kochekov thinks, *my* fantasy, *my* inviolably personal odyssey.

Of course, I have never looked forward to explaining the position to Asta, and the morning's conversation about foreign holidays made matters even worse. In this mood, I was ready to believe that my interview with the Foreign Visits Commission would be a complete disaster.

The meeting was scheduled for three o'clock, and, to comfort and fortify myself in advance against possible success, I made a detour via the little Pelmeniye Bar on Vinokurov Street. It's a steamy, greasy, outwardly gloomy place I haven't been inside for years, but the service is quietly unfriendly rather than aggressively hostile, the queues are minimal and, above all, the dumplings are served in honest, generous piles. I was looking round for a table when a familiar figure caught my eye, graceful, narrow-bodied, with a mop of unfaded red curls. She was eating in a desultory way, a book in one hand, her fork in the other.

'Lubov Sergeevna,' I said softly across the table. As she looked up from her book, all kinds of emotion seemed to flit across her pale face: surprise, annoyance, humility, irony, even scorn. But the final expression was a hollow sadness.

'I didn't know this was one of your haunts, Arkady Petrovich,' she said, with a ghost of her old crispness.

'I didn't know it was one of yours.'

'I come here for lunch sometimes as a special treat.'

I couldn't quite tell if she was joking or not. 'May I sit down?'

'Please do.' She drew in her feet to make room for mine. I glanced down: black, flared trousers, heavy-heeled, unfashionable shoes.

'It's lovely to see you.' I noticed that the cuffs of her sweater were badly frayed. She blushed and didn't answer.

'What are you reading?'

She turned the book so I could see the title: *Siberian Folk-Ways*.

'Tamara sent it. She's on a young peoples' building project in Verkoyansk. She took some lovely photos, too. It's a pity I haven't got them with me.' She hesitated. 'I read your novel, by the way.' Her voice was careful, a shade deferential. 'I thought it was a bit strange but I liked it. Are you writing another one?'

'No, short stories. I've got a collection almost ready. But what about you? Are you still working at the same place?'

'Yes, different department, though. They demoted me. I spend most of my time washing glasses in the lab!'

'That's tough.' I winced to think of her humiliation.

'That's life.' She shrugged. 'I'm lucky to have got my freedom.'

'I heard that Boba wasn't so lucky.'

'No, she wasn't so lucky. Does it matter to you?'

Before I could stutter an answer, she had changed the subject.

'I heard you got married again. I heard it was the brilliant match of the year.'

'Oh, really? We explode brilliantly too, go off at one another like rockets.'

'Isn't that what artistic types are expected to do?'

'It's worse than artistic temperament, at the moment. I'm going to London, you see, in a couple of weeks' time and I'm leaving her at home.'

'That's very gallant of you. I suppose you intend to get up to mischief in London?'

'How clever you are, dear Luba.' I really thought she was, and tried unsuccessfully to take her hand.

'If you see Elizabeth,' she said neutrally, 'ask her what became of the magazine, if anything. And give her my love.'

'Yes, of course.' I paused, embarrassed. 'I suppose you wouldn't have her address, would you?'

'I've got the rectory address. I don't know if she's still there.'

'That would be better than nothing. I used to have it, but I lost it. So much has happened since those days, so many changes.'

She gave me the faintest of wry smiles. 'But you haven't changed. You're still a child. Perhaps writers have to be.'

I blushed then, remembering the trick I'd played on Taras.

She cleared the scraps from her plate and I began to eat quickly, because the waitress was hovering like a vulture, and I wanted to pay for us both.

We took the metro together back to the centre.

As we came out into the street, a cold March wind was blowing. 'I mustn't forget to give you that address,' Luba said, her teeth chattering. She rummaged in her handbag and pulled out a small, tattered book. 'Oh no, that's not it, that's Boba's.' She looked at me, shocked, like a child who's just burned itself playing with a box of matches.

'What is it, may I see?'

'Just a diary.' She hesitated before relinquishing it. 'It's interesting, especially what she wrote just before she died, when she was trying to fight off the effects of the drugs they were giving her.' She spoke in a soft, level, neutral voice, though all the while she kept her head down, hiding her eyes.

Impulsively, I said, 'Let me keep it a while. I may be able to do something.'

'In London? No, Arkady. You shouldn't run any risks, in your position.' She took off her glasses, rubbed the back of her hand across her eyes and replaced the glasses in a single swift gesture. 'You've got too much to lose.'

'Please, let me try. I always felt ashamed for not doing more.'

'You had your life, we had ours,' she said neutrally.

'Yes, but now I could do something. Wouldn't Boba have wanted me to?'

'Of course she would.' Luba looked unhappy. 'If you're sure you want to and you'll be careful. But listen, I don't want you to take it out of the country. It would be better to do the translation before you go, and just take that.'

I hesitated; I already had more than enough to do before I left. But Luba's old determination asserted itself.

'I'm sorry, Arkady, I don't feel I can let you have it on any other terms.'

'All right, then. I'll do the translation before I go. And don't worry, I'll guard the diary with my life. I know how much it means to you.'

'No, you don't, Arkady. But when you've finished reading it, you might begin to know.'

'I'm honoured that you trust me.'

'Here's the address,' she said evenly. But as I took it from her I noticed that both our hands were trembling.

'Luba?'

'What is it?'

'Can we meet again?'

'Oh yes, of course. Let's meet in a month, same time and place, and you can return the diary.'

I touched the side of her face, wanting to kiss her, but she moved away. 'I'm sorry, but please don't. It isn't the old days. We're worlds apart now, and always will be.'

'I don't want anything from you, Luba. Only friendship.'

'Do you really know the meaning of that word – where a woman's concerned?'

I was offended, but I tried not to show it. 'Give me a chance! Doesn't this prove my friendship?' I held up the diary.

'Perhaps,' she said coolly.

An angry impulse urged me to give it back to her. But Luba had begun to smile at me sadly; I saw the tired little creases round her eyes and thought, She's already taken punishment enough.

'You'll see.' I slipped the little diary into my pocket and walked away. Neither of us said goodbye.

Ever since the Foreign Visits Commission OKed my trip to London and I made it clear that neither Taras nor Asta was, by my own choice, invited to accompany me, the three of us have been at war. The shrieking stage is over, it's true: Asta and I are now having 'reasonable' arguments. With Taras the war is more subtle. He contrives to exude a frank, though slightly wounded, puzzled charm in his direct dealings with me, but he feeds Asta with ammunition – much of it derived from my past love affairs – to add to her own perfectly sufficient supply. The provocation has mostly come from that side: until now I have kept a remarkably cool head. But today both of them have gone too far.

I got back from a morning's work in the library (1000 words for the *Star* and, since it was Saturday, I'd made a start on the translation I'd promised Luba) to find a curt note from Asta saying she and Taras had gone to the studio. I remembered now – the occasion was a champagne lunch to celebrate the completion of *Maybe It's Because I'm a Muscovite.* This was a simple little documentary of city life, modest of budget but lush of sentiment, and guaranteed to bring Taras fame and fortune. Its chief interest, from my point of view, was that it included some footage shot while Asta and I were getting married (Taras had obtained special permission to film in the Palace of Weddings by means of various bottles, preview tickets etc., in the right quarters), and that it was I who had I sweated over the boring script – what script there was. I ought to have been at the lunch, for God's sake – wasn't I scriptwriter and co-star? It's not unusual for my wife and her lover to slip away without giving me a second thought, but this morning's act was deliberate.

I stalked the flat moodily. I opened various small doors in the kitchen and slammed them again, unable to raise an appetite. Accusingly, I strode into Taras's bedroom – dim-blue and fuggy and rumpled and laid back as jazz. My irritation mounted to such an extent that I was tempted to liquidate his hi-fi system, or his polyester floral shirts, at least. Then all at once the sight of a pair of maroon leather Gucci slippers and a bedside bottle of liqueur (why the fellow's disgustingly white teeth aren't rotting stumps by now, I shall never know – I suppose they are made of the same impervious substance as his brain) gave me a more original idea.

Having finished the job to my entire satisfaction, I thought it might be a good idea to get out of the flat. My feet automatically took me in the direction of Vinokurov Street and the Pelmeniye Bar. I imagined Luba sitting dispiritedly at her lonely lunch, and how I would wittily tell her the story of my revenge and make her laugh. I was also looking forward to showing her what I'd completed of the diary translation.

The bar was crowded, but I knew at once, instinctively, that Luba wasn't there, and a surge of disappointment swept over me. I ordered a plate of dumplings and ate them without tasting them, my eye constantly on the door where I hoped, vainly, as it turned out, that Luba might still appear.

I lingered as long as possible in that now charmless place, then set off back to the library. I was just crossing the road towards the metro when who should emerge from its ever swinging doors but Asta and Taras?

They were swaying against each other and giggling, both obviously tipsy. Asta, fur-clad, looked panther-like, Taras merely comical in his ski suit and pom-pom hat. Involuntarily, I glanced down at his fashionably booted feet. Like a criminal caught in the beam of a militiaman's torch, I saw all the details of my crime flash in front of me, but it was as if I were merely watching a film of someone else. I told myself that it was hardly a crime, just a childish prank. But Taras would consider it a crime, of course: Taras, who loved fancy Western clothes even more than he loved himself, would consider it murder. Double murder, in fact. I fixed a stupid, surprised grin on my face, and watched a similar expression form on the rosy mug of my enemy.

'Well, now, fancy meeting you,' he gurgled.

Asta, her panther eyes flaring, butted in sweetly, 'Are you spying on us, darling, by any chance?' She turned to her paramour. 'He's spying on us, my husband is, Tarasenka. What shall we do about it?' He enfolded her protectively and continued to grin at me.

'I could say the same about you,' I suggested reasonably.

Taras looked puzzled, and scratched his head through the woolly hat. 'We're not spying, old chap. Matter of fact, we're just on our way from a champagne lunch at the studio to a private screening of my latest film.'

'The film I scripted and acted in?' I asked pointedly.

'That's the one. You could come along if you liked' – Asta at once fixed him with glaring eyes and went through a frightful series of grimacing and head-shaking – 'but there are no seats left, it's invitation only,' he added hastily.

'We don't want you anyway,' said Asta. She made a pouting face at Taras. 'Did you know he's going to London without me? Don't you think he's got a bloody nerve?'

Taras nodded enthusiastically. 'You already told me, dearest. And I agree: it's a bloody nerve!'

I lost my temper. 'You're the ones with a bloody nerve,' I said. 'Taras is probably too stupid to behave any other way. But you,' (I glared at Asta) 'you spend all your waking hours and a good many sleeping ones with this booby, and have the audacity to resent it when I do something on my own.'

Asta's nose reddened as it always does before she cries. 'But I always, always longed to go back to London.' She sniffed.

Meanwhile, Taras was clawing at his scalp again. 'What did you just call me?' he asked, more puzzled than threatening.

'A booby,' I said in my clearest tones. 'But perhaps that's too flattering. How about if I called you a prick instead?'

In my last moment of perfect vision, I saw the cloud of puzzlement lift from the man's face, to be instantly replaced by simple, unaffected rage. Then a lump hit the side of my nose and everything exploded into a wet, glittering, stinging scarlet and silver.

With very little sense of aim, I swung my own fist. It came to a halt against something gratifyingly warm and solid.

'Stop it, stop it, you idiots!' Asta sobbed as Taras and I tried hard to wrestle one of us to the wet pavement.

A second later we were wrenched apart by two passing busybodies.

'That's enough, young man, that's enough,' squeaked Taras's restrainer, a wiry old grandfather who obviously prided himself on physical fitness.

'I'll call the militia,' growled mine, less tolerantly.

'Look at his nose. He should go to hospital.' A woman pointed at me from the crowd. I struggled to free myself while the peasant who had pinned my arms behind my back, convinced I wanted to take another punch at Taras, growled on about the militia and tightened his grip. 'I only want to go home,' I shouted. 'Let me go!' After a dozen or so repetitions of this, and some nudgings from the crowd ('Let him go, he's bleeding, he could bleed to death' etc.) the grip was infinitesimally relaxed. At once I pulled away and escaped into the metro at a run.

'Whatever happened to you, you poor darling?' cried Lenina Andreevna as soon as she opened the door to me.

'I was in a fight with Taras,' I said thickly.

'Oh,' she said, 'that was bound to happen sooner or later. Come on, you poor darling, let me patch you up. I hope you gave as good as you got,' she added as I followed her into the hall.

Bathed, anointed, bandaged, fed first strong tea, then good French brandy, I soon felt like a tsar – particularly as I had draped myself in my posthumous father-in-law's silk dressing gown while my bloodied shirt swirled in the washing machine. I was certainly in no hurry to leave – though it did briefly cross my mind that there was still time, if I wanted to smooth things over, to try some kind of salvaging of the slippers before Taras got home. But I didn't want to smooth things over, I decided; it was only fair that I should have the *coup de grâce*, for hadn't I received the bloodiest blow? (Taras, I was sure, hadn't bled a drop.) So I stayed on for dinner, and then Lenina put on some music and got out the brandy again, and it was too late to do anything about the slippers now. At the back of my pleasant, hazy thoughts a single, alert nerve waited for the phone to ring.

At 10.15 it did. I clenched my fists while Lenina went and answered it. She came back laughing. 'That was Taras. He wanted to talk to you. He was positively incoherent with rage. He said something about you ruining his slippers! I told him you weren't here. Well, I don't want him coming round and picking another fight.'

'Thank you.' I patted her cheek. 'You did the right thing.'

'Maybe you oughtn't to go home tonight.'

I had had the same thought myself. 'If it's no trouble . . .' I began.

'Of course it's no trouble.' Lenina Andreevna stood up, stretched, and took the band from her hair so it tumbled in pale scrolls over her shoulders. She lifted it up, wafted it out, gathered it to her cheeks. Maybe it was dyed, but it looked silky and alive. I caught a faint scent from it – camomile, perhaps.

'I'm tired, I'm going to bed.' She leaned towards me, kissed my cheek. 'You're a good boy, you put up with a lot from my daughter. But, you know, talented people have to have a certain licence. Of course you know – you're a talented person yourself,' she went on softly. 'You know where the spare room is. And where I sleep, if you want anything.'

Though she spoke softly I heard every contradictory nuance: the question, the challenge, the plea, the caress.

I was in a labour camp somewhere in the east, shovelling great heaps of snow. As I dug I uncovered three sticklike corpses, huddled together, frozen. They were a bluish-yellow colour, like the figures in one of Asta's Picasso imitations. I bent down to examine the faces; one by one I recognised Ilya, Rivka and Boba. To my horror, Boba's eyelids opened, and she began to sit up. Her bones creaked like thawing ice. There was a terrible expression of vengeance on her little, yellow, skull-like face.

I made stifled groaning noises, then managed to shout out 'No, no' so loudly that I woke myself up. Thoroughly frightened, I shouted again, jumped out of bed and ran for the light switch. At the same time, the bedroom door was pushed open, and a hand reached out to me. I noticed that it was not so old and veined as I had feared, not yet rotting, and I grasped it.

'There, there, don't be afraid,' Lenina Andreevna said, drawing me into the passage where rosy light spilled from her opened bedroom door. 'Only for tonight, and never again.'

From Boba's Diary, Moscow, 1978

19 April, 3 p.m. We had the visit we've been waiting for. I was typing Lara's piece on 'Why the Soviet Authorities Extol Motherhood', and Luba was making borscht, her quick version, with grated beetroot. All the other pieces we've been collecting for the third issue were spread around the room. What a catch! They took everything, and 'accidentally' destroyed the typewriter ribbon while removing the page I was working on. That's a serious matter, as it happens; it was our last, and they're not easy to get. The young fair-haired one read a few lines of what I'd typed, and looked me up and down and said, 'Anyone could see you'd never make a mother – no tits for a start.' His fat-nosed friend fell about laughing. 'What's so bad about motherhood?' he asked Luba, who said she had two daughters of her own, and he should read the essay all through if he really wanted to know our arguments. Big nose said it wasn't necessary – he'd already read enough – and waved a copy of issue 2 in front of us. Luba and I looked at one another, we had the same thought: was it the copy that Joey had been carrying?

'So which of you two beauties is the editor?' asked Blondie, staring at Luba. 'We share it equally,' I said. But he kept staring at Luba. 'She's the boss, isn't she,' he kept saying, 'you just carry out orders?' 'We don't work like that,' we said, but he didn't want to hear. 'You can speak for your friend, anyway,' big nose said, as they took Luba away for questioning.

I can remember enough of a lot of the pieces to be able to reconstruct them. But I can't do anything without a typewriter ribbon. It's no use sitting here biting my nails. I'll fetch Luba's girls from school and then do the rounds of my friends to see if I can beg, borrow or steal one.

11 p.m. No use trying to work any longer. I'm at my wits' end, and just hoping that I'll get a call from Luba to say she's all right. I can't ring her at home. My phone's still OK, by a miracle, but hers has been cut off. I know she'll ring here. When she can.

It's been a nightmare evening. After taking Luba's kids home and breaking the news to Borya (he behaved as if it was all my fault and practically threw me out of the flat), I decided to come straight back here – I suppose I had a premonition. Gena from across the landing met me with the news; those bastards had come back, broken in and taken more papers and notebooks from the file (thank God I had the diary with me in my handbag) and, worst of all, hammered the typewriter to pieces. So now I didn't just have to search for a ribbon but a whole machine! I didn't know whether to laugh or cry.

I took some of Gena's valerian powders and calmed myself down. This is the time to be like steel, to say, 'You won't stop me all the while I can move and speak!' No use throwing yourself on the bed and howling . . . Work, woman, work!

I was afraid of laying trails to the doors of my friends at a time like this, but I was desperate for a typewriter. Who to try? Lara would be at the factory by now; she does a night shift. Raisa was a possibility. I tried her apartment; she was out.

Who else did I know? Not many people have their own machines. Writers, of course. But the only writer I knew was Arkady Petrovich. I remember Luba saying they'd been friends, and he was sort of sympathetic to our cause. I decided to go and see him.

I suppose I seemed crazed. But it seemed to me at that moment that I *must* get the third issue out as soon as possible. Anything could happen. I'd read all the material and it was still fresh in my mind. I was still at liberty. Tomorrow, all that could change. I was prepared to sit up all night. It was for Luba's sake too. She was going through heaven knows what, but she'd at least trust me to keep things going. And when I saw her again I'd be able to say – here it is, the third issue; they didn't stop us! That was all I could think about as I dashed along Gorky Street.

His girlfriend, Anastasia Vladimirovna, answered the door and hurried me into the flat. Arkady Petrovich was there, and a visitor. I didn't know if it was safe to talk in front of him. We sat round drinking, gossiping about nothing. At last I plucked up courage and told Arkady Petrovich I needed to borrow his typewriter. 'Just for tonight,' I pleaded. 'Mine got broken.'

He frowned and said, 'Look, I'm very sorry, but there's this article I've got to finish by tomorrow. It's press day, and I was going to burn the midnight oil, like you. On top of that I'm in the middle of a novel,' he said, not looking at me. 'My deadline's only a month away, and I'm working all out. But surely you must have other friends?'

I said I'd try to think of someone. As he saw me out he said if I wanted a ribbon at any time, he knew how to get hold of one – just tell him the size.

'I'll remember that; thank you very much,' I said. I could hear Anastasia and the other fellow roaring with laughter in the living room.

'You're being careful, aren't you?' Arkady Petrovich said softly.

'Yes, of course, I'm always careful,' I said coldly, not looking at him.

'I've been scribbling these notes ever since I got home. I've got a terrible headache, I want to take some more powders and go to bed, but I can't, I might not hear the phone.

22 April. My first words to Luba were: 'They smashed your typewriter and I haven't been able to get another one.' I burst into tears.

And I should have been the one comforting Luba! In fact, she was in good spirits. They hadn't treated her too badly. They'd tried to get her to sign a statement (composed by them) about the aims and intentions of the *Noviye Domostroi*; she refused. 'We don't support wife-beating either,' they said. 'Why are you so afraid of publishing your magazine?' 'We're quite prepared to publish the next issue officially,' said Luba calmly. 'Would you officially like to help us?'

The copy they got hold of doesn't seem to have been Joey's, thank God – they made no mention of our attempting to publish abroad. They simply said, when Luba refused to sign the statement, that in that case they'd ask her permission to invite her back for further questioning.

The relief of it – we both felt madly happy, all of a sudden. 'D'you realise winter's over? It's the first warm day,' said Luba. 'Let's take the girls and a bottle of wine and go to the park.'

We ran races with the girls and played rounders. Then we spread our coats and had the picnic. Tamara is just like Luba, and almost grown-up. She wouldn't play with Katinka, but wanted to sit with us, discussing our plans and having a taste of our wine. But we finally got a moment to ourselves; Kat came running back from the lake with news of some black swans, and Tamara wanted to go and photograph them. Luba took the opportunity to tell me that she and Borya were thinking about divorce. He didn't like living with a dissident – and a feminist dissident was worse still. It was a long time since they had been lovers. Luba didn't want that sort of relationship, and Borya had looked elsewhere, she was pretty certain. I got up my courage. 'Have you ever thought you could love a woman?'

'In a sexual way?' Luba was surprised, I think, rather than shocked. 'I don't much like being touched by anyone,' she admitted. I'd noticed that, of course.

'It may be because no one has ever touched you in the right way,' I told her. 'When I was working in a hospital in the Far East I learned massage from one of the nurses. It's the most terrific sensation!

'It's very relaxing, too, mentally as well as physically. Would you like to try it? I'd be very gentle, and I'd stop if you said no. You'd always have the power of stopping me.'

'OK then, you can try it some time.' Luba was amused. 'You seem to want to save me from divorce!'

'No, I just want to massage you,' I said.

'Go on, then!'

'Not here, silly. I need this special oil for a start, and you'd have to take your clothes off – you can lie under a sheet, of course. And it's good to have music playing – I've got this cassette of Arabic music that's good for atmosphere . . .'

Before I could finish, the children had run back. Or at least, the little one had. Tamara was some way behind, walking slowly. She looked flushed and miserable. 'I've got a headache,' she said. 'I want to go home.'

I suppose it must have been because of the wine we'd let her drink. Anyway we packed up and Luba went straight home. She's promised to come for her massage on Tuesday. And she also thinks she might have got hold of a typewriter by then. There's a very nice girl at the polyclinic who writes romantic novels in her spare time.

Luba said I should have known better than to try to get help from Arkady. He's gone up in the world now, he's with Asta and he's got too much to lose by being loyal to old friends.

24 April. Luba came for her massage, and brought the typewriter. She'd been going to stay the night and dictate while I typed – we've found that's the quickest way of working – but Tamara's still ill. She thinks it's a bad attack of flu and she wanted to get back. She liked the massage, but she would only let me touch her shoulders, neck and arms!

25 April. She rang at five, very upset, to say Tamara's been rushed to hospital with meningitis. I wanted to go straight round, but she said no, Borya was in a foul mood, the best thing I could do would be to get to work on number 3 because Yana wants her typewriter back this weekend. So I got out my precious notes and began. I also went round to Lara to see if she'd kept a carbon of her motherhood piece; it's so frustrating to have only the first page and a half, and I just can't compete with her wonderful acid style. But her mother-in-law opened the door and was very short with me. She insisted Lara wasn't in, though I saw a light coming under the bedroom door and thought I heard Lara's voice, talking to her husband. It occurred to me how the KGB could have got hold of that copy. Lara always said the old girl hated her and thought she wasn't good enough for her Avram, and Lara hated her back, of course; they were always rowing. I shall rewrite the whole piece, and print it under a different pseudonym from her usual one. So another friend falls by the wayside.

29 April. Luba came, straight from the hospital. Tamara's a lot better, sitting up and taking food though not allowed out of bed.

She's coming home on Friday if all goes well. Then she'll go with Borya to his mother's in Yaroslavl, to convalesce. Borya can travel in to work from there. Luba says she doubts if he'll come back to Moscow again. Things are quite impossible between them – he even blames her for Tomka's illness!

I thought I wouldn't suggest a massage, not tonight, when she's got so many worries, though it's good for tension. But Luba herself suggested it. I was very gentle. This time she let me touch her legs and buttocks. But it was because she didn't care, not because she wanted me to. I stopped halfway through and sent her home to bed.

I'm happy, I can't help it, in spite of everything. Luba accepted my invitation, and she and Katya are coming to stay till Tamara's finished convalescing. Tomorrow I shall go out and buy bedlinen. And I want to get some plants, a picture and a mirror. I shall make them each a beautiful 'corner', Katya's in the bedroom, Luba's in the living room, because we'll often be up late working.

6 May. They're settled in. I'm happier than I've ever been in my life! Katinka's a darling. And I've never seen Luba so relaxed and happy.

12 May. Tomka visited. She looks taller, and quite rosy. Borya has bought her a flash attachment for her camera, and she took lots of pictures of us. When it was time to go she said she wished we could all go with her. I wished there had been room for her to stay, I could see it was a wrench for Luba to part from her. Luba was right; Borya has asked for a divorce. It was in the letter Tomka brought. Luba didn't let on to the girls. She said she'd wait until they'd got a bit more used to the idea of Mummy and Daddy having separate lives.

9 September. This must be the place they took Luba – half an hour's drive south, palatial rooms. I'm between interrogations – the militia have to have their tea break, poor dears, after working so hard. I don't think my interrogator is the same one who grilled Luba; hers was tall, fair, like a Nazi, she said, and at least gave the impression of courtesy. Mine is a snouted, black-eyed pig. He hates me – it's personal; he really thinks I am his enemy, his wife's enemy, his daughter's enemy, his country's enemy. He's been showing me the photographs – I nod and smile, they're rather good. Women with their arms round each other, he spits, what sort of filth is this? After an hour or so of puritanical loathing, his salaciousness leaks out: tell me, what do you do with each other in bed?

I'm not clever like Luba; I can't play tennis with these questions. I only ever want to tell the truth, in any situation. But the truth about me and Luba is too complicated for him. I can't deny there was something erotic in it – for me. But we never even slept in the same bed. I was teaching her to love me, or trying to. Those smiles and embraces meant love on my part, friendly affection on hers. I refuse to lie about my love, and so he spits, yes, literally spits at me, and asks for the graphic details of my 'affair'. We haven't discussed the magazine at all. Above all, I feel insulted; what is this image they're trying to create? An empty-headed little pervert with no ideas or ideals, involved with feminism just for the erotic thrills?

I don't think he's going to let me go, with the polite request for my permission to let him 'invite me for further questioning'. I think it's big trouble.

How did he get the photos? Borya? I don't believe he'd do such a thing. Maybe Tamara was careless, took them to school, lost them?

11 September. 'If we put you in the women's labour camp it'll be one long holiday for you, won't it? It's too good for women like you, isn't it? If I made the laws, I'd have women of your sort sentenced to death. But I only carry them out. And the law has compassion, in cases like yours. It gives you the benefit of the doubt. You are not evil, but sick. And the sick must be treated . . .'

12 September. 'I have examined the patient and found her to be suffering from severe delusions, of both a sexual and a reformist nature. I recommend a course of daily chlorpromazine, preferably to be administered intravenously.' The woman in the next bed had a convulsion and Sister left her notes on the locker for a moment, so I was able to get a glimpse of my medical report. I am in White Pillars Psychiatric Hospital; there's a wood near here where Luba and I used to pick mushrooms. I don't know how long I shall have to stay. They will try to dose me out of my mind, but I won't let them.

10 December. I am Boba I do not know how long I have been here I am not ill I don't think so but the drugs I am writing this to keep my mind working I am Boba I am Boba I am Boba they had pictures of me and they said two women two women arm in arm two women laughing they had Tamara's pictures they said you are ill you must be rehabilitated they say I shall be here for a long time maybe not Luba will write won't she dear Boba I am waiting I am also waiting I can hide the pills but sometimes it's a needle and then I can only sleep they sew me into the darkness with their needles but I am Boba still dear Luba write to me I am waiting I am Boba.

Maria Borisovna Kadashevsky
English translation: © Arkady Petrovich Polyakov

From Arkady's Notebook, London, 1984

Democracy: our first impressions

There was time, just before we left the hotel, to tune into a few minutes of the BBC's *Question Time in Parliament*. It was Lev's idea; he had issued the invitation to me the previous evening, to come to his room and sample English democracy for the first time.

But we lingered so eagerly over the English breakfast that we found we only had one minute left for the democracy (this subsequently dwindled to half a minute, as Lev twirled the dial frantically from right to left).

There was a sudden lowing, as of newborn calves. Then a voice called out in a disagreeably sneering way: 'Order! Order!'

'This is it!' cried Lev.

A woman, with a voice that sounded as if it were a bicycle tyre being pumped up and up until in imminent danger of bursting, declared, '*If* the Right Honourable Gentleman were to be invited to the Pearly Gates, he would still without a doubt find something *there* to *complain* about.'

More lowing and bleating, and cries of 'Order, order'.

'Bad temper and democracy are not impossible consorts,' reflected Lev as we rode down in the lift.

'How many parties did you say there were?'

'Three.'

'It sounded like more,' I said. 'I can't understand how they ever decide anything, with all that shouting and sneering going on. It seems to me they're wasting time and ideas, shouting each other down.'

'It's called a debate,' said Lev. 'You oughtn't to make judgements at this stage. It's a great tradition, after all. There must be something to be said for it.' He was being judicious as always, but I could tell he had suffered a blow to his ideals.

Are these the gardens of the institute?

Kochekov stops and looks suspiciously about him; his tone, as usual, is harsh and disapproving. In front of us is a lake, narrow but extending indefinitely to both east and west. The sun draws silver Vs behind a pair of black, dawdling, red-beaked swans, and pencils individually and blackly round the edges of the tulips, massed yellow and scarlet on either side of the gateway we have just stepped through.

'Are these the gardens of the institute?' I parody my editorial guardian in a whisper and clutch at Lev's sleeve. I want to giggle hysterically, beside myself with the ecstasy of a kind of homecoming. Plato Park, your gaze bright and peaceful as the gaze of the girl who first decribed you to me, I already know and love you in every detail!

'No, Mr Kochekov, this is the park. The college is situated inside the park, on the other side of the lake. You can just see it over there, through the trees.' Simon, the young man from the British Council appointed to be our guide, is an affable sort of fellow. Though boyishly short and wispy in physique, he compensates for this with an authoritative, worldly manner and a ringing voice which Lev informs me is either Eton or Harrow, he hasn't quite decided which. He is wearing a cherry-coloured blazer today with a matching tie and cream shirt; every inch the public-school head boy, says Lev admiringly. He has been fluttering protectively and talking loudly ever since our delegation arrived at Heathrow.

He began apologising when we were still in the baggage reclaim. The conferences and readings had been due to take place in the County Hall, but unforeseen circumstances had resulted in a change of venue. Only the Festival Party and the Farewell Supper would now be held at the County Hall. The rest of the week's events had had to be transferred to Sebastian College. 'But, but' – our host firmly swatted at the swarms of objections he imagined were about to fly from our innocently opened mouths – '*but* it is a perfectly *delightful* place, in a perfectly delightful setting, in a *park*, in fact, and *miles* more convenient than the County Hall for the sights of London, not to mention the Prince Regent Hotel.'

Something fired in my brain and started cogs and ratchets and pistons whirring.

'What's he trying to say?' demanded Kochekov, who is far too patriotic to have ever succeeded in mastering more than a few snatches of any other language than Russian. Lev came obligingly to his rescue, and I turned to Simon.

'Sebastian College? What park did you say it was in?'

'Plato Park. They're both named after the Victorian architect Sebastian Plato. I can't think why they named the college after him, though. He wasn't exactly an intellectual, from what I've heard. On top of which he ruined a perfectly good royal park with ghastly statues and pagodas and chunks of kitsch designed to appeal to the worst popular taste. Fortunately, most of 'em have fallen over.'

So we troop into the park, and onto the little wooden bridge, hump-backed, lattice-sided and, I hope, more durable than Plato's other decorative items. Green water winks up darkly between the slats. 'Anyone for a spot of punting?' asks Lev.

'Ah,' sighs Simon tenderly. 'Now, if this were . . .'

The Soviet delegation, I should explain, numbers five participants and one non-participating spouse. We are all male, apart from the spouse, of course, and all variously tarnished by the shades and excrescences of middle age, apart from Kochekov, who, in spite of his soldierly posture and boardlike stomach, now qualifies as definitely old. Karambaev, the poetry editor, is the fattest; Djavar-onok, the poet, the baldest and the youngest. He is tall and thin of smile and quiet-spoken and has brought his wife, Zina, a jolly Czech girl who has already set off on a spending spree in preference to a day of speeches.

We troop along a gravel path that runs alongside the lake. On the bank are cherry trees, so laden with double clusters of rich pink blossom that they cannot lift their branches, it seems, but are forced to spread them horizontally.

Karambaev makes rapturous noises, and pours the contents of a tube of Smarties into his mouth.

The college gate has a small flapping banner which reads: WELCOME TO THE FIFTH SOCIALIST WRITERS' FESTIVAL.

And here she is – Elizabeth's alma mater – hexagonal, grey-white, many-windowed, ready to embrace us with warm, open arms.

'Built in the sixties,' Simon apologises. 'Universities and colleges were sprouting all over the place – red-brick, plate glass, reinforced concrete, Portakabin, you name it. Anyone could become a student then.'

The foyer is already crowded with delegates. The foreign contingents are instantly recognisable. Like us, they wear dark suits and clean shirts and their stomachs and foreheads tend to bulge, as if stuffed with a plenitude of correctness. The natives, on the other hand, are gorgeous dragonflies. Skeletally thin, they are winged in jackets that may be short or long or sleeveless, leather or denim or woollen, armour-plated with bright badges or adorned with multicoloured scarves; their legs, though, are uniformly denim and variously blue. I cannot understand the scarves – on such a sunlit April morning – but perhaps these thin, frail creatures are sensitive to intangible chills and draughts we coarser creatures know nothing of. The women look more sporty and muscular; they're dressed for flying, running, mountain climbing, despite their earrings and bangles. We bask in the light and colour and chatter, frozen creatures allowed for a few hours into a tropical garden, while Simon flutters and darts his eyes anxiously for someone worthy of the honour of being introduced to us, and I, too, glance around me with timid hope.

'They're going in,' trills a woman in a red hat, standing nearby.

'So they are.' Simon looks at his digital watch. 'I'd be surprised if they start on time.'

Nevertheless we follow the red hat that bobs on the tide, and are swept into the amphitheatre and down to our reserved seats in the front row but three. We sit down, we unsnap our briefcases, we rustle our prepared papers, we try on our headsets, we hold out our hands to Karambaev for showers of Smarties to keep up our blood sugar (except Kochekov, who swallows vitamin-E tablets from a dark bottle). Twenty minutes later, we glance up, bored, towards the platform where someone – the festival director or merely an assistant dragonfly, who can tell? – is informing us languidly that we are having a spot of technical bother concerning the simultaneous translation, but, 'Do not adjust your headsets, ladies and gentlemen, normal service will be resumed as soon as possible.'

'Resumed? We haven't had any service yet,' grumbles Simon, who is by no means elated that his prophetic genius has been confirmed. 'That's typical of this bunch. I'm going to get a cup of their disgusting coffee; would anyone like one?'

The buzz in the hall has risen to a gentle roar. I notice how the rebellious and introverted Anglo-Saxons among us are disobeying the dragonfly's instructions with vigour; several headsets now lie in pieces on their owners' laps, and many more are being variously rattled, shaken, peered into, breathed upon, twisted and turned. On the other hand, our brother Hungarians and Czechs have begun shouting at one another and clambering across seats. Only we Russians, conscious of our imperial responsibilities, sit with exemplary fortitude, neither destroying our headsets nor exchanging obscene jokes and scandal in loud voices. Kochekov scans the deserted platform like a general the scene of battle; Karambaev munches; Lev and Djavaronok reread their papers (Djavaronok seems to be rewriting his); and I, as usual, have my pen in my hand, my notebook on my knee, and my consciousness at large. A voice suddenly booms hollowly, 'Testing, testing, one, two, three. Mary had a little lamb.'

Lamb, lamb: I collect another coincidence. Simon scurries in with his carton of black coffee. 'It's going to start,' he hisses, in great agitation. 'Does everyone know the running order? D'you all know when you're going on?'

The hall crackles thickly with applause, topped by a rising shriek of girlish cheers.

'That's Ken,' says Simon. 'Leader of the GLC. He'll make a speech first, of course. That's Eric.' (More applause, thicker still, with a slightly wilder note of girlish cheers, as one of the dragonflies trips on to the platform.) 'He's the festival director. He'll make a speech too, I'm afraid. I don't know who that is.' (A mere sprinkle of applause, no cheers.) 'Labour MP, shadow minister for something or other. Well, let's hope they manage to be amusing, if they can't be brief.'

'I like this GLC,' announced Kochekov while we were eating vegetarian pizza in the college refectory. 'But this Eric, no. I no understand a word even wearing those ears!' He smacked the sides of his head and frowned severely at Simon, as if he held him personally responsible.

Lev signalled agreement, and turned to me. 'All those references to *1984*,' he said, 'when 95 per cent of the audience hasn't read it – someone ought to have told him. And if they had read it, it would have been even worse.'

'The point, I think, is' – Djavaronok smiled thinly – 'that he wasn't saying these conditions apply in the countries of the Eastern bloc, but in Western Europe, specifically England under this present Tory government.'

'Yes, and it was total rot,' said Simon. 'He may have had his grant cut, and all the hassles he was talking about, but the fact remains that the festival's on; it wasn't banned, and no one's going to arrest him, though he'd probably be overjoyed if they did.'

'I liked the Cuban beauty queen best,' I said hastily, changing the subject. ('Beauty queen' was a concept I had acquired from reading Lev's *News of the World* yesterday: SHOCKING REVELATIONS OF FORMER BEAUTY QUEEN had been one of the lead stories, from which I had learned additional useful Western concepts such as 'drug smuggling', and 'Miss World'.)

Kochekov pricked up his ears. 'The Cuban? Ah yes, very fine paper. The most correct analysis I've heard yet!'

'You will excuse me, won't you?' said Karambaev, suddenly rising. 'I've something, um, some work to attend to this afternoon. I'm sorry I shall have to miss your excellent speech.' He bowed solemnly to Kochekov, but there was an infinitesimal twinkle in the solemnity. Kochekov nodded, masticated and looked inscrutable.

Soon after, I followed Karambaev out into the sunlit quad. I consulted for a moment the little park map helpfully stapled to my copy of the schedule and compared it with the street map in my shiny new *A–Z*. Fox Street ran in a straight line on the east side of the park. The rectory, number 4, would be at the northern end. But it still wasn't far. I simply had to walk for half a kilometre or so, diagonally, go out through the Fox Gate and take the first turning on the left. My heart was racing. Elizabeth, Elizabeth, is it possible . . ? As I walked, I combed my hair and sucked vegetable fibres from between my front teeth.

It was in the middle of the rose garden, among the stumpy, flowerless bushes with their dried-blood-coloured talons and leaves, that I discerned a spiritual warning or at least a dampener. It emanated from four tall, grey statues crowned with laurel wreaths and wearing long robes. Curiously I read the inscription: 'The Guardians of the Republic: Wisdom, Courage, Intelligence, Self-Control.' The only one I could distinguish was the last. The others had all raised their hands and turned their heads in stilted conversational gestures, whereas Self-Control stood with his hands at his sides, impassively staring into the middle distance. The inscription also read, in tiny gilded italics: 'By Sebastian Thomas Plato; in honour of his Namesake, the Great Philosopher.'

As I came out into Fox Street I could see already what I thought must be the rectory, and my heart began to hammer. It turned out to be a furniture depository in the guise of a church, but the rectory stood at its side like a little brother, clad in the same pocked grey stone and trying to look equally solemn and disapproving. The leaded windows gave away no secrets. The front lawn needed cutting, though not badly, and the privet hedge was slightly overgrown.

A sense of the complexity of Elizabeth's life, and my exclusion from it, swept over me. I would pull the bell, wait, and who would answer? A complete stranger? A bent, old man who'd refuse to recognise me? Or who'd tell me his daughter had moved to Scotland, and was married with four children?

I stood for a long time, then looked at my watch. That decided it; there were only ten minutes till the conference resumed, and I was first on the programme. I told myself it didn't matter, I could try another day, and turned back towards the Fox Gate.

*

'I'm Jean Bone: delighted to meet you!' A large, firm, pale hand like the blade of a cricket bat was thrust towards me, barring my way as I tried to cross the crowded foyer to the coffee machine.

It was the enthusiastic, red-hatted lady I'd noticed earlier.

'Pleased to meet you,' I said nervously.

'I'm the literary editor of the *Saturday Post*. London's Liveliest Weekly Newspaper – you must have seen our advert, it's on the back of every other bus. I must tell you, Mr Poly-er, I thought your paper this afternoon was really brill.'

I muttered self-deprecatingly, since it was obvious that 'brill' was a term of approbation, even though it sounded somewhat abrasive, regarded onomatopoeically.

Jean Bone came to the point. Her readers, she said, were extremely interested to know what it was like to be a poet in the Soviet Union today, and she would be fantastically grateful if I would grant her five minutes of my time for an interview.

Faint alarms sounded in my head; this was the bourgeois press, of which I had so often been warned in the weeks preceding my trip.

'I'm not really a poet, I'm a novelist,' I said nervously.

'A novelist! That's even better!' shrieked Bone. 'I thought you must be a poet because of what you had to say about rhyme – I do *so* agree, by the way. But a novelist suits us down to the ground – he's more of a mouthpiece for the ordinary folk, wouldn't you say?'

I told her that I was honoured but that I didn't think I was at all worthy to be a mouthpiece for ordinary folk. Cunningly, I suggested that a distinguished older writer would be more appropriate, for example, my esteemed colleague Leonid Borisovich Kochekov, to whom I would gladly introduce her.

Jean Bone shook her head and poked a roguish finger at me. 'You won't wriggle out like that, young man. Youth is what the *Post* is all about – the young in years and the young in heart. We're a very forward-looking paper. That's why we're so interested in the fresh responses of a distinguished but youthful writer like yourself.'

Though I pride myself on both a sense of irony and caution, I find it hard to resist flattery, particularly when the flatterer is an unusually fresh-cheeked and authoritative middle-aged woman whose dedicated gaze and incontrovertible handshake would not have disgraced a member of the Central Committee. I was pleased to be thought distinguished – and even more pleased, at nearly thirty-eight, to be thought young. Surely one careful little interview couldn't hurt?

'I'd have to get my editor's permission, naturally,' I said, still playing for time.

'Of course. But let's make the appointment now, in case our paths don't cross again. I'll give you my card so you can ring me if there's a problem. When are you free?' Jean Bone shone on me the shrewd steady, professional gaze of one who has softened a great many ironists and self-preservers during the course of her career.

I drew the creased conference timetable from my pocket. A bizarre jumble of events additional to our daily official chores had been crammed in to keep the delegates out of mischief. They ranged from *No Sex Please, We're British* (tonight) to Highgate Cemetery: the Historic Tomb of Karl Marx (Friday). Wednesday alone was an all-leisure day, though there were optional trips to Madame Tussaud's and the London Zoo.

Ms Bone and I agreed that the waxworks and the zoo could be given a miss. 'After all, you'll see some waxworks when you come to our office. And you'll certainly be in a zoo.'

Ms Bone's laugh, like her handshake, was irrefutable, and lasted a long time.

Karambaev did not reappear at teatime and was still missing when Simon, prefectorially counted heads in preparation for our outing to the Garrick.

'Mr Kochekov isn't here, either,' he said, frowning at his watch.

'Leonid Borisovich isn't coming,' I told him. 'He's got a paper to prepare for tomorrow.'

'He's not interested in British sex,' added Lev.

'Then it's just Mr Karambaev. Mr Karambaev,' boomed Simon. 'Has anyone here seen Mr *Karambaev*?'

I volunteered to go and try his room.

I could hear faint noises from inside but he was a long time answering: I had to knock twice before he called out to me to wait a second, and finally opened the door. He looked hot and dishevelled, and exhaled in my face a cheesy compound of crisps and beer. I soon realised that his expansive gestures and broad, side-to-side swaying motions were not sufficiently explained by the beer. He was trying to stop me from seeing into the room. My focus instinctively sharpened. There was a metallic gleam about the bed, a blue-and-silver gleam that stirred in me a curious longing, and memories not of moonlight and midnight and southern seas but of . . . caviar. Yes, that was it! The bed was awash with small jars, dressed in the traditional blue-and-silver labels of Russian caviar.

'What are you doing, Petya, preparing a light supper?'

Karambaev groaned. 'You'd better come in. Quickly, quickly, this is a no-go area.' He waved towards the opposite door. 'Big brother,' he hissed, 'keeping an eye on me!'

'He doesn't seem to have cramped your style so far.'

Karambaev noiselessly shut the door behind us. 'We've known each other a long time, Arkasha.'

'Yes, indeed.'

'And I can trust your absolute discretion?'

'If it weren't for my absolute discretion I wouldn't be standing here in the Prince Regent Hotel, London, England.'

'Well, then. You might not find it easy to believe that this little lot has nothing to do with personal gluttony. I am merely an agent.'

'What kind of an agent?'

Karambaev's voice came from far behind his front teeth. 'The commercial kind. It was the boss's idea. He decided to go in for a spot of private enterprise with me doing the legwork. But I've been toting the damned things around all day and none of the shops will take them, however much I knock down the price. It's because I'm a Soviet. Everyone thinks it's a commie plot to poison the British bourgeoisie! I don't know where to go next – I've done Harrods, Fortnum's, all the Oxford Street food halls. This damned book's no good,' he added, petulantly swiping crumbs from the opened Yellow Pages that lay on his dressing table next to a tooth mug of beer.

'Look. Foam Products Latex, Foam Products Plastic, Food

Importers, Food Processing, Food Products Prepared, Footware Components! Not a food hall in sight,' Karambaev whined.

'Try under Grocers,' I suggested. 'But not now, or we'll miss the play!'

'Hang on, hang on. How d'you spell Grocers?'

Wearily I told him. Karambaev leafed through the pages. 'You're right. I always said you were a bloody genius. Lists and lists of them!'

I strode to the door and flung it open to get him moving. 'Come on, or they'll go without us. You can do all this tomorrow morning!' Then I froze: Kochekov was coming round the corner. He had seen me and, I reasoned, it would only make matters worse to dodge back into Karambaev's room and shut the door. I called again in a nonchalant way for Petya to hurry up.

'I am hurrying,' he shouted. 'I've got to lock up all these damned jars of caviar – I don't want them walking off without me!'

'Good evening, Leonid Borisovich,' I said loudly. Kochekov nodded in token courtesy. He looked stung, whether merely at the sight of me or in response to Karambaev's declaration as well, I couldn't, and hardly dared, guess.

'I greatly admired your speech this afternoon, Leonid Borisovich!'

Kochekov gave a curt nod, turned on his soldierly heel and swung into his room.

'What's that?' Karambaev, hearing the door slam, jumped to attention. 'Oh, good grief, that wasn't?'

'Yes, it was, I'm afraid.'

'Did he hear what I said?'

'I'm not sure. But he certainly saw me.'

'Oh, my God! It was supposed to be a state secret. I'll probably be sacked from the union for this.'

Karambaev was absent the whole of the next day, still attempting, I suppose, to persuade the retailers of central London that he was offering genuine, cut-price Russian caviar, not genuine, cut-price Russian axle grease. (My suggestion – that he should eat a small sample in front of them – had given him a renewed sense of purpose.) In the meantime, I succeeded in avoiding Kochekov without appearing to do so, thanks to the fact that the conference had been divided for the day into small seminar groups, and he had gone with the elect – editors and publishers – while I mingled with the riff-raff – fiction writers. I observed that Miss Cuba had also joined the editorial group, and my initial jealous pang was swiftly subsumed in the generous hope that she would act as a soothing, cheering influence on my boss. This indeed seemed to be the case, for at suppertime he shared a table with her and the other South Americans, his thin lips stretched in a bemused grin and his cheekbones bright as cherries. What wonderful things love can do, I thought, and lingered for a long time over my instant coffee, considering whether to ring Elizabeth or to return dutifully to my room and work on my paper for the final session (provisional title: 'Disposable Words').

My hesitations seemed peculiar even to me, and proved to me what an odd fish I really was. I wanted so much to keep Elizabeth as an imaginative possession that I was almost ready to forgo the attempt to rediscover her reality. As well as being afraid that she was now unreachable anyway, I suspected that, if I did find her, I should not be able to contend with the emotions – and the terrible sense of possibilities – she would arouse. After all, the end of my London trip was already in sight, and the end was Moscow, Asta, work. In view of such a denouement, the climax of the story could only be a hillock, not an alp. Supposing I should feel so shaken by Elizabeth's presence that I felt I should have to throw myself in the Thames rather than leave her? Supposing I were to discover that she had not simply been a wistful diversion for me all these years, but that she really was my great, impossible love? Of course, there was a sense in which I wanted to discover exactly that: I longed for authenticity, even romantic authenticity; I was sick of living on the slummy outskirts of compromise. The trouble was, I had lived there so long I probably couldn't survive in any purer environment.

On the other hand, there was the practical problem of Boba's diary. Though I had browsed through countless women's magazines whenever I got the chance, I still couldn't decide on the best place to send my extract. The less glossy, more radical magazines would be more likely to publish it, but their circulations were surely tiny. It was possible that Elizabeth had contacts on one of the better publications; at the very least, she could probably help with an editor's name or private number.

The dining room had almost emptied. I was alone: Lev and Djavaronok had gone, by special invitation, to a lecture on translation at the Royal Society of Literature and Zina was watching *Goldfinger* in her room. Meanwhile, Kochekov and the South Americans had ordered more cups of coffee. It would be easy enough to slip off and make my phone call.

Notes for my final paper: Disposable Words

Ladies, gentlemen and comrades,

Since arriving in your fascinating city (no, keep it simple) since arriving in London, I have discovered cornflakes, the Body Shop, Yevgeny Zamyatin, musical (what do they call them?) loos, bitter ale, graffiti, the bad *News at Ten* (pause for laughter), McDonald's hamburgers and and and tea bags. I have bought my wife a rose-pink *footballka* (no, sweat shirt) a rose-pink sweat shirt on which her name has been printed by a youth wearing a gold ring in his nose. I have sat through two and a half hours of British humour and succeeded in laughing two and a half times (good, they like you to insult them – pause for prolonged laughter). I have been searched by security guards on the suspicion that I am an Irish terrorist (no, freedom fighter), I have looked out for unattended packages while travelling on your wonderfully complicated metro.

Ladies, gentlemen and comrades,

I have been dazzled, bewildered, impressed, depressed and, above all, I have been informed. I have lingered in bookstalls gleaning strange facts from *Spare Rib, Cosmopolitan, Prediction, Knitting, Playboy* (no, delete), *Time* magazine and the *Investors Chronicle*. I have tried to follow the competing arguments of the politicians on the radio and in the press. Journalists have told me that the invasion of the Falklands was a great act of British heroism and that it was a disastrous mistake. I have been advised that the unemployment figures are rising but really falling, that I should eat 33 grammes of fibre per day, that there is no place like Selfridges. I have even learned that Comrade Chernenko is seriously ill (pause for nervous laughter, horrified gasps etc.). No, delete.

Which brings me, ladies and gentlemen and comrades, to the subject of this paper, disposable words. It seems to me that yours is a city of words – words that seem eloquent and informative but which turn out to be as disposable as the paper they're printed on. Big, front-page stories live for a day, then vanish unconcluded. Everyone is allowed to state their opinion, but no one cares what it is, or acts on it. Your slogans are existentially trivial, aimed merely at persuading people to buy things. Words are not solid blocks with which to build society, but playthings to jingle, roll, toss in the air, kick in the gutter, sew onto your jacket, decorate a bus with, sprinkle like salt on your french fries, and flush away with your Babysoft toilet tissue (no, delete).

Ladies and gentlemen and comrades and fellow word-spinners,

For writers in such a society it seems to me that the possibilities are endless but meaningless. (The possibilities are meaningless but endless?) The pos – no, delete.

At this point, I decided that I had overreached myself, that my paper was itself the product of an inflation-prone society. I crumpled it up, discarded it, took a fresh sheet and stared at it, my whole mind suffused with grey despair. The real reason that I hated words was that, half an hour ago, the universe had said no to me.

I had walked into the phone booth on an open, starry path, the clutch of tenpenny pieces already sticky in my hand. Everything and anything could happen. The future was horizonless, the world only half created. I dialled slowly, my finger shaking: I was a kabbalist, and this was the number that held the secret of life.

At first, nothing happened. I stood and listened to nothing happening. It was like peering into an abyss. I dialled again, very slowly, a beat between each digit. And then a loud, angry, extended note shot into my eardrum like a bolt into a lock. I tried several more times and each time came this black-hole sound, this horrible signal of negation, antimatter.

Coming out of the booth I walked straight into Lev. He saw the look on my face and asked me whatever had happened. 'Calm down, go back and ring the operator,' he said. 'She'll tell you if the number's unobtainable.'

This was a new word in my vocabulary. (It is fixed there now – hateful and unforgettable.) I did as Lev suggested, and indeed discovered that the number – Elizabeth's number – had no official existence. There was a long pause, during which the operator leafed through her directory and I held my breath. But there were no Lambs living at the address I had given, she told me in a tone of crisp finality: and if I didn't have the right address, she couldn't help me.

I went back to my little box of a room, my little box of a self. I regretted that I had tried to earth my fantasies in this way, because now I had simply destroyed them. Elizabeth was lost among the mysteries of the universe. I had no place to imagine her: not the rectory, Plato Park, Sebastian College; not even London or Moscow. Elizabeth floated with the Great Unseeable – the microbes, the atoms, the distant galaxies, the vast mass of human and animal life on this and perhaps many other planets. She was unborn, perhaps she was dead. My tears flowed uncontrollably: yes, she could even be dead.

Red bus to the Lubianka

Yesterday it seemed the worst thing on earth – the thought that Elizabeth could be dead. But today, a mere twenty-four hours later, Elizabeth's death seems a pale unreality; even Lev's offer of a Harvey Wallbanger in the Regency Cocktail Bar to steady my nerves is about as attractive as the offer of a cardboard lettuce. I myself am almost dead – with fear.

Of course, I realise now that I should have got off the bus as soon as I saw the scarlet eartips and boardlike back in front of me, and headed straight for the safety of the waxworks. But the iron was in my soul, the Carlsberg lager in my belly. I had spent lunchtime with Lev

in the Red Lion, off Oxford Street, drinking myself into that gl
insouciance which seemed somehow appropriate to a confronta
with the editress of London's Liveliest Weekly Newspaper. Lev ha
sipped his tomato juice and quoted Pushkin.

'I really don't see the point, Arkasha. It seems to me that you're risking the necessary in the hope of acquiring the superfluous!'

'It's an expression of independence,' I told him with dignity. 'For one week in my life I am a citizen of the free West, and I shall behave like one.'

'The free West? Don't kid yourself!' Lev got up. 'Anyway, I'm going to meet Comrade Marx and Comrade Lenin in wax. I shall prostrate myself before them on your behalf. Take care, for heaven's sake. They're villains, you know, the capitalist press. Don't let anyone push you into a printing machine; I don't want to see your secret thoughts splashed all over the front page tomorrow.'

His brotherly words came back to me as I cowered behind my copy of the *Morning Star*, lowering it every so often so that I could check that Kochekov was still in his place at the front of the bus.

We had reached the junction with Tottenham Court Road when Kochekov leaned over and began to fidget with the briefcase or whatever it was on the seat beside him. For an instant he glanced back and seemed to look straight at me. Then he attended to the case again. He was going to get off – he would walk up the aisle towards me, and if he hadn't seen me before, he would certainly do so now. I scrambled down the stairs, almost falling, and jumped for the pavement, while Kochekov sailed on towards High Holborn.

Once more I had a chance to change my mind. I stood in the swirling crowd in a daze of ugly fantasy. Kochekov was sitting at the desk in Jean Bone's office, grinning maniacally and holding out a pair of handcuffs. He was on his knees planting a small electronic device under her door. Another number 15 was coming along the road, with LUBIANKA in white letters on its forehead and Kochekov, his face a blaze of malicious glee, in the driving seat.

Then LUBIANKA dissolved into LIVERPOOL STREET, I told myself not to be so cowardly and jumped onto the bus. I went to the top deck and stared brazenly about me. Of course, not even Kochekov had the power to be in two places at once.

Anyway, I told myself, Kochekov himself had committed a peccadillo or two during this visit. Possibly we could come to a gentleman's agreement, and organise a kind of moral exchange between thirty jars of caviar and Jean Bone.

In such a lamentably unrealistic mood I boldly gave my name to the security guard and rose to the twelfth floor of Pressco House.

'You're the Russian gentleman come to see Miss Bone,' said the girl at the reception desk before I could open my mouth. How did she know I was a Russian gentleman? Was it my plastic shoes, my untidy hair? Had Kochekov already tipped her off? 'Please take a seat, she won't be long.'

I receded obediently into a very soft, very green bucket-shaped chair, and picked up from the glass-topped table at my side a copy of the *Post*.

It was a cheery sort of tabloid, with headlines much like those in Lev's *News of the World*, concerning beauty queens, drug-smuggling stranglers etc. The main difference was that the *Post* had a special page called Lively Reads. The lively reads of last week's issue included 'Tips from the Mrs Beeton of Curries' and 'Jean Bone talks to Adrian Mole'. Mole, I discovered, was not an author but a character, a fact I found vaguely reassuring. Gradually I was drawn into the simple, bright, chatty world of lively reads. I even began inventing headlines for myself, imagining my name as 'a name to look out for', my pen as 'scintillating', my books as 'musts'. I wasn't a tired old Party hack like Kochekov but a bright, young author who understood Western ways: my place was here on page 10 of the *Saturday Post*.

'Well, now, Mr Poly-er,' boomed a voice above my head. 'How nice. Have you got clearance from your boss and all that?'

'Yes, fine, no problem!' I jumped up and followed Jean Bone into a tiny office, every inch of which was books. Even most of the floor was books. I trod delicately between the shiny, toppling piles. There was no need to worry, I told myself: all this was only a dream.

I acquitted myself carefully and well. Even if he had been listening, Kochekov would have heard little to turn his ears frostbite white or wasp-sting purple. Since she hadn't read my books and didn't know much about the Soviet Union, Ms Bone's questions were largely innocuous and irrelevant. I talked a lot about my first impressions of England – *Question Time in Parliament*, Carnaby Street, bacon and eggs, pubs etc., and patriotically lamented the 'things I missed most' – the smell of April and the taste of kvass. When sketching out the plot of my latest publication, I was at pains to point out that, while set in an imaginary advertising agency in an imaginary bourgeois state, it was far from Utopian. My only lapse was the momentary suggestion that the socialist-realist manner of prose writing had had its day. It was more fruitful, I said, to use satire, as I had done, to attack the other camp. 'The West has numerous subjects fit for such dystopian satirising,' I concluded piously.

'You seem to be very well informed about the West – for a Russian.' Ms Bone smiled sharply.

I seemed to sense a warning tingle in Kochekov's eartips. 'If my fantasies have any truth in them, it's purely by chance,' I answered swiftly.

'What about a quote from one of your poems to round things off?' she suggested, when we'd all but finished. 'In English, of course.'

I rattled off a quatrain from a ten-year-old effort called 'The Dryad' (a love poem to Luba, actually, but no one was to know) and Ms Bone jotted it down in Speedwriting. 'That was most beautiful,' she said sincerely. 'We can offer you a small payment of £10. I'll ask Lindy in a minute to raid the petty cash – it'll be easier than getting Accounts to send a cheque to you in Moscow.'

I thanked her warmly: it was a useful supplement to my minuscule daily allowance. And so I stood clutching my two five-pound notes and an armful of shiny new books which Ms Bone said I could have because they were 'only going to Gastons', flushed with my sense of achievement and my hatred for Kochekov's ears and all other inhibiting devices. Ms Bone was thanking me again, clearly wondering why I hadn't taken my cue the first time and departed, but meanwhile a wild idea was going round and round in my head and finally forced itself to my lips.

'I was wondering – do you have any jobs in the literary department?'

A strange light passed across her face and left it very slightly altered, as if she'd had a minor stroke.

'For yourself? Are you planning to remain in London, then?'

I realised at once that I had blundered, and attempted to retreat.

'No, no, I meant in general – the unemployment problem and all that.'

'You're not wholly contented with life in Russia?' Ms Bone's eyes had narrowed and she gave me a penetrating, journalistic stare. 'Off the record, of course?'

I shrugged. 'Nowhere's perfect. Are you wholly contented with life in England?'

Jean Bone worked her stare into a frown, then into a faint smile. 'I could give you a bit of reviewing, your English is certainly good enough. But there's nothing else at the moment. A lot of journalists are out of work at the present time. I really think you'd be better off going back to Moscow, Mr Polyakov.'

'Of course, I *am* going back to Moscow!' I felt like shaking her till that horrible, knowing little smile fell off her face.

'I've got a wonderful wife, a wonderful daughter and – ' I almost said 'a wonderful mistress' but swiftly inserted 'an excellent job'.

She uttered her impressive laugh. 'Of course. I understand.' She shook my hand with great warmth, and opened the door for me. 'Don't forget to buy the *Post* on Saturday!'

As I walked to the bus stop I found myself breathing heavily. The rush-hour swirl made me feel panicky; I wanted to grip something to keep myself from being whirled in directions I didn't want to be whirled in. I stared round furtively, convinced that Kochekov was somewhere in the crowd, trailing me.

I stood at the bus stop, my head sunk into my collar. I felt a great yearning to escape this grimy, couldn't-care-less of a city, to be back on the broad, open-featured, innocent streets of home. A tramp came and rummaged in the yellow bin that was belted to the stop. He pulled out a carton with a straw in it, and raised it to his lips. My disgusted pity rose like bile. If the bus hadn't been coming, I would certainly have thrust one of the five-pound notes into his filthy paw.

I slid past the doorman of the Prince Regent Hotel, subdued but resolute. I would go straight and work on my paper: from now on, I wouldn't put a foot wrong. I was about to scurry into the lift when Kochekov intercepted me.

'Arkady Petrovich. I'd like a word. You know where my room is, don't you?' He pierced me with an ice-grey look.

'Yes, I think so,' I said.

'Number 110. Please be there in exactly half an hour from now.'

It didn't take me long to realise that Kochekov was as uneasy as I was. He stalked about the perimeter of his room (a double, I noted: the rest of us had singles), his hands locked beside his back, intermittently cracking his knuckles. Extraordinarily, his first words to me were identical to Ms Bone's: what did I think of London?

I was unnerved; it seemed to me he was checking my honesty. Yet I dared not say to him what I had said to Ms Bone, i.e. that I found it exciting, if a shade decadent. I didn't even dare say it was decadent, if a shade exciting.

'Well,' I began.

'Yes?' Kochekov cracked his knuckles impatiently.

'Well, er, the streets are rather narrow, compared to Moscow.'

Kochekov frowned. 'Of course of course! But the shops. Tell me, what do you think of the shops?'

'They're very well supplied,' I said nervously.

Kochekov cracked and nodded. 'Yes, yes. That's undeniable.'

'Yes, I agree.'

'But, on the other hand,' he began after a pause, 'there are gaps, wouldn't you agree?'

'Gaps?'

'Gaps in the market. *The market*,' he added satirically. 'Of course, I'm speaking their language now. But my point is that certain products are not freely available, whatever the propaganda says.' Kochekov cracked decisively. 'For instance, um, certain foodstuffs.

And even, you know, well, perhaps you don't.' He stared at me, his eyebrows twitching. 'I'm talking about patriotism, actually, Petrovich. You see, I feel I have a certain mission towards the West. To show them that communism isn't the evil they think it is. That it can benefit them. That it has produced many good things – for instance, Russian caviar. Do you understand me, Petrovich?'

'Oh yes, I think so.'

He caught my eye, and went on, 'And you agree that my analysis is correct?'

'Yes, I do.' I realised the time had come to press home my advantage. 'But I'm not sure that everyone would share such a progressive view.'

Kochekov stood to attention. 'I take your point. Some people – myself, Karambaev, indeed, you – are enlightened about these matters. But others might not understand.'

'No, they mightn't.'

'I'm an old man,' said Kochekov with just a trace of self-pity. 'Planning to retire in under ten months' time. You weren't aware of that, I believe? Of course, I have a considerable say in who is appointed to take my place on the *Star*.'

I said nothing: a small shiver ran the length of my spine.

'It would have to be someone I could trust.'

Another shiver, 'You could trust me,' I said almost inaudibly.

Kochekov bent his head slightly. 'Excuse me, I'm a little deaf these days. What did you say?'

'You could trust me, Leonid Borisovich. Absolutely. Please don't doubt it.'

Kochekov was smiling, but he still looked perplexed. 'When you saw me on the bus today,' he said confidingly, 'it was only, you know, the same sort of thing. When in Rome, etc. I was sure you'd understand.'

'Oh yes, I do,' I said sincerely, making an immense effort not to burst out laughing. So the great Kochekov thought that I, his minion, had been shadowing him!

At last his features relaxed. 'Splendid! I have no doubt that the union will be delighted to offer you the post of editor of the *New*

Literary Star – in nine months from now!' He held out a veined tremulous hand and I grasped it with real warmth.

'Thank you, Leonid Borisovich!'

'Not at all, Arkady Petrovich,' he said with a trace of his old asperity. 'I'm glad to see we understand one another so well.'

Caviar, kitsch and Miss Cuba

We were eating our last lunch in Sebastian College refectory: shepherd's pie, chips and sliced carrots, followed by saucers of raspberry jelly under whose surface, like iced-in fish, lay flaky cubes of pineapple and what looked like more sliced carrots, though on closer acquaintance they turned out to be very hard slices of banana, dyed rosy by the jelly.

For once, these gems of English cuisine did not provoke us to hilarity. The thought that our London jaunt was nearly over and that by this time tomorrow the soles of our feet would be passing high over Czechoslovakia, possibly never to tread westward again, had a drugging, somnolent effect. We were suspended in a sense of unreality, each of us struggling inwardly with the knowledge that, by this time tomorrow, the red stars of the Kremlin would have risen once more for us; and the bright neon of Piccadilly and the cold blue moons of Whitehall would shine on as if we had never sighed over their lovely decadence.

Kochekov alone had been sprightly and conversational during the meal. No doubt the little chat that he and I had had yesterday accounted partly for this. He was also probably genuinely pleased to be going home. After all, his life, like mine, did not lack for Western-style comforts, and, unlike mine, they had been purchased with honest, uncompromising labour. He had always been true to himself. Even if he had lived in Miami Beach, Kochekov would have written socialist realism.

Yes, anyone could see that Kochekov was uncharacteristically high-spirited. But who could have been prepared for the moment when he raised his right hand and called our table to order, his broad smile roving over the dejected faces like the rays from a lighthouse over drifting oil slicks?

'Tonight, as you know, our esteemed comrade, GLC, is going to entertain us with a party at his Country Hall. But may I first invite you to a small farewell party of my own, by way of appetiser? A caviar supper, to be precise.' He twitched a wry, minute grin in my direction. Karambaev, who was sitting between us, immediately spilled his glass of apple juice, but some quick action on my part with the paper-napkin dispenser prevented any drips from soiling the Kochekovian khaki.

A murmur of approbation went round the table; glances were exchanged that read: What's the catch? Or is the old fellow human after all? Even Djavaronok wiped a crumb of New Zealand cheddar from his ascetic lip and smiled that he hadn't tasted proper caviar for years.

Karambaev, fully recovered, announced beamingly that we would need various accompaniments – bread, butter, vodka etc. – and that he would gladly do the shopping, provided we all contributed our small change.

'Ah yes, Petya, I believe you're quite an expert on the local grocery stores,' Kochekov said in a low voice, and thumped Karambaev rather heavily on the spine.

'Not only the local ones, Leonid Borisovich – I am an expert on every grocery store in Greater London,' gasped Karambaev.

Kochekov got abruptly to his feet. 'I shall extend the invitation to a few of our colleagues,' he announced. 'We must not be selfishly individualistic about our great culinary heritage: no, let us show the world that we Russians know how to live!' I watched as he marched across the hall and stopped with a bow at Miss Cuba's table.

The conference was packed for the final session, the tone of which I found disappointingly parochial. My own paper, a revamped version of 'Disposable Words', was a success, but it inspired nothing like the animated debate produced by a rambling apologia by one of the English delegates for what he called 'community arts'. He had scarcely finished when all the English writers jumped up and began to hurl at each other unseemly comments about their union. All of them hated it, though apparently for different reasons. One person shouted that it gave too much money to ponytailed poets who couldn't string two rhymes together: a ponytailed poet shouted that it had never given him any money in his life and what was wrong with poetry that didn't rhyme? Pandemonium broke out and Eric called in a fussy voice for order. Then a portly chap in a commercial-looking suit stood up and declared that poverty was essential for creative nourishment, and besides if a writer were good he'd make money anyway. There were cries of 'Bullshit' and 'Shame' from the back of the hall. The foreign contingent watched in silence and waited hopefully for these secretly hot-blooded Anglo-Saxons to come to blows. Yet again, order was called for and grudgingly resumed as an elderly dramatist (one of the kitchen-sink lot, muttered Simon) tottered to the microphone to mumble obscurely for half an hour about the two golden ages of Elizabethan drama. Finally, Eric summed up with a speech that ranged chronologically from the signing of the Magna Carta to the Prevention of Terrorism Act. He was briefly halted by someone shouting that this last had nothing to do with literature; but fought back strongly with the argument that it had everything to do with it. Certain acts of Parliament, he went on, meant that the freedom of the individual was being eroded and it would take with it the freedom of literature. Simon beside me groaned; Kochekov muttered about selfish individualism, a nearby Swede quoted Marx on necessity, and the fat man in the pinstripes shouted 'Shame'. Only when Eric said that East and West must sink their differences and join together in fighting for world peace was everyone apparently satisfied, and the conference allowed to subside as the loudspeakers blared into a full orchestral arrangement of 'The Red Flag'.

What happens next in the narrative of this limited picaresque becomes increasingly hard to remember. The first few sentences are crystalline. We tramped for the last time over the little wooden hump-backed bridge. Karambaev sprinkled the remains of a packet of salt'n'vinegar crips into the water in some ritual act of farewell obscure to me but pleasing to the ducks; cameras were produced and the ends of reels used up on hollow willow trees, ice-cream vendors, cloud formations and flowerbeds.

Back at the hotel, we had a quick wash and brush-up, and then, without delay, made our way to Kochekov's room, each clutching, as advised by Karambaev, a pillow to sit on and a tooth mug to drink from. Karambaev had set the vodka to cool in Kochekov's bath, and removed the lids from half a dozen of the shiny jars. A biscuit-tin lid full of melba toast sat on the dressing table and a soap dish of butter had been ledged on the hot-water pipe that led to the hand basin. On the TV, a young blonde policewoman was inching, pistol cocked, along the parapet of a high block of luxury flats somewhere in LA. Lev's eyes lit up the moment he came into the room. He drew a chair close to the set and crouched there with a glazed, oblivious smile.

Kochekov decided to pour us all a drink though no one else from the conference, apart from the eager young Simon, had yet arrived. The vodka was blue label, and better than most of the stuff on sale at home. The caviar, needless to say, was rich and glorious. 'A snort of Baltic cocaine,' said Simon. 'Who says the Russians don't appreciate luxury?'

From the vantage point of the morning after it seems to me certain that we will never be invited to London again. I am sorry to say that none of us ever made it to the official farewell party, not even Kochekov who, well in his cups by nine o'clock, spoke constantly about how we must be off, what a good fellow this G. C. Hall was, how we'd only have one more and then get a taxi, etc. The rest of us wholeheartedly concurred, including Miss Cuba, and yet we were unable to move (I believe Djavaronok tried to stand up once).

'It would be a pity to disgrace ourselves in front of all those British dignitaries,' remarked Lev. Everyone at once congratulated him on his good sense.

'Yes, we're absolutely too drunk to move,' said the giggling Miss Cuba, and thus Kochekov subsided into beaming inanimation. The rest of us then decided for some extraordinary reason to dance. Djavaronok's wife volunteered to teach us some Bohemian frolic whose name escapes me but which, as I remember, involved a good deal of joining hands and bumping heads and falling about merrily onto the floor.

I also remember that at one point Kochekov, speaking his best but still execrable English, tried to sell Simon a set of *matrioshka* dolls which he had conjured from under his bed. Ducking discreetly down I discovered a whole open suitcase full of them. Another area of private enterprise which he had tried to explore, I thought to myself with a grin: Kochekov certainly had the instincts of a good capitalist even if his sales technique left something to be desired.

'These beautiful doll is very soul of *russkiye narodi*,' he drooled earnestly.

'Kitsch, my dear chap, no, thanks,' said Simon firmly. Kochekov looked depressed for a moment. Then he brightened and turned to Miss Cuba. He would present her with twenty dolls, he declared, in exchange for a single kiss.

'Twenty is rather much,' said Miss Cuba with a charming frown, 'but I will kiss you for just one set, OK?'

It was a very proper kiss but Kochekov's whole face went purple with delight. I think this party must have been the nearest he ever got to an orgy.

And now it is 29 April, departure day. With the iron discipline of the true Soviet man I rose at six o'clock and had a cold shower. I then set off for the newsagent's and a last look at Plato Park, dropping into a pillar box on my way the extract from Boba's diary, addressed to the magazine called *Spare Rib*. And so I am sitting at this moment on a damp lakeside seat with a small thermos of coffee, a fat, still-folded copy of the *Post* and a faint headache, meditating on the eternal theme of '*sic transit gloria mundi*'. The sun is shining hard on the moist grass, and promises the warmest day yet. It is strange to think that before the sun has risen to its full midday height, I shall have descended into the afternoon glow of another world. A little cloud of depression hovers on the crisp blue horizon but I dispel it by reminding myself of Kochekov's promise. Arkady Petrovich, editor of the *New Literary Star*. With a tremor of pride I turn to page 10 of the *Saturday Post*.

The story of someone

see him as if from long distance; a curled black ant of a man whose elbows and knees jut out oddly, brokenly. I creep nearer and observe the details: the purple shirt whose open collar is a half-size too large, the matted hair, the speckling of grey-black bristle on the lower jaw, the wild light in the eyes, the bulky shapes of the camera, the suitcase and the flight bag crowding at his feet.

There's no question that this man is at odds with his innocent, bright green landscape – and also with himself. You can tell by the way he scratches first his head and then his crotch, crosses and uncrosses his legs, almost gets up, and turns his head sharply every few seconds. It's as if he believed that even the sun points its long fingers at him, and the wind hurries by with rumours to amass like clouds behind his back.

He is clearly thinking very seriously about moving on. He looks nervously to the right, where a thin, white dog and a tracksuited girl are out for a run. He looks to the left, and is momentarily terror-stricken by a little straggling, thoughtful, gossiping army of Japanese schoolchildren, some of whom are clutching footballs. He looks at his watch, then straight up at the sky. He is right in his calculations; at Heathrow, an Aeroflot plane has just begun climbing into the sky without him.

Under the jet's retracting wheels, the park tilts and slides away, and at one of its oval windows, two shaky fingers splay in the English V for Victory. Magazines are opened, sweet papers rustled, no words are said. There is a wound in the body of the five-man Soviet delegation and four men are quietly losing blood because of it. But magazines are opened, sweet papers rustled, no words are said.

Someone, antlike again, has picked up his suitcase, flight bag and camera and is making his way across the park in the direction of Camden Town. He doesn't know that's where he's going, yet. He knows only that he must avoid going south; avoid Baker Street and the wailing cop cars and the stalking ghost of Sherlock Holmes; avoid the Prince Regent Hotel where there are eager whispers among the doormen and the chambermaids concerning a KGB kidnap and a cache of stolen caviar; avoid the British Council office and the County Hall; avoid Fleet Street and the Gray's Inn Road like pestilential swamps. It is better by far to go northeast: northeast, after all, would bring him home, eventually, if only he could walk far enough, if only the suitcase weren't so heavy, if only the sea were not so deep . . .

He walks along a sunlit road, straight and dotted with tidy, domestic little trees that drop a ball of shade at precise intervals. On one side are houses, on the other a high brick wall from behind which echoes the business of trains. He goes on tiptoe to check; yes, these are big, serious trains, not the little silver subterranean worms he is accustomed to, but brontosaurii, with a vast tangled network of rails to guide them. Surely, therefore, a station must be somewhere near. It occurs to him that he had better avoid this station. Stations are where people look for fugitives; he doesn't know who might not be looking for him.

He turns left, away from the railway and downhill into the High Street.

The haunted feeling loses some of its urgency. People are getting on with their own business, preoccupied but casual; he feels safe and self-forgetful with the herd. After all, he knows the herd's language; he has learned it from books and speaks it even better than most of the herd does. Though his arms ache with the weight of his luggage, hunger and thirst have begun to make stronger claims on his attention.

A faceted spinning top of brownish meat, revolving slowly in a shop window, stops him and wafts a wonderful, greasy odour at him. He puts down his things, pats his pocket for small change, picks up his things, struggles inside. But he misunderstands the young Iranian behind the counter, and lets him drip too much chilli sauce into the pouch of sliced meat and cabbage. He eats half, discards half, and then discovers that the building he's leaning against, with its skirting of bottle-green, urinous tiles, is a pub.

While he's sipping his half-pint at the bar, a small, scarlet-faced, potato-nosed man, who has been observing him from behind, comes and stands beside him so close that their sleeves touch. He looks down pointedly at the Aeroflot flightbag. 'You're not from around these parts, then, my friend?'

The foreigner stares frightenedly into a pair of blue slits that seem to be shining at him from the far depths of history. 'No, I'm Greek. From Greece. On holiday.'

'Oh yes, I see.' The head nods but the shine in the eyes is steady, a light behind a mask.

The Greek swallows down all his drink and hurries out, trembling and at odds with his own limbs again.

Something has caught his eye in the jumbled window of a shop called Help the Aged. It's a large, plaid shopping bag with a black plastic trim, resting on a frame with wheels. He goes inside and pays a helpful, aged lady 40p for the bag and 50p for the frame. Then he lumbers with all his belongings into a tiny alley called Meryl Street. (The last T of Street has, for some strange reason, been inked over and turned into a P.) He unzips the plaid bag and forces into it his whole flight bag. Having zipped it up, a better idea occurs to him. He removes the flight bag and tips into the plaid bag a compound of the following: notebooks, pens, sponge bag, an extra sweater, an I LOVE LONDON T-shirt and a perfectly cellophaned box of Milk Tray from which both layers have miraculously disappeared, to be replaced by two paperbacks by Zamyatin and Voionovich respectively. He sighs, hesitates, then discards the flight bag into a conveniently placed dustbin. He removes the plaid bag from the frame and somehow persuades his modest-sized suitcase to sit there instead. The plaid bag is perched lengthwise on top of that. Delicately, he propels the contraption back and forward over the cobbles. He thinks that if he goes slowly it will be all right.

But where is he going, why this desperate attempt to stay mobile? The sun has already taken on a lazier, rosier gleam. The life of the High Street is slowing down, turning home. No one can walk behind a luggage cart for ever. (Though he has seen pictures of people straggling with all their possessions across snowy landscapes, looking as if they had walked, and would walk, for ever.)

He glances at his watch; he wants to know if the plane has landed. It has, if it was on time. A shock of frightened grief jumps into his throat. The dear, grey city rushes behind his eyes, and, in a tiny, corner frame, a black-haired woman is sliding out of the bed and into the kitchen to prepare his evening meal. Or perhaps she isn't: perhaps the bed is occupied by two people, one of whom is the black-haired woman, pleasantly oblivious to the hour of the day. But still, he ought to be there.

Or at least somewhere.

As he trundles along he formulates a strategy. It concerns a frail, innocuous-looking old lady who has just begun to cross the street in his direction, and a dog whose loss he wishes to report at the nearest police station.

How sad his request has made the old lady. Her glassy eyes droop, her mouth droops as if she had swallowed a bitter almond, her white head quivers on its stalk like a dandelion puffball. Nevertheless, her grip on his arm is surprisingly fierce.

She wants to know what kind of a dog. Is it a little brown one? She saw a little brown one up by the butcher's in Chalk Farm Road. Dead, squashed by a car. People ought to look after their dogs properly.

'No,' he says hurriedly, and remembers the girl in the park. 'Not a little brown one but a big, thin, white one.'

'One of them pedgirees, one of them, what d'you call it, greyhounds, was it?'

He is relieved that she has removed her claw from his sleeve, though he quails slightly at the inexplicable accusation which glitters at him from beneath the drooping eyelids. 'Not much of a pedigree,' he assures her. The puffball of her head trembles more rapidly; she lifts her claw to indicate, roughly, where the police station is, and croaks a complicated set of instructions twice over. She adds that she hopes that they'll be able to help him, 'But don't expect nothing, they're not like them old bobbies what went out of their way for you even if you was only a kid what'd lost tuppence halfpenny.'

He crosses at the lights, turns left by the flats as she told him, and goes into a yellow-brick building with a blue lamp outside. (He leaves his luggage at the door, confident of the blue lamp's lofty thief-deterrent powers.)

'I wish to request political asylum,' he tells the bored-looking duty sergeant, uttering at last the phrase which he has elaborated in at least twenty different versions during his hours of wandering.

A spark of something that may be malevolent or merely humorous enters the sergeant's pale-blue eyes.

'Political asylum, sir?'

'Yes. I am a Russian dissident.'

'A Russian, sir? A dissident?'

The pale-blue eyes flicker innocently. The policeman wants to play, but the 'Russian' doesn't. He produces his passport, together with his air ticket, from his top pocket. The policeman pretends to read the passport. Then, with a sigh, he gets up to fetch the officer in charge.

The officer in charge is Djavaronok in disguise – tall, pale, ascetic, youngish and very probably bald. His eyes are pale-blue like the sergeant's, but more astute. He regards the 'Russian' closely for a few minutes after listening to his story. Then he invites him behind the desk flap and down the corridor into his office.

The 'Russian' notices as soon as he sits down that there is a copy of the *Saturday Post* on the officer's desk, opened at the sports page.

'Where did you learn your excellent English, Mr Polyakov?' the officer enquires, a degree more affable now he has escaped the public glare of the front desk.

The Home Office doesn't work Sundays

'Excuse me, please,' I said, and began to flick over the pages of the tabloid weekly which the officer had been peacefully reading until my noon-shattering interruption.

I pointed to the item concerning me.

'Ha, I see.' He read quickly, with small grunts, uttering aloud certain phrases with an ironical inflection I found reassuring.

'"Arkady dreams of living in the West . . . he seems to be hooked on all things English . . . would love a job on the *Post* . . . his last book was a fantasy about the glitzy life in a West End ad agency." No, you don't sound very patriotic, do you? Is there any truth at all in it?'

'I did ask about the job, it was supposed to be off the record. The rest of it's grossly exaggerated.'

'It seems to me that there ought to be a way round it with your people – assuming that they even read the piece, of course.'

'They will,' I assured him. 'They read everything.'

'OK, but wouldn't they be more than willing to be persuaded that the article was a fabric of lies? It would be your word – the word of a trusted Soviet citizen, as I presume you are – against the word of the notoriously unreliable capitalist-imperialist press.'

He opened his desk drawer absentmindedly and pushed it shut again with the heel of his hand.

'Or is there in fact more than a little truth in the idea that you've fallen for the Western way of life?'

He pulled a small packet from his pocket and offered me a very small cigar, wrapped in cellophane.

'Think about it, Mr Polyakov. The point is that before we can help you, as we're certainly willing to do, we need the assurance that you are committed to making your life in the West. It would waste a lot of our time and money if you were to change your mind a week later.'

He lit up our child's cigars; we sat back and looked at each other through the smoke.

'I won't change my mind,' I said, thrilling to the confidence of my words. 'I believe I have more to contribute to a flexible, democratic society than to a stagnant, totalitarian one.'

He smiled, if a shade wryly. 'Very well, then. So be it. Tell me more about yourself. Beginning with your date and place of birth.'

After taking notes on me for ten minutes he ushered me into the lift. 'Down to the bowels of hell.' He pushed the button marked B.

I smiled nervously.

'You've chosen a bad time to defect. Five o'clock on a Saturday afternoon, and the Home Office doesn't work Sundays. Never mind. We'll get you sorted out first thing on Monday.'

He waved me into a small, bare room with a WC in it.

'Not exactly the Prince Regent Hotel,' he agreed, following my horrified gaze. 'Imagine you're sleeping in the bathroom.'

'I never had to sleep in the bathroom, not even in Moscow.' I tried to smile, but couldn't.

'Please understand, it's merely a convenience – oh dear, wrong word – merely a *useful fiction*, to keep you here until we can make proper arrangements. We certainly don't want you to feel you're a criminal.'

'Are you going to lock me in?'

'Certainly not, old chap. Now, why don't I go and light the samovar?' He chuckled appreciatively to himself. 'Do you take sugar, Mr Polyakov?'

Despite his promise, later that night while I was dozing on my prison bed, a young constable came in and told me that they'd be bringing down some Saturday-night drunks, and the door had better be locked for my own protection. Such a commotion of roaring and cursing ensued that I suppose I should have felt glad to be locked in. But I didn't; and when the noise died down, I still couldn't sleep; that bolted door loomed all night in every cranny of my consciousness.

The following week was hectic, self-important and disorientating in the extreme. When not gliding across the Thames in the back of an estate car I was sipping weak tea in offices and waiting rooms annexed to offices, soothed by the womanly gossip of typists and typewriters and the prospect of being the centre of interest to yet another smooth-talking, note-taking official. I discussed myself in especial detail at the Home Office and at the Ministry of Defence, where a gaunt, sardonic young man left me in no doubt that I was the most disappointing Soviet defector he had ever had the misfortune to attempt to debrief. Thus stripped, to some extent, of my illusions, I was dispatched to my last office, a paper-strewn attic belonging to the Committee for Refugee Aid. Here, one of those gracious, gentle, Help the Aged type of ladies which England abounds in (so much more reassuring than the grim, assertive Baba Yagas at home) gave me a generous clutch of notes from a tin box and the address of a 'very nice B and B' in Eversholt Street.

The Pompadour, spelled Popado on account of the m, u and r having fallen out of line and slid down the building's face like crooked tears, has turned out to be a five-storey block painted a drizzling cream and flanked by Susie's Sauna on the right and the Peking Fish Bar on the left. The manager is a harassed, greasy-haired, pop-eyed little man, himself rumoured to be a refugee of many years' standing from one of the Baltic states. His name is Max Freestone, but, perhaps not wishing to be reminded of the paradox of his surname, he likes to be known as Mr Max.

There was a faint but pervasive smell of burning in the Pompadour's stale air, but no visible evidence of an imminent conflagration, so I refrained from comment as Mr Max gloomily welcomed me into the reception cubbyhole. He turned his dandruff-flecked, gloomy shoulders and unhooked a small key attached to a hefty, smuggle-proof metal slab.

'Room 13. It's all we got. Maybe lucky for you,' he added, without conviction. 'Third floor. Look for the door that's got no number.'

I carried my baggage up myself. No, there's no number on the door between 12 and 14: only a large knothole just above the latch, stuffed with old newspaper, as yellow and flaky as sawdust.

As I slammed the unnumbered door behind me, a shred of the paper was dislodged and floated to the floor. I picked it up and read, in tiny, faded print: 'Easter Monday top-of-the-table clash with Tranmere.' I began to feel panicky. Most of the words, individually, are comprehensible, and yet the phrase simply does not make sense to me as a whole. Keep calm, I told myself, be patient, you're not naturalised, not Archie Pollock, yet.

('Do you intend to naturalise, Mr Polyakov?' 'Pardon?' 'Apply for British citizenship?' 'Oh yes, definitely. I didn't know you could apply for things like citizenship, is it expensive? OK, I'll even change my name if you like: what about Archie Pollock?' 'That really wouldn't be necessary, Mr Polyakov. Not unless you want to, of course.')

I stood and surveyed room 13. I like it; unlike Mr Max, it's obviously trying hard to be cheerful. There's a soft, bright blue carpet underfoot, scattered with yellow lozenges and moons. The bed has a blue cover, the curtains are dark gold with diagonal rainstreaks picked out in Lurex thread. There is gateleg table whose wooden surface is cosily printed with the white rings of numerous previous refugee coffee cups, beer mugs etc. And a small trolley with a red Formica top, just the place for a typewriter. Chairs of every size and degree of upholstery, five of them, invite me to be sociable.

I looked at myself in the spotted dressing-table mirror, chastened my hair to a semblance of good behaviour and went to the window. Not much of a view: a dark tiled wall belonging to Euston Station, a bit of blue sky. I pushed open the window. The soft roar of London gushed in like a warm, oily, dirty sea. It occurred to me I might be happy. In fact, not just happy; elated.

The joy of the domophobic at being finally homeless . . .

I meet some of my fellow residents and their prejudices

Later that evening, I traced the faint burning smell to a narrow bead curtain in the basement passage. From behind the curtain came voices, a furious sizzling noise and a haze of smoke. I poked my head through the strands of tinkling plastic. A powerful memory came back to me – of the shared kitchen in the old, communal apartment we lived in when I was a child, before we moved to the spacious, three-roomed luxury of our flat on Gorky Street.

Two women brooded over the stove. It was the younger of the two who was responsible for the sizzling. Another woman, with clumpy, henna'd hair, sat smoking at the metal-topped table, at the far end of which stood a boy with Arabic features, beating an egg in a chipped mug. In the far corner, a long-haired Indian was ironing shirts.

He looked up. 'Hello, what can we do for you?' he asked. (Rajit's great dream, I later learned, was to run his own tobacconist's and he was practising hard to perfect the genial manner he felt essential to the British shopkeeper.)

'I smelled burning,' I said apologetically. 'I thought there was a fire.'

The old woman turned from the stove. Her face was perfectly white except for two bright cheek spots, and she was shawled and jewelled in a style more appropriate, I thought, for dining out than for cooking.

'Is no surprise. The English don't know even to fry the egg,' she said, and gestured with her ladle towards the young woman with the frying pan.

I watched in alarm as, scarlet-cheeked, the latter twisted off the gas tap, seized the frying pan, stamped her foot on the pedal of the bin and emptied the frying pan into it. She replaced the pan with a bang on the stove and rushed past me with a sob and a frenzied rattling of the bead curtain.

'Dear, oh, dear, you upset her again, contessa,' Rajit remarked placidly.

The contessa ignored him. 'You want use it?' she asked me, indicating the free burner.

'I haven't got anything to cook,' I said feebly. 'I didn't know there was a kitchen here.'

'Where you think we eat then?'

'You want some toast?' called Naseem, pausing in his egg-beating. 'Here, pass it to him, Joanie!' He threw half a wrapped sliced loaf along the table to the henna'd woman, who held it out to me with a rather sour look of pity.

I felt dazed and almost tearful myself. The little scene over the frying pan had given me a sharp attack of homesickness. I could smell stewing cabbage and burnt onions, and see the weary look of triumph on my mother's sweating face as she emerged from the kitchen with our hard-won supper, a tray of cabbage soup and cutlets, slamming the door conclusively behind her.

'Come here, I'll show you,' ordered the contessa. 'The grill don't work too good because no one ever clean it.' She snatched the plastic bag from me. 'You like one pieces, two, three?'

In a while we were all assembled round the table with our respective feasts. Naseem had thoughtfully laid out jars of ketchup and brown sauce, and a drum of salt. He had prepared himself something he called 'luncheon-meat scramble'. Rajit had abandoned his ironing and produced from the broom cupboard a crock of home-made yoghurt, tenderly swathed in a woollen scarf. Joanie continued to smoke, impassively flicking her ash into a large scallop shell; she said she'd had two fry-ups already. The contessa added a final splash of cooking sherry to her soup, then came and determinedly squeezed her chair between Joanie and me.

'I stay to talk with new guest,' she declared magnanimously, and pressed my hand. 'You're from the Poland also, I am right?'

'No, I'm from the USSR.'

She withdrew her hand from mine as if from a blazing coal. 'Russian? You? I never have believe it.' She peered at me darkly.

Naseem, though, leaned forward so excitedly he almost fell into his dish.

'What you want to leave Soviet Union for? Best system in the world,' he cried.

I wasn't prepared to admit to Naseem, or anybody else, the accidental element in my defection. By now I felt thoroughly at home in the dissident role. Each day brought me a keener awareness of the possibilities inherent in my adopted society and the restrictions of the one I had left behind.

'It's not so wonderful,' I said, and proceeded to set a few facts before Naseem, while the contessa beside me urged me on with grunts and gurgles of surprised approval.

Naseem, however, simply grinned and asked me where I'd picked up my bourgeois propaganda. Though he had never been to the USSR he knew beyond a shadow of doubt that it was the socialist utopia, and his greatest ambition was to go and live there.

Food shortages, he scoffed: had I ever been in the northeast of England and seen the rows of boarded-up shops – and the shops with nothing but a few cans in the window and empty shelves behind them? As for personal freedom, my problem was that I was an aristocrat, just like the contessa here. Maybe I wasn't descended from the Romanovs, but it was obvious that I belonged to the intelligentsia – a class which was aristocratic in its demands for special treatment. Ordinary socialism would never be good enough for the likes of us.

Best of all, Naseem said, playing his ace, was that the USSR has no unemployment.

'But here you can get paid for not working,' I protested. 'To a Russian, that's a miracle.

'You call it getting paid, what you get on the dole?'

I bit into my butterless toast. 'It's not riches, but at least you don't starve.'

Joanie cleared her throat sharply and announced that England was the best bloody country in the world and foreigners what didn't like it should go back where they came from.

'It's a fine country, but not for jobs,' said Rajit peaceably. 'Most of the people in this hotel are unemployed – including you, Joanie dear.'

'Ah yes, but my job was special, weren't it?' Joanie blushed. She sank her fat face coyly into her chin and dug her elbow into my side. 'Tell him, Raj, what I done!'

'She was the Queen Mother's look-alike. She opened garden parties and made speeches and launched ships – she did everything, didn't you, Joanie dear?'

Though the contessa scowled and shook her head, I understood that the revelation was intended to win approval. So I responded in an appropriate fashion, and tactfully refrained from asking Joanie why such a post was no longer attainable. Clearly, in her present state, she would have made a poor showing at anything queenly.

A general conversation was started for my benefit, concerning the other residents. In the course of it I learned that the girl who'd got upset over the burnt egg was my next-door neighbour at number 14. It struck me that she might make a not unpleasant neighbour, but Rajit swiftly cast a gloom of doubt.

'We call her Silent Cynthia,' he told me. 'She's an ex-nun. They threw her out of the convent, but I don't know what she's supposed to have done. She never speaks to anyone, hardly.'

The contessa tutted to herself in a scandalised way.

'It must be something bad because she's always praying,' Joanie said confidentially. 'I heard her one night crying out for God to forgive her. You'll hear it too, where you are, loud and clear,' she added to me with a look of joyous malice. 'You can come and tell us what she says.' She jabbed me with her elbow, and winked.

'Who's the other side?' I asked nervously.

'Number 12? That's Mr Phythian,' said Naseem. 'Nice old man, keeps gerbils.'

'No, it ain't. Number 12's the one-parent-family now,' said Joanie firmly. She dug her elbow so hard into me this time that I winced. 'Know what a tart is, Archie?'

'They don't have them in the Soviet Union,' Naseem said quickly.

'Yes, we do. I know what a tart is.'

'Well, then, you better watch out for yerself with her next door. Dresses like a punk, too, an' all.'

'Her hair, my God!' cried the contessa, lifting splayed fingers above her lacquered, silver coif.

'And the family?' I asked nervously, thinking of a film I'd watched earlier in the lounge, *The Godfather*.

'Little boy. She don't have him, though. He's always round her mother's. Disgustin', innit? She's here on false pretences. The council pays her rent 'cause she said she was a one-parent family, lying bitch. I'll report her, I will, one of these days.'

Although Joanie's language was violent, I noticed she always preserved a small, high-pitched rather impassive delivery, presumably a throwback to her days of queenly speechmaking.

'Don't take any notice of Joanie,' Naseem said to me as we trudged back upstairs. 'It's Mr Phythian at number 12. He's very nice, very quiet, except the gerbils sometimes, you know.' He pressed the flat of his finger to his nostrils and rolled his eyes.

It was silent on my corridor, contrary to my now fevered expectations. I sniffed the air outside room 12, but could detect nothing except the pervasive Pompadour odour of burnt fat. Then I hesitated at the door of room 14.

Not a sound. I looked at my watch. It was only half past nine; I didn't think Silent Cynthia could be in bed. I tapped on the door.

'Who is it?' whispered a muffled voice.

'Arkady – from the next room.'

There was a shuffling from inside, and Silent Cynthia opened the door just enough to put her head round, wide-eyed and open-mouthed. I suspected she was wearing a dressing gown though it was hard to be sure. She was rather plain but fresh-complexioned, with a thick, brown, childish fringe sliced neatly to her brows.

'I'm sorry if you'd gone to bed. I just wanted to tell you that the kitchen's free now, no one's using it.'

The poor girl turned red. 'Thank you, that's kind of you.' Her voice was rusty and faint as if being played on an old gramophone record.

We stared at each other, embarrassed.

'I know how difficult it is to share a kitchen,' I said. 'When I was a child in Moscow my mother shared with four other families and there were always arguments and scenes.'

Silent Cynthia hung her head. 'Thank you,' she whispered again. 'But I won't go down now, I'm rather tired. Please excuse me. Good night!' She shut the door swiftly and soundlessly before I could think of anything else to say.

Slightly aggrieved that she had shown no interest in my Moscow childhood and at the same time anxious that my interruption had offended her, I crept to my own narrow bed. Soon after I'd fallen asleep I was awakened, not by oratory but by a faint, regular squeaking. I recognised it in seconds: Masha had once kept a hamster, with a wheel in its cage. Gerbils and Mr Phythian, not the One-Parent Family, I said thankfully to myself. I fell asleep again, and dreamed vividly and confusingly of all the flats I had ever lived in.

A curious relationship sprang up between Cynthia and me in the subsequent few days – touching, enigmatic, tantalising. It began with the discovery of a bottle outside my door, containing something dark and bearing a handwritten label: ELDERBERRY WINE. I recalled having heard a few moments earlier the soft hiss of Cynthia's door and a creaking of floorboards outside my own, though I had thought nothing of it. Immediately I knocked and called, but there was no reply from her room. Romantically, I imagined her holding her breath on the other side of the door; though of course it was quite possible she had simply gone out.

I tracked her down the following night to the cooking facs. She was on her own but she still looked flushed and harassed. Not unexpectedly, she was wielding a smoking frying pan. She started on seeing me, and began to apologise for taking up the stove. 'Please, I only came to thank you for the wine,' I said. 'My auntie Varya used to make her own wine, out of wild berries. A lot of Russians do. It's very nice to taste it again.'

'It's quite potent,' Cynthia whispered, scarlet-faced.

'That's fine with me.' I tried a hearty chuckle while Cynthia frowned at her lace-up shoes. It occurred to me, rather unkindly, that she might well have alcoholic tendencies, and that her motive in home-brewing could simply be to give herself the spiritual exercise of resisting powerful temptation.

When she held out the frying pan, which was heaped with not very burnt chips, and asked me if I'd like some, I was delighted. Eagerly, I fetched two plates, anticipating a tense but fascinating unveiling of souls.

Before I could protest, Cynthia had scooped three quarters of the chips onto my plate.

'It's far too much, what about you?'

She began to laugh, and gave me another huge scoopful. Then, to my disappointment, she gathered up her own sparsely filled plate. 'Excuse me, but I prefer to eat alone in my room.'

The next night, I arrived home from my wanderings to find a stack of slightly tattered paperbacks outside my door. On the top of the pile was a copy of *Dr Zhivago*. Again I tapped on the door; I even rattled the knob and shouted 'Cynthia!' several times. But again, there was no response. I decided I'd resort to similarly oblique methods of communication – a spray of lilies of the valley, perhaps, tied charmingly to the doorknob?

The vision was swiftly put to flight as Mr Phythian suddenly popped his head out of his door, like a haggard fledgling from an egg.

'Break it down if you like, go on, break it down,' he said mildly.

I said gingerly that I hoped I wasn't disturbing him.

'No, no, no, make as much noise as you like, please do. It won't get you anywhere but there's nothing like persistence.' Mr Phythian's voice was all politeness and reason, but there was a gleam in his watery round eyes that I found unnerving. I tried to retreat inside my room.

'Wouldn't you like to know why you won't get anywhere?' persisted Mr Phythian, spinning his mental treadmill and fixing me with his mad eyes.

I humoured him. 'I presume because there isn't anyone there.'

'Exactly, exactly!' He bobbed about excitedly. 'Miss O'Reardon isn't there. How astute of you to realise!'

'Yes, well, if you'll excuse me.' I made another attempt at retreat.

'Wouldn't you like to know where Miss O'Reardon is?' he cried.

'If you insist,' I said, hoping to sound a note of discouragement.

Little Mr Phythian stepped right out of his door and came so close to me I could smell his gerbil odour of damp straw. 'Look here!' He nudged me, then, with no further warning, broke into an extraordinary, bouncing kind of dance. His baggy trouserlegs flapped, the floorboards trembled. I watched in horrified admiration. The footwork was complicated as well as energetic, and I was afraid the old man would trip over himself. Fortunately, he was forced to stop quite soon because of breathlessness.

He wheezed enthusiastically. 'That's. What. She does. Every. Wednesday.'

My head cleared. 'I see, you mean she goes dancing.'

Mr Phythian stamped his foot. 'No, no, no. Doesn't go dancing. Teaches dancing. Irish jigs. To the working classes, you know. You approve of all that, of course,' he added slyly.

'Miss O'Reardon's Irish?' I said incredulously. I suppose I'd imagined that all Irish women had the pale, ethereal, fine-boned looks of dear Keloway.

Mr Phythian glared pityingly. 'No, of course she's not, she's Chinese!' The force of his own wit proved too much for him. Wheezing and neighing and shuddering, he backed into his room. The unpleasant noise continued intermittently for the next half-hour, eventually driving me out into the murky twilight to search for that beacon of comfort and sanity, the British pint.

My father: vegetable or mineral?

Brooding over my glass that night in the Railway Bell, I found my thoughts again returning to my father. The scrawny pathos and malevolent wit of a certain kind of masculine old age (e.g. Mr Phythian's) did not appeal to me, and I hoped profoundly that he had matured with greater dignity than the mad gerbil-keeper. After all, my mother had always told me I would grow up to be exactly like him. Her tone had not been encouraging.

I had never had much luck when I tried to remember him before. But now, thanks perhaps to my encounter with Mr Phythian, or to the gloomy, sodden, remorse-inducing atmosphere of Anglo-Saxon inebriation, my subconscious mind began to liquefy and yield up an image or two.

A clock face: pallid, plump, with black hands and golden numerals. The time is a quarter to seven: father gets home from work just as the large hand tips the ten. I wait for him, trying to see the hand move. I succeed. It travels in tiny little jumps. This is disappointing; I would prefer to think it's impossible to see the hand move, as father said.

What did he do at the Institute of Metallurgy where he worked? Stupidly, I still don't know; when I write my letter of contrition to Leningrad I must ask, though I suspect that mother doesn't know either. As a child I thought it must be a hard, glittering sort of job, involving trams or tin cars or knives and forks. It puzzled me that he didn't look metallic too; he was more vegetable. Beetroot or potato, according, I suppose, to how much he'd had to drink.

A brown five-kopeck piece. That was what he gave me, as a reward for tenacity, when I told him I'd seen the clock's hand move. Did he promise to raise it to twenty if I managed to see the little hand move? No, I think I'm embroidering too much.

But the box was real. A small, red, cardboard box with yellow squiggles on it. And inside it a little picture, cut neatly out of a newspaper. Slightly creased from over-handling, it depicted a smiling woman in a crown. Her Majesty, the new queen of England, said father dryly. Heaven knows where the picture came from. I clearly remember that mother used to get angry whenever he showed it to me in his noncommital way, eliciting my unfathoming admiration (though actually it was the red box I admired most, and next to that, the crown – which I knew glittered with brightly coloured diamonds, though it looked plain white in the photo). Father, when scolded, would merely chuckle and say – what did he say? Yes, I remember:

'It's a fact of history, Ninochka. You can't hide facts.'

Oh, but you can, Father; didn't you know that our native country is one massive concealment of fact?

Perhaps you did, and that was why you vanished.

No one seemed to want to talk about my father's disappearance – and I wasn't the kind of child to ask pointless questions. But I didn't give up on him for many years; often, surreptitiously, I'd glance at the clock around a quarter to seven in the evening. I certainly didn't believe, as morbid old Auntie Galya said, that he had thrown himself into the river. Even Mother favoured the notion of some kind of survival – drunken, disgraced but, in its Russian way, heroic. Whatever he was, Father wasn't dead. He was working at the Space Institute, maybe, on a project so secret he would never be allowed to go home. Or maybe he'd run away to sea, and was shipwrecked like my hero, Robinson Crusoe, on a desert island. One day he'd find a cunning way to escape, though. And the beetroot would shine at the door: I'm back, Ninochka, give us a kiss! (A request with which, for once, my mother would eagerly comply.)

In a sudden burst of indescribable emotion, it occurred to me that he could have ended up in London. I gazed wildly round the saloon bar; there were several candidates of sufficiently advanced years and reddish demeanour . . . but what was the point? I could hardly go round to each one suggesting myself as a possible son. No, it was ridiculous; these were the fantasies of an eight-year-old, not a man of nearly thirty-eight. I calmed down and ordered another beer, with a vodka chaser. But, by the time I'd swallowed three more of the same, I felt emboldened to try a small experiment.

With another of those tiny English vodkas in my hand, I swung round on my stool, raised the glass high. 'A toast!' I cried in my most declamatory voice. 'To Piotr Yurievich Polyakov, late of Moscow!'

The effect was not electric; or if it was, it was that of a minor power cut. Most of the drinkers swiftly averted their eyes and sipped at their pints. A beefy younger man, however, raised his glass and bellowed something like 'There you go!' And a pink-haired girl feeding the fruit machine turned and stared at me with a look of such viciousness that I hastily turned to face the counter. Unfortunately, a man sitting opposite in the public bar seemed to have heard what I said. 'Commie bastard,' he shouted, shaking his fist at me through the forest of uncollected glasses.

The fresh-cheeked young Gestapo officer behind the bar now came at me with a scowl. 'That's enough, you, this is a quiet pub and we don't want no trouble. If you can't take your liquor, we don't want you here. Clear off home!'

'I was merely drinking a toast to my father – it's his birthday,' I said with dignity. 'I'll have another vodka, please, a large one.'

Foolishly, the Gestapo officer turned his broad back and ignored my request. I decided on second thoughts to take his advice and clear off 'home'.

A missing h and two mysterious visitors

I woke up the next day feeling depressed as well as embarrassed by the episode in the pub. I decided to put all thoughts of my father out of my head and employ my imaginative powers in a more productive way. If I wished to make any impact on Western literature it was time I started writing – or at least translating some of the things I'd brought with me. I'd been preparing a collection of short stories for publication in Moscow; there was no reason why, with a bit of de-censoring, they shouldn't find favour with a publisher here.

The main problem was my lack of a typewriter. English being for me an essentially literary language, I find it impossible to know if I've expressed myself well in it unless I can see the words in type. I pondered a while – then decided to try my luck at Refugee Aid. It seemed a bold project to an ex-Soviet, raised in a society where the state provides everything you need, and what it doesn't provide you don't need, even if you think you do. But I was learning that English society is different. Bourgeois, imperialist, decadent or not, it is a kindly society, I think; it actually likes you to ask it for money, and sometimes even gives it to you before you've asked . . .

'Of course you need a typewriter, dear, of course you do!' The two old ladies in the front office clucked and fussed and scurried away to confer with the director. But if I had expected – or, rather, timidly hoped – that a modest sum of money would be pressed into my palm,

I was mistaken. Instead I walked out onto the Bayswater Road, the delighted owner of a portable typewriter. 'It was just standing idle in Mr Robinson's old office,' explained one of the old dears. 'When he left he never bothered to take it with him.'

When I got home I found out why. The machine's Japanese manufacturers had obviously been unfamiliar with the Roman alphabet, for the key marked h turned out to type g, and the key marked i to type g. There was no h to be found on the keyboard, not even under ½ or @. A very un-Russian letter, but a thoroughly English one, that h, I knew, would be greatly missed.

I was giving the machine an undeserved rub-down with methylated spirits and thinking less genial thoughts than formerly about the charitable English, when there came a tap at my door. Silent Cynthia! I cheered up at once, but it turned out to be Rajit.

'Hullo there, Not drinking that stuff, I hope!' Rajit humorously indicated the purple bottle.

'Not yet,' I said wearily.

'I won't keep you, I can see you're busy. I've just come to tell you about your visitor.'

'My visitor?' I stopped rubbing at the inky letters. 'What visitor?'

'I don't know. A man. A Russian man, I think. I was on reception – I always stand in for Mr Max on Thursday afternoons – and this man came in and asked for you.'

My heart was dancing wildly. 'What was his name?' I heard my voice go shaky.

'He didn't say.'

'But what did he want?' Rajit's Buddhist serenity could be very annoying at times. Realising my impatience, he gestured apologetically. 'I'm sorry. You see, he didn't say very much at all. Just asked me if you lived here.'

'What did you tell him?'

'I told him, *of course*,' said Rajit proudly, 'that there are many peoples in this house and I am not the boss and I don't know all of them. Maybe you live here, maybe you don't. Probably you don't.' He looked at me anxiously, gauging my reaction. 'That was the wisest thing, don't you agree?'

'Did he say he'd come back later?'

'No, he didn't.'

'And how did you know he was Russian?' My pulse rate was almost normal.

'Because of his voice. Like in spy films on the telly.'

'What did he look like? Was he old?'

'Quite old, but maybe not very.' Rajit frowned. 'Bald, I think. Shortish. Nothing special.'

'Did he look at all like me?'

'No, not at all. Why, do you have relatives here?'

'I don't know. I don't think so'

'I hope it wasn't the KGB,' said Rajit with a sudden grin.

'So do I!'

'Maybe you know a little top military secret or two,' he hinted shyly.

'I certainly do not. You've been watching too many of those spy films, Rajit.'

After he'd gone, though, I began to sweat; supposing he was right? Surely it was more likely to be some kind of undesirable official type than my father, who, I had to admit, could be anywhere on this dark earth, above it or below it. I told myself I had nothing to fear; I knew nothing about our Soviet defence systems, I wouldn't have been able to tell a missile launcher from a vacuum cleaner. But what if they thought I did, and tried to kidnap me anyway?

For the next few days I scarcely left my room. I requested Mr Max to admit no unidentified visitors asking to see me without warning me first. I fed myself from my store cupboard, exercised by means of occasional vigorous sessions of knee bends, sit-ups and Irish jigs, and worked, mercilessly tapping and cursing at my h-less keyboard, from morning till midnight.

The knock at my door came late one evening when I was about halfway through 'A Dream of the Moscow Metro'. I had travelled with the delectable English tourist Clarissa Brown from Rechnoi Station to Kakhovskaya, from Yugo-Zapadnaya to Sokolniki, from Sochelkovskaya to Filyovsky Park. I felt dazed, hypnotised, entranced, and almost too exhausted to feel afraid. Almost, but not quite. I ducked down behind the red plastic trolley. Another volley of knuckles. I held my breath. They had come to take me home. At least I would see Moscow again before I died.

The door burst open.

'You in there?' demanded a strident voice.

I peeked over the top of the typewriter. Could this be a disguise? It was female, probably; it was black and gold and shining; it was dreadful to behold. I gulped: of course, the One-Parent Family. Crimson-faced, I scrambled to my feet.

'Excuse me . . . I was looking for . . . please come in. How do you do?'

I held out my hand, but it was shaking so much I quickly withdrew it. I had been spared the attentions of the KGB only to be confronted with a different kind of threat – a lesser one, of course, but more incomprehensible.

'You a writer or something?' The hairstyle pointed bright orange fingers at my poor little crippled typewriter. 'The noise goes straight up through the floor; I'm over your head, you know, and this here object's trying to sleep.'

The object turned out to be a very small boy, trailing in his mother's glorious wake, with his thumb in his mouth and one finger up his nose.

I began to apologise profusely, but the Family didn't seem to be listening. She had marched into the centre of my room, and was busily appraising it. I noted that she was dressed entirely in black leather. Her eyes were upswept like those of a samurai and her hair flared from her question-mark skull in brassy cornucopias. She resembled most of all, I decided, some Inca representation of their sun god. Beautiful in a way, even splendid, but armed to the teeth and, frankly, dangerous.

'Your room's even crummier than mine,' she announced.

'Yes, it's very nice, isn't it?' I gabbled in agreement.

She narrowed her eyes at me, then marched over to the typewriter. 'What you writing then?' She stood there shamelessly reading my story, while the object bounced himself gleefully up and down on my bed. 'Stop that, dummy!' She turned to me. 'What's this story about?'

'Life in Russia,' I told her vaguely.

She sniffed loudly. 'You Russian, then?'

'Not much. I used to be.'

The Family ignored this Zinovievian paradox and sniffed again. 'I'm into Russia,' she declared, giving me a quick blaze of her garish smile. 'My granddad was Lithuanian. That's Russia now, ain't it? Can I read the story when it's finished?'

'Yes, of course,' I said in dismay; I was sure she'd rip it up, militiaman-style, if it was not entirely to her liking.

I apologised again for having disturbed her.

'Oh, it was him' she said, giving the child a friendly cuff. 'This little object. Kept on whingeing, "What's that noise? I can't sleep." Weren't it, eh?'

'No, it weren't,' he declared boldly, making violent snatches at her sun rays.

'He'll be at his nana's, thank God, the rest of the week, so you can bash away all you like as far as I'm concerned!'

'That's terribly kind of you!'

'That's terribly kind of you!' she mimicked, in a voice quite different from her usual snarl. 'I say, you do talk awfully posh for a Russian!' She paused at the door. 'What's your name?'

I told her.

'That's an effin' mouthful.' She scowled. 'I'll call you Russky, OK?'

'OK.'

'I'm Treeza. But you can call me Tel!'

With a last sniff and a cuff at the little object, Tel slammed my door. A few minutes later I heard Silent Cynthia slam hers and throw some kind of heavy object against our party wall. She had seen my visitor leave and was jealous, I decided. A little flow of pride tingled through my shot nerves. I must remember to get her that bouquet.

The search is on

My apparent success with two such very different young women emboldened me to the extent that I almost forgot about my imminent arrest. The following day I went out and lurked around the flower stall by Euston Station. I was embarrassed that I didn't know the English word for lilies of the valley, the flowers I had set my heart on. There didn't seem to be any such blooms on show, but possibly the stall man was concealing some because, as often in Moscow, there was a shortage of them. I wandered behind the stall a few times, and tried to get a look underneath it, too.

The stall man's eyes followed me even while he was serving other people; I could see he didn't trust me.

'Can I help you at all?' he finally said.

His politeness startled me. 'Don't worry, please,' I said.

'I'm not worried, guv'nor,' he said, much less pleasantly. 'It's you what looks worried.'

'I'm looking for some flowers,' I told him.

'Are you now?'

'Yes. But I don't know what they're called. They smell very nice and they've got leaves like this.' I drew a shape in the air.

'Really? Got leaves, have they? And a nice smell?' He winked at a woman who was buying roses. 'Not many flowers like that, is there, lady?'

'They've got blossoms like little white bells.'

'Oh, he means lilies of the valley! Don't you?' cried the woman.

'Do I?'

'You should know, guv'nor. Bloody tourists,' he added under his breath

'Have you got any?' I persisted, ignoring the insult.

'Lilies of the V? Yep, got some in my back yard.'

Aha, I thought. I lowered my voice discreetly. 'How much?'

The stall man rolled his bloodshot eyes in a peculiar way.

'They're growing in his garden, love,' the woman said, trying to explain. 'You don't buy them, you have to grow them. Have you got a garden where you come from?'

'No,' I said sadly.

'Have something else,' offered the stall man. 'Them's nice, if you want white flowers.' He pointed to a bucket of carnations.

'How much?'

The man hurriedly picked out a bunch of them and displayed them to me. 'There. Lovely, aren't they? Just what the missus ordered, they are. Fiver the lot. And cheap at the price. Just look at all them buds!'

'Fiver the lot?' It was an idiom I didn't know.

The man sighed and splayed a grimy hand. 'One, two, three, four, five pound notes!'

Dismayed, but afraid to back out, I opened my purse and gave him the required sum. I had nothing left now till my next giro came. But Silent Cynthia was worth it, wasn't she?

No sooner had I got back, flustered and weary, to my room, than Tel barged in. 'Where've you been all day? I told you to finish that story so I could read it!'

She wasn't smiling. My God, I thought, the Writer's Guilt personified. This woman could be just what I need.

'Sorry, I had to go shopping. I'll do it this afternoon.'

She gave a noisy sniff. 'See you do! I'll be back!' The hairstyle pointed all its sharp fingers at me before disappearing.

When she was safely back in her room I gathered up the moist bouquet, and, with a sharp eye on the gerbil's door, laid my offering noiselessly, reverently, at Silent Cynthia's.

'So who was she, then, this English chick?'

Tel had read my finished story and pronounced the verdict (presumably favourable?) that I was not so dumb as I looked. In return, I had brewed her a glass of Russian tea, with lemon and a spot of Rajit's Oxford marmalade. This she slurped from a spoon with childish relish.

'Why does she have to be anybody?' I answered boldly. 'Writers make people up, didn't you know?'

'I bet it was your girlfriend,' she persisted obstinately.

I sighed.

'*Weren't it your girlfriend, that blond chick?*'

'Well – all right. For a very short time, a very long time ago.'

'Tell us, then!' Fascinated, she pressed me for every detail. And when I'd finished, she was gaping with disbelief. 'D'you mean to say you actually *walked past* where she used to live and you never even *knocked on the door*?'

'But I'm sure she doesn't live there now. And ten years is a long time,' I replied.

'Don't you fancy her no more?'

'I do, of course I do.'

'You're afraid of losing your illusions, that's what.'

'I left my illusions in Moscow.'

'Oh yeah? I reckon you brought 'em with you.'

She looked at me piercingly and I blushed, thinking of the carnations outside Silent Cynthia's door. They weren't there now, I'd checked. But I felt that somehow she might have guessed.

'What do you mean?' I asked timidly.

'Elizabeth, for a start. And this dump.'

'What about this dump?'

'You said you liked living here,' she accused.

'Well, in a way I do. Why not? It's a start!'

'A start? It's a bloody dead end, mate, that's what it is!' She drained her tea with an expressive slurp. 'So when you going to call on that rectory place?'

'I'm not.'

'Oh yes, you are,' said Tel.

'Actually I don't go out very much. There's a slight chance that I might be kidnapped.' That ought to impress her, I thought.

'You're joking!' She peered at me to divine whether I was. 'You ain't rich. Only the poncy rich get kidnapped!'

'I meant by the secret police.'

'Ooooh!' Her mouth became a little black hole. Then she suddenly seemed to grow. Her rather flat chest swelled, her shoulders broadened in a creaking of black leather, her eyes flashed massive samurai blades.

'Them bastards,' she snarled, 'them bastards better not try. Just let 'em. Just bloody let 'em!' She raised her clenched fist at me, and even that looked huge and inflamed. 'See what they'll get!'

Suddenly her scowl dissolved to a broad grin. 'Don't you worry.

I'll come with you, and I'll beat up any bugger who so much as gives you the eyeball!'

She rose to her feet and loomed over me. 'I'm off now but I'll be back,' she warned. 'Same time tomorrow. See ya!'

As we approached the rectory (an incongruous couple who nevertheless failed to attract any attention from the passers-by – no doubt they felt it was in their best interests not to see us), I found myself hoping profoundly that Elizabeth wouldn't be there. I hoped nobody would be there, in fact. Tel was an even more terrible apparition than usual, draped in swatches of what looked like real bullets, her hair-horns gelled to points that could pierce the human diaphragm, silver saw-blades painted along both cheeks. I believe there were small offensive weapons stowed in her pockets. If Elizabeth or her father, even, answered the door, I would die of embarrassment. Unfortunately the rectory was a blaze of light.

'Wait for me by the gate, Tel,' I pleaded.

Tel refused. 'What if one of them bastards jumps out on you?'

'I'll scream and you can rescue me.'

'They could have taken over the whole house. Killed the occupants an' all and set up their headquarters. And they've got guns and bombs and machetes and they're waiting for you like big black spiders in a nasty, sticky web!' She spoke with unconcealed relish.

'Don't be silly,' I said, with more conviction than I felt. 'Do as you're told and wait for me here.' It was the first time I had talked to her as if she had been a child, as if she were Masha. Strangely enough, it worked. She slunk sulkily back to the gate.

I braced myself and tugged the metal bell pull.

A mild-looking woman, young, fair-haired and just for a second – but no more – curiously like Elizabeth, opened the door. She listened sympathetically to my garbled story. But she had never heard of the Lambs; the rectory was divided into flats now, she said, and she was just a tenant. I asked her if she could tell me the name of the landlord.

She looked blank. 'Well, now you've got me.' She thought for a while. 'I suppose it must be Camden Council.'

'Can you give me his phone number please?'

'Whose?'

'The landlord's. Camden's.'

The woman smiled, and began to say something. But all at once a cloud came over her pretty brow and she took a step back from me and slammed the door in my face.

'She thought you was a nutter,' Tel explained later, between raucous screams of mirth. 'You're really pissed off about it, aren't you?' she added, seeing my expression. 'You're really pissed off about not finding Elizabeth.'

'I suppose I am a bit,' I said Englishly.

We were in her room, drinking horrible instant coffee from mugs that stood on webbed green feet, a bit like Baba Yaga's cottage. I had almost refused to come in when I saw the swastikas festooned around the walls, but she had persuaded me that it was only because she liked the shape. 'I was born in 1965,' she argued. 'You don't expect me still to be bothered about that old war? Even my mum don't remember it!'

I felt more old and Russian than ever, but I let her drag me in and sit me down on a gigantic cushion that seemed to be stuffed with dried peas.

Tel, sitting on a very narrow and steely chair, stretched her black legs in front of her, raised her feet on her boot-heels and revolved each of them slowly, the right one clockwise, the left one anticlockwise. For some reason, I found myself erotically stirred by these activities.

'I've got an idea,' she declared. 'I'll tell you how to get it together with your ex.'

'OK, fine,' I said, watching her feet as though hypnotised.

'I'm not kidding!' she said earnestly.

'Tel,' I said softly

'What's up now?'

'Tel, wouldn't you like to get it together with me?'

It was a stupidly unsubtle approach, as I realise now. But at the time it seemed wonderfully candid, just the kind of plain speaking she would appreciate.

'No thanks,' she said. 'D'you want to hear about this idea or not?'

'Yes, of course,' I said, abashed.

She tilted her chair back at a horrible angle and scrabbled one-handed among the magazines and newspapers stacked slitheringly on her dressing table. With the natural instinct of the chaotic, she pulled out the newspaper she wanted, a copy of *The Times*, and turned it to a page at the back.

'All you do is send in one of these. Such as – will Cinderella, last seen getting into a pumpkin outside Camden Palace, please contact blah blah blah and she will learn something to her advantage.' She pushed the newspaper under my nose.

'Translate, please.'

Tel explained as patiently as she could the process of placing a small ad.

'But what if Elizabeth doesn't read *The Times*?' I said.

'You got to use a bit of psychology, like. You tell me the sort of person she is and I'll tell you what she reads. She's an intellectual, ain't she? Old like you, a bit short on street cred?'

'You think I'm too old for you, don't you?'

'Yes. Keep your mind on the job, Russky. Is she SDP? Does she like David Owen? What about huntin' shootin' and fishin'? Is she a Sloane Ranger?'

'I shouldn't think so.' I didn't want to expose my ignorance further by asking her to explain these extraordinary idioms.

'You don't know much about her, do you?'

'She likes books,' I said defensively.

'Oh, I say, likes books, does she?' Tel put on her upper-class voice.

'And she's a socialist and a feminist,' I added proudly. 'Or was.'

'Did they have 'em in those days?' She looked surprised.

'Really, it wasn't the Middle Ages, you know!'

'All right, keep ya wool on, Russky. I'll tell ya what!' She began scrabbling again. 'This is it! Here, take it, and push off. I want to wash me hair.'

'Is it washable?'

'Haha, very funny!'

'I didn't mean to be funny.'

'You never do. That's your trouble.' Affectionately she knocked her fist against my chest. 'No offence, then?'

'Not at all,' I said, guessing her meaning.

'And listen, don't you put that ad in without showing me first. Understand?'

'Yes, Tel,' I said and meekly retreated, clutching the copy of the *New Statesman* and the remains of my battered but not mortally wounded pride.

Trial by qwerty

Given Tel's lack of response to my ill-judged amorous overture, it was particularly annoying that our fellow tenants decided to think the worst of us. Silent Cynthia was for obvious reasons the most aggrieved. She not only failed to thank me for the white carnations, she actually returned them, yellow and wilted, to my doorway the following week. On the rare occasion we came face to face she would sour her rosy, schoolgirlish looks with a frown, scowl at her lace-up shoes, and remove herself from my company as quickly as possible. As a neighbour she became less and less silent: there were regular bouts of hurling heavy objects at our shared wall. I felt I ought to attempt to clear things up between us, but I was newly wary of frank speaking. I wasn't even sure that I fancied her any more, an angular overgrown schoolgirl with a beefy complexion and an unforgiving temper.

I particularly blamed her for telling Joanie that Tel and I visited each other's rooms. Joanie, though she had abdicated from public life, was still the uncrowned queen of the telly lounge and the cooking facs – her approval mattered. I found myself shivering unhappily at the cooling atmosphere.

'This place is going from bad to worse,' she would say, addressing a neutral onlooker such as Rajit while gazing meaningfully at me. 'Crawling with riff-raff foreigners now it is!'

'I'm a foreigner, Joanie,' Rajit would say with his Buddhist smile.

'I don't mean you, do I, I mean them Russians.' (I was, of course, the only Russian at the Pompadour.)

Rajit would glance at me nervously and say something placatory like, 'I don't think they're going to drop the bomb on us yet, Joanie dear.'

'That's what you think,' Joanie would say darkly, and several faces would turn suspiciously in my direction.

One day, Mr Max asked to have a word with me in his office. I went downstairs in a state of agitation, convinced my mysterious visitor had called again. He waved a sheet of foolscap in front of my eyes, and told me he had received a petition. Against me.

'It's the typing,' he said gloomily. 'It's noise pollution, they say, and it's driving them up the wall.'

I protested that I had always tried to stick to social hours.

'What's social for some isn't social for others,' said Mr Max, opening his hands in a hopeless gesture. 'Lot of our people sleep in the daytime, for instance, and get up at night.'

I suspected that quite a lot of them slept both in the day and the night. Who, I asked, was responsible for getting up the petition?

Mr Max cagily compressed his lips and shook his head. But he admitted that the signatories included Cynthia O'Reardon, Joanie, Mr Phythian and the contessa. (I was surprised that the contessa had not shown more solidarity with a brother Slav.)

Three of them, sighed Mr Max, were threatening to leave. He hated to say it, but one out was obviously better, from his point of view, than three.

I plodded back to my room in a state of despair. If I couldn't type I couldn't write, if I couldn't write, I was nothing and no one. I was used to having my wings clipped by Glavlit, but this was castration! The work had been going beautifully, too; I had started a story about Ilya which I felt marked the discovery of my new, liberated, London voice. The first page sat disconsolately half-typed in my machine.

I paced my hot room and brooded. Suddenly I hated England. I wanted Moscow; I wanted to be among honest, plain-speaking working Russians, not these slippery, slitheringly hostile Brits. I wanted Lev and Luba and Asta – I even wanted Taras. I wanted *Pravda* with all its lies, I wanted a plate of raw herring, I wanted a metro that only cost five kopecks to anywhere – *my metro*, as

Okhudzhava said on behalf of all Muscovites. I wanted my desk at the *New Literary Star* and my table in the dining room of the Writers' Union. I wanted my daughter. Most of all I wanted myself.

Leaning on the raw, baked wood of my window ledge, I swallowed sobs.

Later I heard Mr Phythian go out. That cheered me up a bit: I was pretty sure Silent Cynthia was out too. I tapped on her door to make sure. There was no reply. The only other person in earshot of my typing was the contessa, who inhabited the room immediately below. Surely, on such a fine day, she would be strolling regally in Plato Park, or taking tea with her aristocratic friends?

Lightly, tentatively, I depressed a few keys. No one in the house stirred. I tried a few more, and then, the narrative carried me away. I had reached the bottom of the page when an angry knocking began to vibrate beneath my soles. It was the contessa, drumming with her wooden cane.

I stopped immediately, and flung myself down on the bed. But I couldn't stay in this stifling little prison for another minute. I jumped to my feet: I would take my notebook and go and write doom-laden adolescent poetry in the park.

Then a better idea came to me. I would take my typewriter and *work* in the park.

Of course, I hadn't thought the mechanics properly through. It was easy enough to find a secluded place – there was a bench I always thought of as the honeymoon seat, high and shady and alone among the shrubs of the rockery mount – but to find a workable position was a different matter. I started off with my typewriter balanced on my knees, but I hadn't reckoned on the inconvenient length of my spine. I had always considered my spine to be unusually short: I held it personally to blame for my Napoleonic stature. Now, I discovered that I had greatly underestimated the distance from my chin to my knees, and overestimated the distance from knees to feet. It was painful to have to bend forward all the time, particularly when I had to dip my neck even further at intervals so as to read the longhand script I was typing from. Then there was the problem of keeping the pages from blowing away. The filmy copy paper discovered air currents imperceptible to me. It was necessary to find a small, clean stone, not the easiest thing in a garden composed of large, dirty, immovable rocks.

I decided on a new arrangement. I would sit on the ground with my typewriter on the seat. In that way I'd have a kind of work table, and everything would be more controllable.

Once again, a shadow fell between the conception and the creation. The problem was that the seat was lodged in a growth of some prickly shrub together with more sharp rocks. There was nowhere for my tender ankles to lodge themselves.

I sighed, and repacked my things. There was nothing for it but to go public at one of the seats on the grass near the main path. I went to the kiosk and purchased a can of Coke. Then, pouncing on an unoccupied seat, I arranged myself with my back firmly to the passers-by, my feet sticking out the other side, and my Coke can acting as paperweight, and began to rattle away as loudly and confidently as I could. I was determined not to hear any comments or shrieks of amusement my curious stance might arouse. Girls could giggle at me, dogs sniff at me, children run round the seat to stare at me, but I would ignore them all until I'd finished 'The Music Man'.

'That's a cunning little arrangement, if I may say so!' The voice had a clipped accent which sounded Russian to me. My fingers froze to the keys. This was it! He had caught up with me. My heart raced, then suddenly I felt quite calm. I forced my hands to move and clasp the machine by its sides. Though portable, it wasn't as featherlight as all that. Used with sufficient force, it could deliver a disabling blow. I raised my eyes boldly.

The man was plump and pale: he had a black, spadelike beard and sharp brown eyes. His smile exposed nastily pointed canines. Even his nostrils were sinister – such round, clean little holes. He was a cross between an overweight Count Dracula and V. I. Lenin.

'What are you writing?' he asked, with blatant lack of ceremony.

'What's that got to do with you?' I riposted.

He gave a little convulsive jerk, as if he had just been switched on;

his plump hands flexed their fingers. I got a firmer grasp on the typewriter and began to lift it.

'Oh, nothing, of course. It was just curiosity; professional curiosity, I suppose, because I'm a publisher. I'm very sorry to have disturbed you.' With a sheepish look, he began to move away.

A publisher? I let go of the typewriter and scrambled to my feet. 'Hey, wait a minute! He turned, warily. 'I'm sorry, I didn't mean to be rude, I mistook you for someone else.'

'That's all right!' He smiled nervously as I approached him, fortunately not enough to show his sinister teeth, or I might have changed my mind about him again. 'I'm sorry, perhaps I should have introduced myself first.' He dipped into his top pocket and handed me a small card. I read the name 'Demszky and Dayland, Ltd', followed by a promising-looking address in West 1.

'I'm Demszky, as you've probably gathered.'

I took his extended hand, still half expecting a poisoned needle concealed in the palm, though of course I had by now identified Mr Demszky as Hungarian rather than Russian. But all I felt was moist, human flesh.

I declared my name, and Demszky knitted his waxen brow. 'That rings a bell! Didn't I see an article about you in one of the papers? I was talking to Gerard, my colleague, about it the other day. He's the one for fiction – I'm cookery and gardening. It was you, wasn't it?'

'I'm afraid so,' I admitted.

'It was a silly piece of journalism,' Demszky went on candidly. 'But I remember I liked the poem.'

We went back to the bench and sat ourselves down. 'And is it my business to ask you what you're working on now?' Demszky asked with gentle irony, glancing over the page in my machine. 'Could I even perhaps be allowed to read it?'

I felt myself flush. 'Yes, of course. But I'm afraid it won't make much sense. There aren't any h's, you see. The typewriter's faulty.'

'So how on earth do you manage?'

'I pencil them in afterwards.'

'Goodness gracious, that isn't very satisfactory,' exclaimed Demszky in his elegantly consonantal English.

I was now so well disposed towards him that I began to describe my other, worse typing difficulty in plaintive detail.

Mr Demszky agreed that it was quite absurd for a writer to be in such a position. He took up my sheaf of finished pages, saying that he could probably supply the missing h's in his head. After a protracted five minutes he handed them back to me. 'It seems very good,' he said. 'The sort of thing Gerard ought to be looking for. Why don't we make a date for you to come into the office? Maybe we could even find a spare typewriter for you to use.'

'Wonderful, wonderful,' was all I could say.

'Perhaps you'd better ring first. On Monday, not too early. You've got my card.'

Wonderful Mr Demszky, wonderful park, wonderful England!

The letter arrived the morning I was due to visit Demszky and Dayland's. Headed paper, an address in Leicester (Leicester – remember to look on the map). Plain, clean, slanting hand. Real ink, not biro. Faint, wonderful, girlish scent – lime flowers, lilacs?

Dear Arkady,

I saw your advert in the *New Statesman* and wrote to them for your address. It was nice of you to think of looking me up while you're visiting London. I've moved to Leicester now, but I come down once a week to do a Russian class at the Euston School of Languages.

Would you like to meet me outside the School on Tuesday 18 June at 12.30? I enclose a little map and the address. You needn't bother to let me know. I'll look out for you anyway.

Hoping to see you,
With best wishes,
Elizabeth

I rushed upstairs to pour out my gratitude to Tel. 'Oh sod off, Russky,' she said pleasantly. 'Wait till you've met her before you come on with the romantic drool.'

Back in my room I dabbed on more aftershave, grabbed my *A–Z* and set off for the legendary village of Soho.

I spent the whole day in a little cupboard of a room, one among many in that rabbit warren of offices occupied variously by a firm of solicitors, a picture library, a dentist's, a nursing agency and Demszky and Dayland, Publishers.

'I trust you'll be inspired by our Dickensian surroundings,' said Gerard Dayland in a way that made me suspect he hoped rather the opposite. It seemed to me that I was one of a positive herd of East European lost sheep that the soft-hearted Demszky had given shelter to at some time or another, and even talked him into publishing on occasion: as such, I was only barely tolerable. However, although he sighed wearily and deeply, he agreed to cast an eye over my stories.

I worked through lunch – an extraordinarily long lunch, by Moscow standards. Dayland and Demszky left the premises at 12.30 and returned, with flushed complexions, at ten past four. Dayland's attitude towards me had warmed considerably, I observed. He lingered in the doorway of my cupboard, exhaling rich fumes and a slightly unreal enthusiasm.

'So what d'you think of the Smoke? Swinging city, eh?'

I agreed that it was.

'This part of it especially,' Dayland said enthusiastically. 'They say it isn't what it used to be. The old carpers and grumblers. Don't know what they mean, myself. Atmosphere – that's Soho. Pure atmosphere. I wouldn't work in any other part of London.'

'I don't know it very well,' I confessed.

'Don't know Soho? Then you're half-educated, if I may say so. Well, well, well. Why don't I show you round the old village some time? Doing anything tonight?'

I hesitated; I knew, of course, what was coming next and it didn't greatly entice me. However, expediency warned me I needed to get Dayland on my side; he was, after all, the fiction man. Besides, it was all experience – the lack of which I'd lamented so bitterly once by the Moscow River.

I told him I was free, and accepted his offer of a night on the town with suitable emotion.

'Good chap,' said Dayland, staggering slightly. 'Excuse me now, I've got a meeting at five.'

At ten to, Demszky said a bleary goodbye to me, and Dayland began to brew coffee. The meeting began on time and, judging by the spurts of girlish amusement that issued from Dayland's office, was an unusually pleasant one. I tried not to disapprove; it was no use clinging to the Soviet work ethic in such a hedonistic society. Better to enter the spirit of it too. I read a magazine and clock-watched, anticipating my evening out with heightened intensity. It got to 6.30; then, at ten to seven (that numinous time) my door burst open and Dayland appeared, closely followed by a black-skinned girl in a white safari suit.

They both regarded me pleasantly, as if I was some not altogether toadlike museum exhibit. The girl smiled at me warmly and held out her hand, having been introduced as what sounded like Salary or Celery Fitz-Jones.

'Salary has written us a wonderful book – it's going to be a bestseller.' Dayland chortled.

'Oh, you must be joking,' Celery demurred with a charming, throaty giggle.

'I'm certainly not,' protested Dayland, 'I never joke about money. Or literature,' he added as an afterthought.

'What's it going to be called?' I asked conversationally.

The couple exchanged glances.

'*Millet*,' said Salary firmly.

'We're still discussing the title,' said Dayland, equally firmly.

'This man is a real live Russian dissident,' said Dayland, changing the subject. 'You've heard of Solzhenitsyn, haven't you, honeybunch?'

'Oh yes, I think so,' breathed the lovely Celery.

'This is the new Solzhenitsyn.'

'You must be joking,' I said, and winked at Celery.

To my disappointment, Dayland did not protest. This proved that he thought of me neither as money nor as literature. What as, then? asked a small voice within.

'Well, now, if you'll excuse us,' Dayland said.

'Yes, bye-bye,' said Celery charmingly, shaking hands with me again. 'One day we must read each other's books.'

So collapsed my hopes of a night on the town and, possibly, of publication, too. I slipped dejectedly through the narrow streets, casting frightened, envious glances into the hot little mouths of strip clubs and blue-movie theatres. Several times an acned young proprietor tried to lure me inside, but I hurried on by. I was not yet ready for these wilder, more libidinous manifestations of capitalism – at least not without Dayland's worldly experience as my protection.

Despite the not-quite-promising start I returned to the office several times that week. Though Dayland did not repeat his offer (his relationship with Celery, flourishing far beyond decent, professional limits, seemed to take up all his considerable free time) he seemed more civil to me than before, and was glad to exploit my presence by giving me a bit of (paid) proofreading to do. Demszky too gave me some fetching and carrying and photocopying, though with a more apologetic air: to him, at least, I was a real writer. Though I hadn't yet acquired a publisher, as I'd hoped, I had acquired a job, of sorts, which was almost as gratifying. It satisfied me to be working for my bread again; the bread itself was useful too. It meant, for a start, that I would be able to afford a pair of Levi's, a new shirt in one of the colours from my Turkish cucumber tie, and a haircut at a unisex hairdresser's (though my heart trembled at the thought) in honour of my meeting with Elizabeth.

As the day drew closer I felt almost unable to bear the excitement, the hope and the sheer terror that I would be a disappointment to her. (It never occurred to me that Elizabeth could be a disappointment to me: I knew absolutely that she couldn't be.)

Demszky, sensitive to my moods and baffled by the hairstyle, finally asked me what was brewing. As soon as I had told him he exclaimed, 'That's a good story. That's a *real* story. Start writing – don't let it slip away.'

I shifted in my chair. 'Don't you think my other stories are real stories?'

Demszky sighed. 'I like them, of course. But Dayland thinks they're – well – a shade predictable. Not so much the ones you wrote in Moscow, but the later ones. The so-called dissident ones. And I have to say, Arkady, that I tend to agree with him. The trouble is, we've been there before.'

Some distant vein inside me burst, but I kept my voice low and reasonable. 'But listen, Gabor, even if it's been said, it needs to be said again, and more loudly. No one in the West really knows what's happening. You know, of course, but plenty of others don't.'

'Yes, yes, yes,' said Demszky sadly but impatiently.

I willed my voice not to break. 'My closest friend, the one I wrote about in 'The Music Man', got twelve years simply for standing on a street corner with a banner defending the right of his fellow Jews to emigrate. He wasn't even a refusenik! So what if Western readers have been there before? Let them go there again and again, until they understand what the bloody Soviet Union's all about!'

'I don't deny your heart's in the right place,' murmured Demszky.

'You're just thinking of the commercial aspect. You and Dayland, you only care about making money!' I was conscious that my hopes of publication were spiralling rapidly towards zero.

'No money, no more books,' said Demszky mildly. 'But that isn't the whole of it. Truly, I think these stories of yours are good, but they're somehow stilted. In a way, you've censored yourself in reverse. You've done precisely what you objected to doing, quite rightly, when you were in the Soviet Union. You've written for the sake of the message, not for the sake of the writing. The muse objects to political exploitation, Arkady. I believe you know that already in your heart.'

I did know it, though I couldn't yet admit it. 'So you think I should just write personal trivialities?' I said bitterly.

'Do you really believe the story of you and Elizabeth is trivial?'

I shrugged. 'I don't know.'

'Anyway, on Tuesday I think you will find out,' Demszky said. I shivered. Demszky patted my shoulder. 'Don't worry. I feel it's a real story, and a happy one. And remember, even if it's not so happy, it can still be a story.'

I nodded sadly. I couldn't bring myself to tell him – I had barely faced up to the fact myself – that I knew from the letterhead that Elizabeth was married.

Plato Park

It was a fiercely hot day. All the Plexiglass windows of the Euston precinct were burning and sizzling, their undersea blueish-green shot with laser-sharp crosses and stars. I could scarcely breathe with the heat and excitement.

I recognised Elizabeth at once – the brown dress, the moonlight hair – as she swept out of the School of Languages with a quick glance to either side as if she wasn't quite sure that she wanted to see me.

I ran towards her. 'That's the same dress you wore in Moscow,' were my first silly words.

She looked surprised. 'This dress? No, I bought it a few weeks ago.'

'It's just like the one you wore to Lenina Andreevna's party.'

'Is it? I'm afraid I've put on weight since then.' She laughed self-consciously. 'Anyhow, it's nice to see you again – welcome to London!'

She held out her hand, which I clasped in both of mine: I wanted to kiss her, but I wanted to gaze at her too, and it seemed more prudent to content myself for the time being with gazing.

'You haven't changed at all,' I said, but it wasn't quite true. I'd have recognised her anywhere, of course, but something about her had changed. She didn't look any older or less slender – it was simply perhaps that her grey eyes held more, knew more than they had when she was twenty.

'I like your jeans,' she said, and it was my turn to feel self-conscious; I realised at once that they were far too blue, far too clean and a little too tight.

'My first Levi's,' I said. 'Better late than never.'

'Oh, jeans are ageless. I shall still wear them when I'm ninety.'

Did I look old to her? Involuntarily I patted the unisex fuzz on the top of my scalp. 'I'm not quite ninety yet,' I said ruefully.

She blushed. 'Of course you're not. You haven't changed either,' she added kindly.

'Shall we go to the park?' I said. 'Have you got time? I've brought some wine and sandwiches for a picnic.'

'Lovely! Much better than a pub on a day like this.'

'So why are you learning Russian?' I asked her, in Russian, as we walked along.

'Because I'm going to the USSR!' The words – and the way she said them – brought a pang to my heart. Her hand flew to her mouth. 'Oh, that was wrong, wasn't it?'

'You used the wrong aspect of the verb,' I said gently, and repeated the phrase correctly. She copied me exactly, like an obedient schoolchild. 'Excuse me, please!'

'Of course! Let's say *tui*,' I added. 'We're old friends, aren't we?'

'Would you mind, but I'd rather speak English?' She laughed nervously. 'I haven't been learning very long – and there's an awful lot I don't know.'

'When are you going?' I asked, reverting to English at once.

'September. Will you be back by then?'

Did she hope I'd say yes? I couldn't tell.

'I'm not going back,' I said. 'I didn't leave officially, you see; I'd probably be shot for treason.'

'Treason!' She looked at me with horror. 'Arkady – you're not a spy, are you?'

'Wouldn't you be seen in the street with me if I said I was?' I teased her.

'Yes, of course, it's just it's scary – and sort of unreal.'

'Don't worry, I'm not! Shall I tell you the whole crazy story?'

When I'd finished, her eyes were wide and sad. 'How awful for you – never to be able to go back.'

'It isn't awful. It's the best thing that ever happened to me.'

She looked confused. 'But you're married, aren't you?'

'How did you know?' We turned into the park, between flower-beds so bright it hurt to look at them.

'Joey said. I hope you didn't mind.'

'Not at all. It wasn't a very close marriage, we were on the verge of breaking up anyway.'

We crossed the lake in silence.

'You're married, too, aren't you?' I finally said.

She looked at me sharply.

'I noticed the heading on your writing paper,' I explained.

'Oh yes, that. I'd forgotten.'

'Well?' I persisted.

'Well what?'

'You are married, aren't you?'

'Yes!' She sounded irritated, but I had to go on.

'Have you got any children?'

'No!'

I relaxed, just a little.

'I don't think motherhood is for people who've never had mothers,' she explained seriously. 'I mean I had a mother, of course, but she died when I was five. My auntie Bonnie brought me up, but she died, too, when I was fourteen. I used to think it must be something about me!'

'Poor Elizabeth, I've never realised.' I wanted to pull her into my arms and comfort her.

'I had a good father, anyway,' she said briskly.

'Is he' – I wanted to say 'still alive' but changed it to 'keeping well?'

'Daddy died four years ago,' she said calmly. 'He and Joey were living together, you know. They were very happy. They sold the rectory and went to the seaside – Bournemouth. I never see Joey now,' she added. 'I didn't get on with her – I suppose that's only natural.' She laughed – not an honest laugh, I thought.

'Is *your husband*' (hateful phrase, but I had to ask) 'going with you to Moscow?'

'No, he's not,' said Elizabeth and the positive tone in her voice greatly cheered me. 'It'll be the first time I've ever been abroad by myself. Isn't that ridiculous – at the age of thirty-two?'

'Not to me. I'd never been abroad at all at thirty-two.'

We had reached the Royal Garden. The long, straight paths blazed like wheat between the brilliant emerald banners of the little lawns. Geraniums poured from the white urns that flanked our path, their bitter perfume so powerful at times that I could taste it.

'When I was a kid, Auntie Bonnie used to bring me here and sometimes we played ball. You're not supposed to – but Auntie Bonnie was a bit odd in the head, she didn't care, and I thought it was fun. We were expert at catching. The ball never went into the flowerbeds, however high we threw it.'

'I wish I could see you as you were then.'

'I don't. We must have looked a funny pair! I was little and scrawny and she was little and fat. We used to sit over there by the fountain and eat ice creams when we were tired. Auntie Bonnie loved sweet things. She used to buy us four – one for each hand, she said.'

I laughed. 'Let's go and sit there now. It's a funny thing,' I went on, 'but this park is a kind of magnet – for both of us. You went to college here, and now you're at the language school not far away. I came here for the Writers' Festival and now I'm living just the other side. I think it's bewitched, don't you – some places are.'

'I used to think it was haunted – the rectory, too,' she admitted, with a little frown.

'Well, then, there you are! We can't both be wrong. And whoever's haunting it seems to want us to be together.'

Elizabeth didn't reply.

'I think it's still cold, it was in the ice compartment all morning.' I unwrapped the dewy wine bottle from its newspaper swaddling.

'Not too much, please, I've got to think this afternoon,' said Elizabeth as I filled our paper cups.

'To you and to me!' We brushed the cups together and drank.

'Do you remember that bottle of cognac we shared?'

Elizabeth's smile, bright and shy, was the truest I had yet seen. 'Yes – at Ilya's Cavern. How is he – is he still singing?'

I hadn't expected the question. 'Oh, he's fine.' I hesitated. 'I don't see him much, he went to the Far East.' My face went hot with shame; I didn't even understand why I had lied. All I knew was that, at that moment, I couldn't talk about Ilya. Perhaps it was because the equilibrium between us was so frail I couldn't risk disturbing it: perhaps it was an odd little flicker of loyalty to my cruel motherland. I swore to myself that I would tell Elizabeth the truth at another, more appropriate time.

Her smile and her colour had faded rather. 'That's a pity,' she said. 'I thought I might have looked him up in Moscow.' She hesitated. 'I suppose he got married – he had lots of girlfriends, didn't he?'

'Oh yes, I think so.' I fumbled in the string bag. 'Let's eat the sandwiches before they melt.'

We munched in silence for a while. The mood between us was difficult to interpret.

'Elizabeth?' I began.

'Yes?'

'More wine?'

'Just a drop.'

I poured; the bottle trembled against the side of her cup. 'To your happiness!'

'To yours!'

I pressed the small, pearl hand curled in her lap. 'Elizabeth, do you remember telling me about *Dr Zhivago*?'

'Yes, vaguely.' Very gently, she slipped her hand free, and used it to brush a strand of hair from her cheek. 'Why?'

'Oh, nothing!' I felt pierced by rejection. 'I've read it now, that's all.'

'Did you like it?'

'Yes, very much.'

'I haven't read it for years,' she said regretfully. 'I remember thinking the poems were the best part.'

'So did I.' I got back a little courage. 'Do you remember that poem you quoted to me?'

'I haven't got much of a memory for poetry,' she answered softly.

'Surely you remember "the candle on the table burned, the candle burned"?'

'Mmmm, I think so.' She looked at me slyly from under pale lashes.

'"A draft from the corner puffed at the candle flame",' I quoted boldly. '"And like an angel the heat of temptation raised two wings in the form of a cross!" Do you remember now?'

She was smiling faintly, but she wouldn't meet my eyes. 'It was such a long time ago.'

'It was the most wonderful night, that night,' I murmured.

'It was a long time ago,' she repeated firmly. 'It doesn't seem like real life any more.'

'Ten years isn't such a long time,' I said, wounded.

'It depends on what happens during them, I think. Listen, Arkady, I really must be going, I've got a class at two.'

And then, I thought wretchedly, you'll catch a train back to Leicester, back to your husband, back to your 'real' life.

'Can we meet at the same time next week?'

We were outside the college again, and now the light was quite different – softer, darker, greener.

'Mmm, if you want to.' There was a shadow on Elizabeth's pale face.

'Do *you* want to?'

She looked up at me and the shadow was gone. 'Yes, of course.'

The hot, empty afternoon stretched in front of me. How beautiful and richly significant London was with Elizabeth tucked into its heart! I'd have joyfully stood outside the college until six o'clock, when her classes ended, but I knew she wouldn't like it. It was essential not to make demands on her, and somehow to hold back the great waves of my longing.

Quite unaware of what I was doing, I walked to the park again, made my way to the seat we had occupied – still vacant, still imbued with mysterious energies – and sat down. How bright and innocent it was, this heraldic garden, burning emerald, gold and scarlet under the clear blue afternoon sky! Beyond the sprinkled noise of the fountain rose the occasional squeal of children and, more distantly, the strains of a brass band playing the 'Radetzky March'. I sat there perfectly motionless, listening and not listening, hoping and not hoping, blissfully happy and blissfully unhappy. This was the centre of the universe, the insoluble, cross-shaped paradox – human desire that calls itself, dreams itself into, human love.

At first, I thought it must be gunfire – a salute to the Queen or the Prince and Princess of Wales. But then I smelled something smokily bitter – not the geraniums – and saw a thin, dirty cloud rising beyond the trees. I got up and gazed around me; all the other people in the park were doing the same. Then came a wailing chorus of sirens.

'Oh, my God,' said a young woman, leading her child away from the pond where it had been dabbling. 'It's a bomb, I know it's a bomb!'

'What's a bomb?' the child kept saying. 'I want to see the goldfish, what's a bomb? The child began to cry, and I walked quickly away, up the steps and along the path towards the rose garden and Fox Gate.

Decadence – its pleasures and perils

That afternoon when I went out of the park I got straight onto the tube – I suppose I had wanted to put as great a distance as possible between myself and whatever disaster had occurred. For all I knew, World War Three had begun. But I wanted to be in love in peace – and I wanted to talk about it, if possible, to someone sympathetic. Demszky was the obvious choice, so I took the Bakerloo to Piccadilly, but when I got to the offices I found them locked. It was five o'clock, after all, and neither Demszky nor Dayland was averse to slipping off early on a quiet day.

Disappointed, I wandered the hot, tawdry streets until the pubs opened. Elizabeth would be travelling back to Leicester by now. It was a pity I didn't know which station she went from. I could have loitered there, undisclosed, to catch one last sight of her to sustain me for the seven days I must endure before seeing her again.

At last it was opening time. I went into a small pub in Marshall Street, and there the afternoon's events caught up with me. There was a small black and white TV set hanging above the bar, and when the six o'clock news came on, it was the first item. A bomb had gone off in Plato Park near the bandstand, killing two musicians and one spectator. The IRA 'claimed responsibility'.

It was unpleasant to think of violent death in such a setting, and to know how near we had been to it. But I admit, shocked and sorry though I felt, it didn't touch me deeply. I couldn't imagine that it would involve me in any way.

If I had known then – if I had cared a bit more – but how could I have known? It wasn't till I read that little item in the Sunday *Mail* two weeks later that I began to wonder – and even then I didn't know.

But I'm jumping ahead; this is still my Tuesday night of dreamy though now slightly tainted happiness, my night in Soho, going from pub to pub through the hot, gaudy, glittering night, and then down a little narrow stairway, thinking of the Cavern, beckoned by a girl with the moonlight hair and slender limbs of Elizabeth.

I pretended not to speak any English: that made me different, distant from my real self. Anyway, the girl had an accent that was hard for me to understand, as if she was chewing mouthfuls of gum.

She led me into a little bar, whose atmosphere dappled my forehead with sweat in seconds. Gold sputniks with winking lights orbited just above us, mysteriously keeping time to the music (disco style but, thank goodness, quite soft). There were mirrors everywhere. I saw myself in duplicate – men with tight jeans and thrusting stomachs and eager, heated faces – and other girls like Jacqui, their bare breasts hanging from the scaffolding of their shoulders like peculiar, large eyeballs. I decided not to be embarrassed by these starers; they were unaccusing, honest, even friendly, and looked at each other more than at me.

Jacqui, enthroned on the stool beside me, had a way of hollowing her back and making her bottom stick out so that the cherry slip clung thinly to its cheeks. She ordered large gins and tonics, for which I paid, complained loudly of the heat, and fanned herself with a beer mat. As we progressed with our sipping, she thrust one leg towards me and rested her white wicker sandal on the rung of my stool; her knees fell apart and the cherry slip edged further up her thighs, but I was at the wrong angle to see what she was offering me. It didn't matter; I knew the offer had been made. She didn't pay me much attention otherwise; most of her gum-chewing conversation was with the girl behind the bar, though now and again she sent me a cherry-red flash of smile. Meanwhile, her knees remained open and her buttocks remained thrust out – her offerings to me as the drinks were my offerings to her. She wasn't Elizabeth at all, I realised now; even the hair, though the right colour and length, was wrongly combed. No, she was more like Asta – a fashioned, angular, invulnerable doll.

I muttered obscenities to her and stroked her thigh; she talked to the bar girl about her mum's operation and shot me the occasional smile. It was peculiarly arousing, and when she led me away I was ready to burst the zip of my new jeans.

'You're a good boy – nice and clean,' she said approvingly as I undressed, and it was true; in spite of the weather, I still smelled deliciously from the morning's detailed anointings with soap, shower gel, body rub, shampoo, conditioner, talc, aftershave, antiperspirant and all-day fragrance for men. I flashed her a bright, uncomprehending grin. She came towards me naked (her pubic hair as black as her public hair was gold) crouched and took my penis in her hand. I believed she was going to worship it with kisses. But instead she briskly dressed it in a preservative. 'Good boy,' she said again. I urged her, not too gently, to the bed.

She liked my performance generally, I think, though she looked a bit alarmed when I shouted, 'Elizabeth, my life, I adore you, if you don't leave your bastard husband and be my love for ever I'll throw myself under a train,' etc. I was quick, and therefore cost-effective. She certainly wasn't displeased with the ten fivers I paid.

I felt quite a hero, as I went out through the bar, for all the girls waved to me and chorused goodbye. One of them, with a particularly bright smile, was black and wore a white safari suit. I was almost sure it was Salary.

Mr Max, too agitated to even knock, showed the police officer straight into my room. I was stripped to the waist and doing my morning exercises with a vigour that owed much to my newly enhanced self-image as a success with the ladies of the night. Now my muscles went rigid with dismay. Deep in my heart I had known it was wrong – not merely wrong morally, but illegal. Of course it was! Not even the English could be that liberal.

'The officer just wants to ask you a few questions.' Mr Max was flustered. 'He's Russian, but he speaks perfect English,' he added to the policeman, thus destroying the one possible ploy that had offered me hope.

The policeman helped himself to one of my chairs and sat looking about him; he was a rod-backed Kochekovian type with a florid complexion and a falsely genial smile.

'Don't worry, it won't take a moment,' he said, as Mr Max, wringing his hands and muttering, backed out of the door.

'It's in connection with the occupant of the room next door. Cynthia O'Reardon.' So! She had reported me! Trailed me around Soho in her silent way, spied on my activities and told the police.

I couldn't speak; I just stared in horror.

'Sit down, Mr Molyakov. There's no need to look so alarmed – you're not a suspect.'

'I'm not a suspect?'

'Certainly not so far.' The thin lips twitched away the remnants of false geniality. 'Mr Molyakov, I want you to think very carefully back to the last time you saw Cynthia O'Reardon.'

I was desperate to comply, but my mind was as blankly white as a January field.

'Do you remember if you ever heard, or saw, any suspicious goings-on connected with Miss O'Reardon and room 14? Any unfamiliar visitors, for example?'

'No. She was out a lot, I think. I sometimes heard a few bumps and thumps.' The officer appeared interested by this; at least he began making marks in his notebook.

He looked up. 'That's all? Anything else to add?'

'No.' I felt sure I ought to tell him about the white carnations – surely that was a kind of going-on he'd have liked to make a note of – but I compressed my lips firmly. He stood up, thanked me and told me he wouldn't detain me any longer from my 'physical jerks'. I suddenly felt rather let down, after all, and singularly uninformed about the whole affair.

'Have you arrested Miss O'Reardon?' I boldly asked.

'Not yet. We've got to find her first.'

'But what did she do?'

'We have reason to believe she was involved with the local chapter of the Irish Republican Army.'

Cynthia O'Reardon a secret soldier!

'Goodbye, Mr Molyakov.'

I ran after him along the corridor. 'I've just thought, she taught Irish dancing! On Wednesdays.'

He turned slightly, but did not stop. 'Thank you, we know about that already.'

Cynthia's defection and disgrace meant, at least, that I was no longer the white crow of the Pompadour. Even Tel used the gas stove in Joanie's presence without incurring more than a brief clicking of the queenly tongue. All the residents were united in condemnation of the Irish in general and Cynthia in particular. Hanging, they said, was too good for the IRA.

'They even killed them 'orses, d'you remember? Disgusting, innit?' Joanie breathed.

'They kill innocent *people*,' Tel said loudly. 'Them bandsmen weren't even real soldiers. And what about that poor old tramp what was sitting on the grass listening?'

I waited for Naseem to protest that this was a just war against British oppression but he took the view that they should stick to blowing up places like Houses of Parliament, and then only when the Labour Party wasn't there. ('They're always there, dummy,' shouted Tel.)

The Haven, Oak View, Formality etc.

It was a couple of weeks later; I was browsing through the Sunday papers in the leisurely English way to which I have happily become acclimatised. The press had dropped the bandstand-bomb story and were busy with fresh disasters (the terrorists hadn't been caught, nor had Cynthia O'Reardon been found), but a small headline, FUNERAL OF AN INNOCENT BYSTANDER, on the inside page drew my attention.

> He was known as Little Ivan, [I read] but nobody knew his real name. He claimed to be of Russian origins, and to have escaped from Stalin's Russia on foot over the rugged mountains of the Caucasus. He had lived in England for many years, deliberately choosing, say his friends, the life of a vagabond. In recent

months he had 'camped out' in the doorway of the PO sorting office in Coral Street. He was a fan of the royal family, and loved military music and parades. And that was how little Ivan came to be among the innocent victims of the brutal bandstand killers. His funeral took place at Primrose Hill Crematorium on Friday and was well attended by those who knew him as a colourful figure of local street life. Little Ivan, they say, was a survivor. And his memory surely *will* survive his cruel and senseless death.

I stared at the words for a long time, willing them to reveal a deeper secret. Then I carefully cut out the article and placed it in my wallet next to the photo of Masha. I vacillated between claiming Vanya irrefutably as my father, and suffering indescribable waves of yearning and dismay, and rejecting the ideas as absurd, and suffering corresponding waves of disappointed relief. I don't know what I really wanted: a live but unlocatable father or a dead, locatable one. Later that day I cornered Rajit and asked if he remembered whether or not my mysterious visitor had looked like a 'vagabond'. Rajit answered that he didn't mean to be rude but all Europeans looked like vagabonds to him.

The next day I went straight to the office of the Primrose Hill Crematorium, hoping they might have a record of Vanya's full name. But the young man there couldn't help; 'Ivan' was the only name he had for 'the deceased', 'no fixed abode' the only address. All he could tell me, he said regretfully, was the number of the plot where the rose tree was to be planted. What rose tree? I asked, confused. The young man explained that the deceased's friends had clubbed together to buy a memorial for him. It was the usual practice. Roses were very popular, so were cypress trees. I would see for myself, if I cared to have a look round.

I wandered in this strange garden for several hours, reading the plaques on the Wall of Memory and in the flowerbeds: rows and rows of them glazed an identical reddish-brown and with the same plain style of lettering. Whereas graveyards traditionally express English individualism and class distinction, this was somehow the socialist view of death, rankless and equal. The epitaphs, necessarily very short, were dim little clichés: 'in loving memory', 'sadly missed'.

Everything was exquisitely neat. The plots were divided by cypress hedges and had wooden signs identifying them as the Haven, Oak View, Formality etc. I thought of the small housing estates I'd seen from the back of the police car when we were going to the Home Office. All the flowerbeds, immaculately weeded, were covered with wood chips; I supposed that just underneath lay human ashes. I preferred the wilder parts, where there were tall trees, long grass and buttercups. Were these older, unmarked trees memorials once? As I strolled through the rich, dense summer green, I heard a cuckoo and remembered our old folk custom of asking Kukushka 'How many years will I live?' and counting her cries to find out. I decided not to ask her; death was too near me just then.

There were funerals going on all the time, little trails of people filing in and out of the chapel, dressed in their smartest, darkest clothes, unnaturally silent, stifling their grief. To reach the chapel they crossed a courtyard, where the most brilliant flowers I have ever seen were spread. Some had been shaped into words: I stared for a long time at one that spelled, in lilies and roses, DAD. The mourners paused as they passed to admire their own offerings and, I suppose, be comforted by the awful burning brightness – which, to me, somehow had the incandescence of decay.

Little Ivan would have had flowers like these, I thought: probably even more, and in all kinds of bizarre shapes. I somehow wished I had been part of the tribute – even if he was not my father, he was a fellow Russian, and a fellow dissident. I waited until all the incoming mourners had entered the chapel and the courtyard was temporarily deserted. Then I stopped beside a slightly wilted display, labelled 'In Memory of Esther Alice Wilkinson'. I crouched to the slender bunch of red carnations nearest me and carefully removed a single flower. I was sure Esther Wilkinson would not mind sparing me this little gift, even though it was for a Russian gentleman she'd never met. If the dead survive in any way, they must surely be wiser and more generous than the living.

I found the freshly wood-chipped plot (9 PX in Larchways) where Vanya's rose tree would flower one day, scrabbled a little hole in the soil and inserted the red carnation. As I stood up I noticed the smoke from the crematorium chimney turn from pale grey to black. I watched it until it went back to grey. Whoever it was, I mourned him. I mourned him precisely because I didn't know who he was. I mourned Little Ivan, who might have been my father though he was nameless and without papers, and I mourned Esther Wilkinson who was nothing to me but her name and some garish, wilting flowers. I mourned all the names in the garden, and all the unnamed. I mourned the newly dead, the living, the newly born. And, as I walked back down the path of copper beeches, I had never felt more rich in being alive.

The Temple of the Four Winds

That had been one of Dr Lamb's kinder nicknames for the Euston precinct. Apparently, he had strongly disapproved of its construction, particularly since a rather fine Victorian church had been demolished in the process. For a month of Tuesdays both the phrase and the winds blew ceaselessly through my empty head as I waited for Elizabeth in the shadow of four tall buildings – a radio station, an airline, a tyre company and the Euston School of Languages (all, in their different ways, servants of the winds). I crouched on a circular seat huddled round a billboard, and thought of myself as a tender, shivering animal sacrifice. But I was superlatively happy in my discomfort. My whole existence now was dedicated to Elizabeth and to the art of our curiously strained and reticent, curiously enchanting courtship dance.

Today it was a swift-running, rain-speckled west wind that pushed itself under my anorak and blew me up like the Michelin Man. Elizabeth came out punctually at a minute past one, with a violet scarf wrapped round her head. By now I had got used to the fact that she never looked particularly pleased to see me. Even off guard, her face habitually expressed an anxious sadness. I knew I would always be able to redraw it in gentler lines.

We had planned that, instead of going to her afternoon classes, she would come back with me to the Pompadour. She had agreed very reluctantly, enticed by the promise of a session of conversation practice more intensive than she could possibly receive in a class of twenty. Of course I dreamed that our communications might exceed the merely linguistic. I dared not entertain any very specific hopes. But I was a-tremble with the sense of possibility.

I hurried her to the bus stop (we could have walked but I didn't want her to get wet), hurried her onto the bus, afraid, as all those years ago in Sverdlova Square I'd been afraid, that the harsh city wind would sweep her away. A couple of stops, barely time to get our breath, then I was rushing her up the rubber-carpeted stairs of the Pompadour, praying I wouldn't meet anyone on the way. I settled her into my best chair, a hideous black plastic object whose appearance Tel had tried to enhance with a draped remnant of gold Lurex. Everything was prepared. The wine bathed in cold water in my hand basin (Mr Max had inconveniently taken it on himself to give the communal fridge its annual defrost), the vegetables, cleaned and chopped, gleamed at me through polythene, the anchovies swam motionless in a bowl of rich dressing.

Elizabeth ate with dutiful deliberation, like a little girl. She claimed my salad was delicious, but I wasn't convinced. I suppose I shouldn't have stared at her so much. Her thin elbows stuck out gawkily and looked cold. She was surprisingly clumsy, dropped bits of food from her mouth and spilled some of her wine, with exhaustive apologies. Every so often she glanced at her watch. It was a large, steely, digital watch and looked somehow cruel, nestling in the tiny blonde hairs of her childish wrist.

She would have to get the 4.30 train at the latest, she said, because Gus was bringing some friends round, and she had to prepare.

Behind us, the bed lay under its new, flowered duvet, the freshly changed sheets sprinkled with talcum powder. Neither of us had once glanced towards it: I had even averted my eyes as I spread the delicately scented violet scarf and grey raincoat across it to dry. Once or twice it tried to thrust itself into my consciousness; I told it angrily that it did not exist.

We sat for a long time after the meal, talking stilted Russian over the oily plates. I took my pupil through an entire textbook conversation, from 'May I introduce myself?' to 'When can I see you again?' She had been taught excellent grammar, though her vocabulary was still poor. Her accent was very funny, and utterly charming. I felt as though I was talking with a young child again, and I enjoyed every minute.

We finished the wine and unleashed the brandy (I had bought a whole bottle of supermarket stuff, in memory of our famous quarter). The atmosphere between us thawed and glowed. We had lapsed into English, and somehow the conversation slithered on to those heart-stirring subjects, politics, socialism, good and evil. We talked about the bandstand bomb and I told her about Little Ivan, loving the glow of sympathy in her face. Then she declared that whatever was wrong with Soviet society, at least *that* sort of thing didn't happen. No, I said, but the state commits more crimes to make up for it. I wanted to tell her about Ilya, but found I couldn't; so I told her about Luba and Boba instead. She listened wide-eyed and said very little, except to apologise that her father had never finished the translation of the *Noviye Domostroi*, and to promise that she would return it to me next time. We were talking about other things when I noticed quite suddenly that she was crying.

She let me put my arms round her. To my surprise, she let me lead her to the bed.

Nothing could have diminished my desire for her. But her attitude –somehow both businesslike and curiously uninvolved, now that she had stopped crying – discomposed me. I had wanted to undress her, but she had taken her own clothes off before I could protest, with stunning rapidity. She was wearing a primrose slip under the formal suit. Keeping it on, she slipped swiftly into my bed and lay with her thin arms over the quilt, completely still and open-eyed like a patient waiting for surgery under a local anaesthetic. When I began to fondle her, she closed her eyes.

She feels terribly guilty, I thought; she's probably never been unfaithful to her husband before.

I began to feel guilty myself, and with the guilt came the obligation not to delay. (In fact I believe I heard at one point a small, soft voice say hurry up.) Next door, in uncanny synchronisation with my own movements, Mr Phythian's gerbils were engaged in an unusually vigorous bout of diurnal treadmilling. I was sweating, exhausted, insatiable.

'You're not really enjoying this, are you?' Elizabeth asked suddenly, still keeping her eyes tightly shut.

'It's because you're not. I don't know why, maybe you feel guilty about your husband or maybe you simply don't care for me.' I had not meant to sound such a note of impatient misery.

Elizabeth opened her eyes and gazed at me sadly. 'I do care, but I can't just take up our relationship from where we left it ten years ago. A lot of things have changed since then – for me, anyway.'

'Do you mean feelings – or circumstances?'

'Well, circumstances, mainly.'

Her reply gladdened me. 'Marriages aren't Soviet labour camps, you know,' I said gently. 'If you're in a situation that makes you miserable, you can get out of it.'

'I know that.'

'And you are miserable, aren't you?' I persisted.

'I have been in the past. Things are better now.' Her voice was small, dead, closed. She shut her eyes again, and pulled me closer. 'It must have been terrible for your wife,' she whispered.

Why did she have to talk about Asta at a time like this?

'No, I don't think it's so terrible for her,' I said irritably.

'You just disappeared – and you're never going back,' Elizabeth accused.

So that was it, I thought. She's afraid to give herself in case I do the same to her.

'I tried to tell you before. Asta's very independent, we had an open marriage. She'd got involved with someone else long before I left.'

'I still think it's terrible to just disappear. She might think you're dead!'

'No, she doesn't. I've written to her, explaining everything.' I sighed, and slid out of Elizabeth and onto the bed at her side.

'What's the matter?'

'I would have thought that was obvious.'

She got up quickly and started to dress. 'I'm sorry, I suppose I just wasn't in the mood,' she said.

'What is it you really want, Elizabeth?'

She stood in her formal suit and violet headscarf, twisting her hands with embarrassment. 'To be kind,' she said.

'To be kind to me?' I asked, appalled.

'No, I meant in general,' she answered hastily. 'I didn't go to bed with you to be kind – I really like you. Don't worry, it'll be better next time.'

So the seesaw swung upwards, leaving me suspended, dazed, not quite unhappy. I hoped Elizabeth's problem was that she loved me, but couldn't bring herself to admit it, even to herself.

The following Tuesday, I waited in the square for nearly an hour, huddled under the billboard, paralysed by anxiety and a remorseless north wind. Elizabeth didn't appear. Was she off sick, had she already gone on holiday? Had our last encounter frightened her so much that she was deliberately avoiding me? Perhaps she had sneaked out of a back way I didn't know about. I finally tore myself away, went home and paced the floor.

By five o'clock I was back in the precinct. I had not been able to discover any hidden exits to the School. Some students were coming out: they looked so joyously young I felt as if I had outstayed my time on earth. I picked out a dark-haired girl and asked her if, by chance, she happened to be in the Russian class. 'No, English,' she said, and quickened her step away from me across the precinct. I pressed my nose to the door of the school: even the receptionist at the upholstered front desk was packing up her things to leave. There were fewer classes in the summer months, and they ended earlier. By now, half past five, the building would be empty.

I stayed in the whole of the following day, waiting for a phone call. She ought to ring me, I told myself, we had parted friends, and our Tuesday date was invariable. But then, if she was ill, maybe she couldn't get to the phone, and I should ring her. So I debated the niceties of erotic etiquette like a girl of sixteen. My great fear was of scaring her off with my enthusiasm. Like the sixteen-year-old girl, I had an instinctive faith in the power of nonchalance. Unfortunately, it dissolved every time I heard the distant ringing of the phone.

The next morning I dialled her number. A woman's voice (thank God) said hallo.

My heart pounded. 'Elizabeth, it's me, Arkashka. How are you?'

'This isn't Elizabeth,' said the voice neutrally.

I told her I wanted Elizabeth Coombelands, and recited the digits.

'Elizabeth doesn't live here any more.'

'But she gave me this number.'

'It used to be her number. May I ask who's speaking?'

I babbled nervously that I was a friend from her Russian class, worried because she hadn't turned up on Tuesday.

'I don't know anything about why she wasn't there, and I don't have her new number. But I can ask Gus when he gets home, if you'd care to call back this evening.'

'Gus? Her husband?' I said incredulously.

'Her ex-husband,' the woman said coldly. 'I've been Gus's wife for the last year, I can assure you. Is she pretending she's still married or something? Christ, she always was a bit screwed up, but this is too much.'

I couldn't think properly, but somehow I pulled the essential question out of the air. 'Perhaps I made a mistake. Is she married to someone else?'

'Not as far as I know. As I said, you can ring back later and talk to Gus. I've got to go now. Goodbye.'

Though I didn't want to talk to Gus, I felt more anxious than ever to talk to Elizabeth. I was in a rage of hopes and fears. For some reason I convinced myself for an hour or so that she had committed suicide. Then I calmed down; it was far more likely she had deliberately avoided me. I began to think excitedly that the reason she had deceived me about her marriage was that she wanted to test the seriousness of my intentions. Then gloom descended, as I thought that maybe it had been a feeble attempt at heading me off altogether. If Tel hadn't come down to demand my help with some wallpapering she was doing, I believe I might have gone mad that afternoon.

When I finally telephoned, the impeccable Augustus told me that he did not give out his ex-wife's address to perfect strangers, and if I really was a friend from her Russian class, I should get her phone number from the college registry.

I allowed him the victory, put the phone down and then spent the night bitterly regretting it. I could have explained who I really was. Possibly I could have even got this imperial ex-husband, a rival no longer, onto my side in the matter. But these are social possibilities I can create only when I have a piece of paper in front of me. In real life I am pathetically uninventive. Maybe it's my Soviet training in obedience. Male voices especially produce certain reflexes of humility in me. I know it's regrettable. But I'm afraid the retraining as a dissident, a no-sayer, is going to take a very long time, like a language learned in adulthood – like Elizabeth's Russian.

Next Tuesday I was waiting outside the language school as usual. I licked my finger and raised it to the bitter wind. As I had thought, it was blowing from the east.

My plan was to treat Elizabeth with exquisite delicacy. I certainly wouldn't mention that I had found out about the divorce. I would try to clarify things between us simply by giving her the story-letter, the one I had meant her to have so many years ago. If it showed my human weaknesses, it also showed, I thought, that I truly cared for her. And it would mean that there were no secrets between us any more – none on my part, at least.

Elizabeth was five minutes early. I scarcely recognised her. Her hair had been cut short as a boy's. It was brushed forward, making a slant, moonlit wave onto her forehead. Hoop earrings dangled against her bare neck. She looked beautiful but, as soon as she noticed me, angry.

'I haven't got time for a drink,' she said abruptly. 'I'm sorry, but I really do have to go shopping.'

'OK. But I wanted to talk to you for a few minutes as it's the last time I'll see you before you go to Moscow. Can I come with you a little way?'

I followed her at a cracking pace down to the tube.

'You're going to Leningrad too, aren't you?'

'Yes, for a couple of days.'

'Would you have time to take a present to my mother?'

'I'll try. Yes, of course I will!'

I followed her into the leather shop which was her first port of call, and, while she was trying on jackets, I found some gloves with fur linings. I couldn't really afford them, but I wanted Mother to have them to help her through the coming winter.

I left two Elizabeths: a girl in a russet jacket standing looking at a girl in a russet jacket, the two of them comparing anxieties.

The gloves had been paid for and wrapped. I placed them in Elizabeth's carrier, and kissed her on her cold cheek. 'Goodbye, Lisenka. I wish I was coming with you.'

'Take care of yourself, Arkady. Good luck with the book!'

'The book won't be out for ages, if ever. You'll be back long before then.'

'Is that all right?' The shop assistant hovered near.

'I think it's a bit too short. Have you got anything else?'

'Elizabeth, I just remembered something.'

'What?' She turned impatiently. I pulled the letter from my pocket.

'It's something I wrote for you, about five years ago. I was going to give it to Joey to give to you, but I never did. I'd like you to have it now, before you go. It explains things a bit – not just about me, about Russia, too. You can treat it as a little unofficial guidebook.'

'This one's a three-quarter length,' said the assistant, unclipping another jacket from its anti-theft chain and throwing me a discouraging stare.

'Thank you very much, Arkady!' Elizabeth took the letter and dropped it into her bag. Her smile, nervous but true, went with me as I hurried out of the shop.

A couple of days later, she sent me a letter of her own.

Leicester
19 September 1984

Dear Arkasha,

Thank you for the letter, which I read with many emotions, as you can imagine. I know I owe you one too, and I hardly know where to begin. There are things I ought to have told you – maybe in person – but I lacked the courage and the clear thinking. I wanted our relationship to work out just as much as you did – it would have solved so many things. I tried to hide from myself the knowledge that it was 'almost right, but not quite'. There's an English poem about that, by Stevie Smith; I can't remember it exactly but she says that the almost-right, but not quite, 'in love is wholly evil'. Doesn't that make you shudder – but it's true! I can't explain why – I was never much of a philosopher.

Do you know I am a domophobic like you?! All my life I've had sudden impulses to just take off. It doesn't only affect Soviet citizens, you see. And I've always found other domophobics attractive – Gus wasn't a domophobic, it's true, and perhaps that's why our marriage broke up. We were divorced a year ago; I'm sorry I didn't tell you. Oh, Arkady, where to begin? I wish I could write you a story, but you'll have to be satisfied with a jumble of bare facts.

Round about the time I saw your small ad I'd just received a letter from a boy I used to live with, a hippy type who went by the name of Pelican. Six years ago, after we broke up, he took off for Brindaban, in India, to join an ashram (a religious community). We kept up the occasional correspondence and, when I was depressed not long ago, I wrote to him telling him about my divorce and how purposeless I felt. Eventually he wrote back, and told me that there's a place for me at the ashram, if I want it.

I know a little about Hindu mysticism, from Pelican, and it attracts me. The idea is that human eroticism is a means of divine insight. When men and women unite they become a single godlike One, like Krishna, who, in his highest form as creator of the universe, is both male and female. I have never really found either love or God, yet I still believe in both. On the other hand, there is something ludicrous in the idea of sex as religious duty. Love could easily get left out of it. In fact, people change partners all the time, so Pelican says – the ashram is against pair-bonding. Maybe it's just a glorified brothel, an excuse for screwing around. All the same, I thought it might not be a completely worthless experience.

The important thing is to go somewhere else and not wake up and find yourself back in the place you thought you'd left!

My marriage to Gus was a bit like that, a kind of re-entry into childhood. I had been living with Pelican and, as you know, earning my bread as a trainee copywriter. It wasn't a very well-paid job but I supported us both – Pelican never worked. At the same time, he disapproved of it morally. I did too, really, but I'd left college without taking a degree, I didn't even have secretarial skills, so it was the best kind of work I could get. I worked on English Country Apples and Leopold Bruner Investments – promoting healthy eating and sensible saving! Nothing sexist or indecent or dishonest. But, of course, the basic ethics of advertising are questionable, whatever the product. I wouldn't admit it at the time. I accused Pel of hypocrisy, and we started having the most terrible arguments.

Gus was one of the directors of the company I worked for, quite a lot older than me, but we got on well, and one day he asked me out. So that was how it started. I was defying Pelican, I suppose. Gus was recently divorced, and lonely. He wanted to go back to his childhood city, Leicester, and start his own consultancy. He wasn't short of money. I knew my life with him would be easy and peaceful. He was so old-fashioned – secretly, I think, he didn't really want me to go out to work. I wished Daddy had still been alive, because I think if he'd met Gus he would have forgiven me for everything – not doing my degree, Pelican, all the rebellious stuff he hated. He'd have approved my choice of Gus.

Well, I got the peace, and also total boredom. No, worse than boredom: futility. Gus worked all round the clock, more, I thought, than was strictly necessary, and though I'd looked forward to freedom from the nine-to-five and had planned to do all sorts of things, I somehow couldn't. Some days I was too depressed even to get out of bed.

I agree with what you said about authenticity. I reckon I've been inauthentic for 99 per cent of my life. (I'll tell you about the 1 per cent in a minute.) I think it's inauthentic not to work, and inauthentic to do nothing but earn and consume. It's inauthentic to offer your naked self to someone you don't love, and to receive their naked self. I needn't go into the other, obvious inauthenticities, the daily compromises, but I assure you they do exist even in the free West.

Gus was pleased when I dragged myself out of my lethargy and started learning Russian. He got brochures and wanted to plan a trip. I told him I wanted to go alone. He was hurt, and that began the serious arguments. He was already seeing Sara, as I later found out.

It's odd, though, I hated doing anything without his approval. It was like the sun and made me grow. His disapproval stunted me. I decided not to go away that year, though I went on with my lessons.

It was only when I found out about Sara that I could be really angry and strong enough to leave him. Sara was his ex-wife. I had always been afraid she'd crawl out of the shadows one day. I knew Gus still loved her. He told me once how much nicer and less self-centred she was than me. Well, it's probably true. Anyway, she was his great love. Never come between anyone and their great love – even if they say it's all over and have the divorce papers to prove it, or the death certificate! Great loves aren't divorceable, and they never die.

It was also at this time that I started thinking about Ilya. I came to think of him as the man who could have been my great love.

I don't suppose he told you, but the day our group got back from Peredelkino, he just turned up at the hotel. I don't know how he talked his way past the doorman – as you know, he was the sort of person who could do things like that. He wanted to know if I'd brought any tapes with me. I had brought a few, and in the end I invited him to my room so he could listen to them. He wouldn't go upstairs with me, he said he'd find his own way a few minutes later!

Heaven knows what he said to the *dejurnaya*! Maybe he kissed her or gave her a red rose!

Nothing at all happened – nothing and everything! We said goodbye, I gave him my best Dylan tape. He said he was sorry he didn't have anything to give me, except – and he searched in his pocket – a little medal he'd found. It was a hero-mother medal, and I've kept it to this day, though I've never been a mother or a hero.

I planned to go back to Moscow to see him again as soon as I could save up. But you know how quickly things can change when you're young. I moved out of the rectory, left college and got caught up in my 'glamorous' new job. Pelican was in hot pursuit, as well as one or two others! I did think about Ilya, and I always knew I'd go back to Russia. But I didn't want to go with Pelican. And meanwhile, there were other trips – to India, North Africa, Israel, Greece.

It was after I married Gus that I thought most deeply about Ilya. I realised that he was probably married too. But I thought if I could see him for just a few moments it would confirm somehow that I'd had my moment of authenticity – that day when he left my room and I sat with the little medal clutched in my palm, thinking – he's beautiful, I love him.

And sometimes I'd think: suppose he isn't married. Just suppose that all the time he has nurtured an imaginary love, and given that love my face? I know this sounds like romanticising, housewife stuff, created by a lonely woman standing by her leaf-shaded picture window looking out on an English provincial street full of other leaf-shaded picture windows and other dreaming women. But I've always been prepared to test the dream against reality, even if it means losing it.

Now I've read your letter, I love Ilya more than ever. *I have got to see him again*. I'll visit him if I can, if not in Mordovia, then in Siberia. And if I can't, I'll wait. I won't expect anything; I know, if he ever gets free, he'll probably want to be with Rivka. Why should that alter my love – love isn't about getting things for yourself. Arkady, I'm never coming back to England again.

I know Russia's a cruel country, and nowhere crueller than

Siberia. Air so cold it burns, the soles of your boots cracking like glass, your breath turning to ice dust. Ilya will travel for weeks in prison trains, in wagons so tightly crowded he can't lie down to sleep. Will he have the strength to bear it?

What is Russia? Why do I feel there's more truth in its ice-and-fire barbarousness than in all the seedy, shabby gardens of democracy?

Last night I dreamed of a church – all copper, gold and black, with a great, five-tiered iconostasis, each saint in his own birch forest of candles. The flames flickered on thin yellow cheeks and sombre eyes. I heard dark words: blood, suffering, sacrifice, hunger, permafrost, death. I looked down at my hands and the candlelight burned through them like X-ray film, I saw only white bones.

Around me stood black-shawled women. They prayed silently. Their silence made clouds like incense, and became the ice-clouded air of Siberia. We were trudging along a rutted track that stretched for miles and miles. I could see distant watchtowers and lines of barbed wire. We were all wives – Decembrists' wives, prisoners' wives. Women who took their love to extremes. Some had come to live with their husbands in the freezing dormitories of exile. Others had come to visit them in the camps. Their love lived on starvation rations – a yearly visit, the touching of hands, a food parcel that would be stolen by the guards. I was one of these trudging women of the ice. I had to keep putting my hand over my lips to keep them from freezing.

A man who knew he was loved like that could survive anything.

Can love grow from nothing? All love grows from nothing. You need to know only what a mother knows about her newborn baby in order to love – and that's nothing! It begins with what the Hindus call the meeting of eyes. You recognise someone's existence, and you make your attachment in rays of invisible light. You invent what you must love, and it becomes real. Lovers are constantly creating one another. That's all love is. Fiction. Invention. No one can be human without it. And it begins with that little random spark, that meeting of eyes.

The spark that Ilya and I made continues to burn for me. And I know it's my true thing, my scrap of authenticity. If I try again to snuff it out with common sense, I might as well be dead.

How could I tell you all this face to face? You'd be hurt, you might try to hurt me. (I mean, to dissuade me from what I've made up my mind to do.)

I know you hate Soviet life and love the West. Well, good luck to you if you think you can find authenticity here. As a writer, as a man, you may be able to. For a woman there aren't so many choices. Or, shall I say, there aren't many choices for *me*. I know that the Soviet Union is a cruel country. But at least it has an ideal larger than itself. It may be twisted and distorted, but I'd rather have a distorted ideal than none at all. One day it will become human again. It was under the Tartar yoke for 300 years, but managed to struggle free! The great, true heat of Russia will melt the Soviet state to its own lineaments in the end.

In my dream, the guard refused me entry into the camp, and I was so frustrated that I struck my hand on the barbed wire and made it bleed. I picked up the drops, little hard beads. I told the sentry I would stay there, and freeze to death if necessary.

And I will stay, and wait for Ilya.

I must write to Pelican now. That'll be easier, he won't think I'm crazy. He used to want to live in the USSR too.

Wish me well with my imaginary life, as I wish you well with yours.

Elizabeth

From Arkady's notebook, London, 1984

I had a letter from Moscow two weeks later. It was from Mother. She said she could never thank me enough for the beautiful warm gloves. Would it be possible for me to send a pair for Alla too – she suffered so terribly with rheumatism in her fingers during the icy weather? The English girl was charming; they'd had such a nice chat and it was a pity she couldn't have stayed longer in Leningrad. If only she'd had a daughter instead of a son, Mother added, she wouldn't have been so lonely now – but of course she always knew I'd turn out just like my father.

Francesca Duranti

The House on Moon Lake

'An utterly original book and quite the most enjoyable I have read in a long time'

Listener

'It is not until the terrifying climax that we realise that Francesca Duranti's graceful and literary prize-winning novel is really a horror story of the kind Henry James might have thought of. I found it thoroughly scary'

Nina Bawden

'It is elegant and mysterious – a delicious book. It gave me great pleasure, and I think it is the finest European novel I have read this year'

Mary Flanagan

'*The House on Moon Lake* has won the Bagutta Prize, the Martina Franca Prize and the City of Milan Prize. I wish there were a prize we too could give it'

Independent

Flamingo

Eva Figges

The Seven Ages

'A bravely original book, a panorama of one thousand years of our history through a woman's eyes as uncannily moving as the birth and deaths that stud her poetic pages.

David Hughes, *Mail on Sunday*

'Bold and idiosyncratic . . . . written with evident passion.'

Penelope Lively, *Sunday Telegraph*

'Virginia Woolf would have so welcomed this book, representing as it does the direction she hoped literature would take. Here, at last, palpable, embodied, is that accumulation of centuries of unrecorded lives that she wished for. I read many of its pages in a daze of wonder.'

Tillie Olsen

Flamingo

Ben Okri

Incidents at the Shrine

A collection of short stories

'He seems to have the two great gifts that are required to make a man a teller of tales: first, faultless artistic economy, which shows in his razor-sharp prose; second, an ability to place himself, chameleon-like, in any milieu of society, from the highest to the lowest.' *The Standard*

'The eight dazzling stories in this collection are lyrical, funny and never despairing. Okri demonstrates precision short-story writing without wasting a word.' *Time Out*

'Reading Okri felt to me like talking to someone who has a secret – he made me want to find out what made him write so, but he was not telling.' *New Statesman*

Flamingo

Marguerite Duras

La Douleur

'The work cuts to the bone: distressing and illuminating as the texts are about the nature of war and the self, and the eroticism of grief and violence. How rare and valuable is this account of the last wild, hurtful, murderous days of Hitler's Reich in Paris. Enough to make you change your view of history.'

Fay Weldon

The Lover

Rarely have I read a novel so flawlessly written, so intensely felt that the usual veil between the reader and the writing dissolves. The reality of the fiction is, very nearly, unbearable.'

Spectator

Flamingo

Joan Wyndham

Love Lessons

Love Lessons is the true, unexpurgated record of a glorious youth, begun in the summer of 1939 when Joan Wyndham was almost seventeen and charting the progress of her colourful education in sex, love and life among Chelsea's Bohemian community of the wartime years.

Strictly brought up by a religious mother, Joan throws off her convent past and girlish ways when she meets a dissolute German sculptor at a party and falls wildly in love with him. He introduces her to a noisy, intoxicating society, far removed from her own, to a world of late nights, loose talk and easy sex, and a raffish community of painters, poets and poseurs among whom her innocence makes her a celebrity.

When the diary draws to its close in May 1942, the mood has changed. London is in ruins, old friends are dead and lovers betrayed. The world in which she came of age has gone for ever, but is wonderfully evoked in this fresh and lively journal.

'*Love Lessons* is a unique evocation of a hectic, desperate era. It bubbles along with the energy and freshness peculiar to adolescent girls, and when it ends the reader is left with a terrible lump in the throat' *Val Hennessy*

Flamingo

Jay McInerney

Bright Lights, Big City

'Terrific: remarkable, funny writing, a perfect power-to-weight ratio.'

Thomas McGuane

'In its depiction of youth striving mightily to amuse itself, in the exhuberance of its language and the antic shamelessness of its tale, Jay McInerney's novel calls to mind such classics of knight-errantry as *The Ginger Man* and *The Bushhacked Piano*. It is a dazzling debut, smart, heartfelt, and very, very funny.'

Tobias Wolff

Ransom

'Jay McInerney's book is a pleasure to read. It's cleverly written, it's intelligent, lively and concise. It's very well organised and humorous. And it gives the reader that final buzz – it's serious.'

Guardian

Flamingo

James Rogers

War and Peace in Milton Keynes

In the ordered affluent world of Middleclam, one corporation calls the shots. Cyberserf sells hard, thinks uncomfortably big, and has a new project – a domestic robot targeted on every unsuspecting household in the country.

No wonder that on being revealed to the sales force it throws itself under a table and wraps its arms around its head.

But neurosis has no place in Cyberserf, and should in this instance be correctable. Except that someone has stolen the robot, and a number of only moderately neurotic people are having their lives turned upside down by Cyberserf's ruthless, if admittedly eccentric, attempts to retrieve it. Perhaps it's something to do with an odd button marked 'combat' on that hapless, harmless little machine . . .

War and Peace in Milton Keynes is a hectic black farce set twenty minutes into the future, and a superbly funny debunking of the peculiar obsessions of the get-ahead times in which we live.

Flamingo